D0540592

Please return / renew by date shown.
You can renew it at:
norlink.norfolk.gov.uk
or by telephone: 0844 800 8006
Please have your library card & PIN ready

1l
BTH

NORFOLK LIBRARY ROTATION
AND INFORMATION SERVICE PLAN

John Sutherland is Emeritus Lord North-cliffe Professor at University College London. He is the author of twenty-two books. He writes regular columns for the *Guardian*, *Financial Times* and *New Statesman*.

THE BOY WHO LOVED BOOKS

John Sutherland's childhood ended before it began: when his father was killed flying a Wellington bomber. Half-orphaned, John was abandoned when his widowed mother decamped to Argentina with a new man. He was brought up by an assortment of well-meaning relatives and had an odd, unsettled childhood. He took refuge in books. But then his solitary reading habit merged into a bad drinking habit. *The Boy Who Loved Books* is the story of one man's, often desperate, love affair with reading matter; with drink and with an adored, but absent, parent. And during the shifting twentieth century, when profound changes shook society, it is also a personal account of what it was like to be a grammar-school boy, a national-service man and a redbrick graduate.

JOHN SUTHERLAND

THE BOY WHO LOVED BOOKS

A MEMOIR

Complete and Unabridged

ULVERSCROFT
Leicester

First published in Great Britain in 2007 by
John Murray (Publishers)
An Hachette Livre UK Company
London

First Large Print Edition
published 2009
by arrangement with
John Murray (Publishers)
An Hachette Livre UK Company
London

The moral right of the author has been asserted

British Library CIP Data

Sutherland, John, *1938* –
   The boy who loved books, a memoir.—
   Large print ed.—
   Ulverscroft large print series: non fiction
   1. Sutherland, John, *1938* – —Childhood and youth
   2. Authors, English—20th century—Biography
   3. College teachers—England—Biography
   4. Literature teachers—England—Biography
   5. Critics—England—Biography 6. Large type books
   I. Title
   801.9′5′092

   ISBN 978–1–84782–559–9

Published by
F. A. Thorpe (Publishing)
Anstey, Leicestershire

Set by Words & Graphics Ltd.
Anstey, Leicestershire
Printed and bound in Great Britain by
T. J. International Ltd., Padstow, Cornwall

This book is printed on acid-free paper

For Sarah

Contents

Fair seedtime

William Wordsworth

Fatherlessness

Having a lifelong relationship with a dead father, not to be too Hamlet-like about it, is tricky — more so if that father only exists as faded snapshots in the mind, and a loose bundle of handed-down family lore. Were I to meet my father today, he would strike me as a very young man; immature, even — as exuberantly so as the graduate students I supervise. 'Wet behind the ears' is the expression he himself might have used. Like Housman's runner, Jack Sutherland — the man who fathered me — is forever young, cut off as he was at thirty-ish (I am not even sure of the exact age: family lore is not actuarially precise on the matter). I passed his mark decades ago and have since passed it twice over.

I do have those mental snapshots, some of which are likely to be what Freudians call 'screen memories' — bland fabrications designed to mask other, more painful, recollections that I am frightened to let myself know about. One snapshot is of running through the rain, my feet off the ground like a fairground swing-boat, my

1

hands in the hands of two adults either side of me, whom I know to be my parents. The theme, as always with me, is being cared for; wanted. In a kind of emergency. Unlike those of my later alcoholic life, rain was not an emergency of my own making.

The second recollection is sitting on my father's knee (I cannot, try as I may, see his face) and — on a whim — sucking his thumb. It was brown from tamping the end of his ever-burning cigarette; I can still taste the acrid, bitter, nicotine tang on my tongue. (Not exactly Proustian.) One psychologist helpfully explained the phallic significance to me, forty years later, in an attempt to link it with my alcoholism: oral fixation, suck it and see. I was not entirely persuaded.

The third snapshot, which I fear must surely be a wistful implant from later life, is watching a train carrying him, pulling steamily out of a station (think *Brief Encounter*) — my last sight of him, as he left for Blackpool and thence South Africa where he would die, horribly.

Working-class people have little dynastic sense of their individual forebears. When Alec Douglas-Home (the fourteenth earl) said, in response to the sansculottist sarcasms of his parliamentary opponent, 'I suppose my Right Honourable friend must be the fourteenth

Mr Wilson', he — the Tory patrician — could look back that far. He probably passed a dozen historical replicas of his vacuous, overbred physiognomy when he ascended the stairs every night to his four-poster.

My father, four generations back, must have been one of those clanspeople displaced in the early nineteenth century by the Countess of Sutherland (she too, doubtless, could count back a genealogical fourteen). They were evicted to make room for sheep. Perhaps that predecessor of mine had his roof burned over his head and his few cattle hamstrung to help him on his way to wherever (in his case, it would seem, the urban Lowlands). Half the Scots were pushed north by the Normans, half were pushed down by Irish immigrants (Highlanders, as they came to be called); they were squeezed from both sides by Picts, Norsemen and any number of Celtic tribes. If you go into any lowland Scottish pub on a Saturday night, you feel a collective, unfocused anger: the rage of the perpetually displaced. I always felt it came from a long way back; and I feel it myself — a kind of 'what am I doing here?'

'Here' for my grandparents' generation was the eastern, lowland, prosperous (by Scottish standards) seaboard. My father was, I believe, the son of a middle-management official

(Andrew Sutherland) in the Scottish Post Office, in the 1930s. I will never know or have the energy to follow this information up. Looking up Sutherlands in Register House is as thankless a task as looking up Patels in the Neasden phone directory.

My father was, I believe, brought up in Peebles — on Edinburgh's outskirts. He had at least one sister — Jean — whom I came cordially to hate when I was evacuated to (or, more exactly, dumped in) Scotland during the war. A sour woman, promiscuously unfaithful with the Polish airmen billeted around Edinburgh (to keep them, as Churchill frankly admitted, from violating English maidens and matrons), she strapped me and her other children, dosed us with vile medicines (the tonic 'Gregory powder', specifically) and sent us to school without underclothes, to save herself the less pleasant kind of laundry (which, in a Leith Walk tenement, could be a problem, I grant).

I had, during my childhood, a few relics of my father's existence. There was a tiny, tartan-cloth anthology of Burns's poems (not a poet I've ever much liked). He evidently did not trouble to take it to war with him. There was a Bible, presented by an aunt with pious inscription and instruction ('Be good'), as he took off on the best road a Scot ever sees.

4

There was the commemorative golf ball, between a silver (plated) tripod of clubs, with which — glorious day — he got a hole in one at St Andrews. There were some photographs, all dating from his London years. There was an autograph book with mottos, jokes and sketches, which suggested that he had a set of teenage friends as he grew up ('By Hook or by Crook, I'll be Last/First in this Book', etc). There was an Edinburgh Crystal water glass — the miraculously sole relic of a wedding gift set.

Jack was, by English working-class standards, prodigiously well educated. He 'matriculated', as I was repeatedly told at a time of life when the word meant no more to me than micturition or mastication (and considerably less than masturbation). This equates to American high school graduation, or the O-levels I took in the 1950s. His father was, I picked up somehow, very drunken in a patriarchal misanthropic way. His mother, my Scottish grandmother, I know nothing of. He (Jack, that is) must have loved her. But he left her without any great pang, it would seem.

Jack Sutherland was, family legend had it, eligible for even higher education than matriculation. The Democratic Intellect (in the form of university for the deservingly smart lower classes) was one of Scotland's proudest assets even if it was, by the early 1930s, a fast withering branch of the great Scottish Enlightenment. He was admitted to Edinburgh University. But his father refused to support his studies. It was also my mother's fate when she got a scholarship to Bluecoats School in Colchester, and her parents decided that blue coats (the uniform) were more than they were prepared to invest in the education of a mere girl.

Students at Edinburgh, traditionally, could get by on very little parental support. When I taught there in the 1960s (my father's rueful spirit always just round the corner, accusing me of having had it too easy), the university still had a day off in late winter for what it called Meal Monday. That was the long weekend when undergraduates would go home to the farm or croft, and get themselves a sack of oats to see them through the academic year. The holiday is now, I believe, abolished. Modern educationists would, I imagine, approve of a daily diet of nothing but rolled oats (salted, not sugared).

My Scottish grandfather, apparently, was disinclined to come through with the meal; or the dough. It may not have been entirely a case of MacScrooge or Uncle Ebenezer Shaw. In the terminally slumped 1930s, a 'job' was everything: something between oneself and the dole — the abyss. The jobless were everywhere in the shape of those flat-capped wrecks lounging on street corners, munching dried apple (it expanded in the stomach, giving a spurious sense of fullness), picking up fag-ends from gutters, or — if they had spirit — sewing razor blades into the peaks of their hats with which to do some violent crime. The middle classes realized that the lifeline was work: regular, salaried work. One did not waste time — and four years in higher education was just that: wasted time.

One of the few things I know about my father's Scottish years was that he was a champion amateur golfer. If Sutherland were not such a common name, I could presumably find him in the athletic records of his country. Golf, like university education, is a more democratic thing in Scotland. Even if you drive through the country today you will find funny little links perched on hillsides, or in meadows, in the west and north, nibbled by sheep who presumably have learned, if they wish to continue as sheep rather than mutton, one word of human speech: 'Fore!'

Of course sons who play golf (rather than misspending their youth in billiard halls) must have had a certain middle-class comfort level and status. I remember vaguely seeing my father's bag of clubs (it must have been a twenty-first birthday present, or possibly a prize). What went wrong? Why did he not slip easily into some safe desk job, with a convivial round at the local course at weekends and fifty years drifting towards the gold watch? Something could surely have been found in the GPO.

There was, I deduce, a row. Most likely (as was often hinted) it was about his not being allowed to go to university. Who knows, there may have been other things. He was a very handsome man and, by the standards of that malnourished time, physically imposing at 6 foot 2. There may have been a girl to whom injudicious promises (or more) had been made, some wild roistering. Or simply Oedipal rage and a desire to see the world before he died. Why my mother never met her parents-in-law is a mystery I shall never now solve. Whatever the reason, Jack took the Scotsman's best road and came down to London in 1934, where he was recruited into the Metropolitan Police, A-division. Thereafter, the images are clearer.

This was a period, following the public disorders and strikes of the 1920s and 30s, when policing was physical. Country bobbies may have been fat and laughable, or crazily incompetent like Will Hay (the distant ancestor of Inspector Clouseau). In the city they were urban muscle, Anglo-Saxon storm-troopers. Röhm would have loved my father as a physical specimen. He was a six-foot blond beast — strapping, athletic and literate. And devilish good-looking, in a 1930s, slicked-back way (Brylcreem or Silvikrin was the big issue before going out on a Friday night: the hair cream, of course, substituted for shampooing — fiendishly difficult in working-class houses with only kettles to heat water).

Jack - central and dominating

PC Jack Sutherland rowed, swam, golfed and boxed. And won. And he must have showered more than most — something that doubtless added to his manly attractiveness. One of the legends that came down was that he had gone three rounds with Maxie Baer, on the heavyweight champion of the world's showbiz tour of England. Baer was the last of the Jewish pugilist heroes — a line that began in the early nineteenth century with Daniel Mendoza. Even with his pulled punches, Baer beat the crap out of my father, who apparently nursed his bruises as badges of honour for days after. He had gone the distance.

Jack, like Baer, was a heavyweight (a term which then indicated a weight of some 12 stone, rather than the 17 stone of a man monster like Lennox Lewis). British boxing, at the period, was dominated by welter, light, bantam and feather weights (the poetry of pugilism): fighters chronically malnourished and rickety in childhood who trained on fish and chips and milk stout in between sporadic shadow-boxing and bag-work.

My mother was a featherweight: diminutive, 5 foot 2 standing on tiptoe. (That Essex dwarfishness, and wartime food shortages, cost me a couple of inches in height.) My father would, when angry with her, lift her bodily on to the bedroom chest of drawers to perch there as a kind of 'cutty stool' (that place of shame for women in the Scottish kirk).

I knew the punitive piece of furniture well. That bedroom suite (wardrobe, chest of drawers, three-mirrored vanity table) followed me through my childhood, as we flitted from house to flat to lodging rooms: it was green-stained walnut. And it was while gazing into its triangulated mirrors that, aged five as I calculate, I had my lonely Lacanian moment — the realization that I was I. That image of John Andrew Sutherland in front and to either side of me was a person and I was that person. Everyone, apparently, has this experience.

I would hazard that my father had more personal cultivation than many London constables of his time; sophistication, even. It was with him, for example, while they were 'courting', that my mother went to see Fats Waller at the Palladium, on his English tour in 1936. My mother would do Fats imitations ('one never know, do one?') throughout life, relishing what must have been one of the big moments of her maidenhood. Myself I always found Waller too much the white man's black man. Some versions of 'Ain't Misbehavin'' I like. Not his.

When on night duty, my father insisted on being woken up to hear the quarter of an hour of Caruso on the BBC (a Reithian interlude), played before the 9 a.m. news bulletin recounted Hitler's and Mussolini's latest outrages. Details like that make me think that he would have been an interesting man to know.

And to drink with. It was only later, and by deduction, that I picked up the fact of his addictive boozing. Family lore enshrined stories about a friendly cocktail waiter, living in the same apartment block, who could make — out of whatever kitchen materials happened to be in the larder — never-fail hangover recipes. They were often needed, apparently.

There was one legendary occasion on which my father appeared at the front door, slurred a greeting, and fell flat on his face; another on which he fell asleep and went round the Circle line three times. (Where was he going? We lived in Brixton at that point.) A Colchester relative recalled to me, decades later, my father crooning endlessly, as they walked through the streets, the hit of 1937: 'September in the Rain' ('The leaves of brown came tumbling down in September, that September in the rain'). It was a song which, sentimentally, I made myself love — particularly in the George Shearing version, where the piano and vibraphone combine in languid, melancholy harmony. Rain, brown leaves, early nightfall.

These stories of his drinking were not in any sense moralistic, but *nil nisi* legends of a larger than life man. Now deader than dead.

After their wedding, about which I know nothing (except, so my mother said, that the sun shone — 'happy the bride'), they lived in Brixton. I was born in a nursing home in Norwood, just up the hill. Of that fact my birth certificate informs me, together with my father's profession. I was something under eight pounds, and bouncingly healthy (although my mother smoked throughout her pregnancy: I never have; I like to think it's an intrauterine aversion).

At that period, pre-immigration (other than from places like Peebles and Colchester), Brixton was shabby genteel. It was the favourite boarding place of music hall people (there were even theatres there). It had the capital's first department store, Bon Marché (destroyed in the 1981 riots). It was connected via 'Electric Avenue' with Victoria by Southern Region's third-rail train service.

It was a good place for aspiring lower-middle-class people to live at that period. Among its amenities was Brockwell Park with its 'Lido' — one of the best open-air swimming pools in London. There is a photograph of me, between my parents, in one of the baking hot summers of the late 1930s.

Proud parents

My father's other favourite swimming place, Marshall Street, was a heated, soup-temperature, year-round pool in Soho. Brockwell Lido still kicks into intermittent life every summer. The Marshall Street baths are an empty 'listed' barn which Westminster Council is constantly promising to rehabilitate. I think about my father every time I pass the locked doors.

Oddly, when I moved to London in 1972, I bought a house in Herne Hill, just up the road from Brockwell Park. I recall walking down Railton Road ('the front line') after the race riots in 1981. Afro-Caribbeans, driven to orgasmic levels of violence by oppression and the contradictions within their own community (were they drug dealers or Pentecostalists?), had fought pitched battles with the police, burning and looting their way from pub to pub, torching those which had operated a colour bar.

That night in April 1981 represented the total destruction of the genteel Brixton of my birthplace: and, at the same time, a total demonization ('Scarmanization') of the police, whose uniform my father had worn four decades before. How would he have reacted, I wondered? Head bashing in rage, or head shaking in appalled amazement?

Muddy Roots

How my father met my mother, I don't know and never will. She burned all her letters from him on her second marriage. She too was a runaway. She had been brought up, the youngest girl of four children, in Colchester: once a market town, increasingly a character-less London dormitory. There were three girls, named horticulturally: Daisy, Ivy and Violet Maud (my mother).

My mother loathed the name her parents had lumbered her with (whenever Webster Booth appeared on *Family Favourites*, singing 'Come into the Garden, Maud', she would snap the radio off with an ironic snarl). When she was her own woman, she renamed herself Elizabeth. In childhood she was called 'Lol' — I suspect from her laziness and lolling about. In later life, it was 'Liz'. It was a metamorphosis as much as a rechristening.

The youngest child, Arthur, preposterously renamed himself 'Aubrey' — after 'Sir C. Aubrey Smith', presumably, the absurd English aristocrat and cricketer actor satirized in Waugh's *The Loved One*. Arthur had evidently been entranced by Smith's upstanding performance

16

in *The Lives of a Bengal Lancer*. The new name was promptly travestied by those in his family as 'the boy Arb'. The epithet and name need to be pronounced, bellowingly, in that ugliest of accents, the 'Essex', to appreciate the full horror. 'Essex' was (it has almost disappeared nowadays) the accentual equivalent of mud ('whire yer goin, buoy? Op tahn!'). I have spent a lifetime trying to bleach it out of my own speech.

My mother was brought up in 18 Maidenburgh Street: then a slum, now a listed area, Colchester's so-called 'Dutch Quarter' (misnamed for the Huguenots who fled to the town after the St Bartholomew Night's Massacre). Number 18 is only a few yards from the still standing Roman Wall, and other relics of Constantine's imperial heyday (one of Camolodunum's higher moments — some three centuries after another and prouder moment in modern Colcestrian memory, when the protofeminist Boadicea laid the place waste). My genealogical archaeology is a thin, unimportant layer on some of the richest archaeological cake in Britain. Until the 1890s, the estate which is now Colchester's Castle Park, alongside Maidenburgh Street, was privately owned by the Cowdray family.

All this primeval history lay very lightly on

my grandparents' home. They bobbed through their lives with total incuriosity about the tides which had brought them there. My grandfather was illegitimate. He may well have been half Jewish (as was sometimes whispered), or half anything. And, obscurely, he was, by the standards of his class, well off — or at least propertied. Oddly, however, he never let the fact be known. He may even have forgotten it himself.

At his death in 1957, I opened various trunks which contained sovereigns, ancient banknotes (no longer legal tender) and the title deeds to two houses in Aldershot. There were also dandy trousers and waistcoats from his bachelor days. They were too narrow in the waist and too long in the leg for me ('snakehips', my grandmother muttered bitterly). There was doubtless a fob watch somewhere — perhaps pawned during hard times in the thirties when my grandmother kept bread on the table by cleaning the town hall steps and the local electrical showrooms every morning, at crack of dawn.

Kenneth Salter was, by apprenticeship and trade, a 'presser'. With that strange pride that working people have in their skills, one of the few facts that was handed down about him was that men-about-town, particular about their dress, would come to him, out of hours, to have their clothes 'done', while they waited in their underwear in the corridor of whatever small house he was currently living in. His creases were famous, or so one was told. It was work which was increasingly unwanted in the 1920s and 30s, and he took to labouring. His kitchen retained over a dozen flat irons of different weight, size and shape — as intricate as the tools in a surgeon's instrument bag.

Self and Grandmother, 1940

His wife, Daisy, was a beauty (briefly,

between girl- and mother-hood), from a large family the other side of Colchester. In their early days he drank. Her brothers, I have been told, would beat him up to keep him from beating her — family counselling, Edwardian-style.

On the evidence of the tarred rods and other angling equipment in his shed at the time of his death he was passionate about fishing. His small garden was a wasteland of chrysanthemums which had run wild: he must have been a keen if somewhat single-minded gardener as well.

In that garden, between the back door and the outside lav, was a mound where tea leaves, wet and warm from the pot, would be deposited. It was not a midden, but a game preserve. If you put a stick into the sodden mass, and turned it round and round so as to create small subterranean vibrations, scores of worms (fearing moles in their eyeless stupidity) would writhe out of the ground — tannin addicts all of them, and destined for the fish hook through their leathery skins, and, while still wriggling, the cold jaws of the snatching perch or cunning eel (which would sometimes swallow the bait so voraciously that the luckless worm could be extracted to wiggle on). I firmly hope God is not a worm. OK, if He's a pheasant — I never hurt one of those.

The house in Maidenburgh Street was disorderly and packed to bursting. Beds, baths and washing water were shared. There was no privacy, and toothpaste (the adults did not bother) was a dab of soot taken from the chimney (it is very clean and scours dental enamel very efficiently — I tried it myself, as an experiment, in later life).

There were six people crammed into some 500 square feet. The physical closeness explained the omnipresent terror of TB, 'drinking diabetes' and many varieties of typhoid: diseases about which there were ignorant misapprehensions — as about new handkerchieves, which had to be boiled to protect against nasal cancer, and Craven A cigarettes which were thought to be a sovereign remedy for sore throats. (The brand also offered coupons and loyalty rewards: there were legendary puffers who, at the expense of their lungs — did they but know it — got themselves wind-up gramophones.)

Maidenburgh Street had gas light down-stairs, a coal fire and a cooking range. A stockpot would be simmering on it through-out the week. So too, at various points during the day, would be various flat irons. The grate allowed access for toasting forks and grilling.

Bed mattresses were horribly stained. The horror of them pursued my mother through

Maidenburgh Street: late nineteenth century and mid-twentieth century

life. She was nicknamed in childhood 'Lady Jane' for her finicky refusal to sleep on urinated-on sheets, even when bone dry. The lavatory was outside, in the garden. That was by far the most rational place for it to be, especially in summer. Even in my youth my grandparents still cut up newspapers for toilet use. Chamber pots ('gesunders') were routinely used, privately by the adults, publicly by the children, and, assuming it was just number ones, emptied in the garden (pity the worms).

On Monday, clothes were washed in the copper; the copper stick also served, like Dad's belt (when he came home), for maternal discipline. It was a strangely ossified, anaemically pale wand, blanched by years of scalding water and bleach — something which, doubtless, added to its punitive mystique. The copper would also supply water for the zinc bath, in which the weekly wash would be taken. There was a hierarchy of use; it took hours to heat a full copper. The kitchen was dominated by a huge carriage-springed mangle — a wedding gift, or dowry, brought by my grandmother to the marriage. The mangle was still around in the 1950s, but never used. A new, smaller generation, with rubber rollers and less arm-wrenching cogs, had become available.

When I knew them, the fires had burned out from my grandparents, leaving them withered time-servers, relics of themselves. They must have had some culture, but God knows what it could have been. Inside the house, there was little life of the mind evident. They had no radio until the early 1930s, when they got one of the round, Bakelite wirelesses for the people, powered initially by a large, wet-cell battery. It too was still going strong (from the mains) in the 1950s. Their favourite Radio Luxembourg station was marked on the dial with indelible pencil (otherwise used to mark washing when it went to the laundry).

The Salter children, in the 1920s, had cat's-whisker sets, on which they listened to the Ovaltineys' faint warbling. But their culture was still mainly one of the streets with, for the girls, incredibly complicated skipping, ball and hopscotch games. For the boys there were marbles, cigarette-card flicking and the long wait till fourteen and manhood.

There were few newspapers other than the halfpenny evening paper. 'What do the placards say?' was a regular question asked of those who had been 'up town' — a relic of the times when even the copper required for the *Evening News* was too much.

My grandmother (about whom I shall say

more) was small and unusually (even for a girl of that period) dexterous with her needle. What looks she had were long worn out when I knew her although a certain daintiness survived in her hands. One of the more interesting periods of her married life must have been the First World War when she was left a khaki widow (with the quite likely prospect of black widowhood to come). It was during this war that my uncle Arthur was conceived. He died in 2005, warehoused for death in an NHS hospital the size of a Butlin's Holiday Camp, having believed through life that he was illegitimate. He may well have been; wars loosen morals. He was beaten constantly by his father, being a boy, red-headed and headstrong with it. No maternal uncles came to protect him from the strap. At the same time, the youngest child, he was mollycoddled by the women.

My grandfather returned from the war blinded in his left eye. It stared at one unblinkingly, like a split eggshell. It was the result of friendly fire, apparently (he never talked about it). Some comrade had thrown a snowball containing a sharp-edged stone — or, I later suspected, it had been a scuffle of some kind he was not proud of. He brought back with him shell casings and other ornamental weapons of war for the mantelpiece. My grandmother would

brasso them once a week, on Friday afternoons.

The injury to his eye did not get him
invalided out, but he may have been
withdrawn from the front lines. There was a
picture in their house, later on, of a group of
old sweats with rifles, which suggested he had
seen active service. Doubtless there were
meaningless medals. Once a year, during the
appropriate week, he took out a cloth poppy
from the drawer where he kept it. By the time
of his death, half a century on from the
carnage in Flanders Fields, it had faded
almost to grey. At the time, it seemed to me
comically penny-pinching; now I tend to feel
that he had earned the right not to cough up
the annual shilling.

Among his trophy souvenirs he doubtless
had memories of a vague, slaughterous
hellishness and a quarrel between great
powers which meant as little to him as Ohm's
Law. At one point, for a couple of years
(during my own juvenile fishing mania) I was
fairly close to him. But I never heard him talk
of the Great War.

My eldest aunt, Daisy, I never knew. Decades
later I discovered that she had got herself
pregnant and been shipped off to Australia:
transported, like a Victorian fallen woman.
The whole thing was hushed over. There was

still a male surplus among the Australian population. She married and had a normal life down there. There was the occasional Christmas card. Somewhere, too, there must have been a bastard cousin of mine.

Ivy, terrified by the domestic violence she had seen in childhood between her parents, cowered her way through life. She had red hair, which ran in the family (my beard would be red, did I grow it, and it still have any tint but grey), and a terrible, introverted temper. She was one of those people who, as the critic Terry Eagleton puts it, would want written on their gravestone, 'I never caused any trouble'. She had a horror of conflict, some of which rubbed off on me during the years when it was her turn to take care of the superfluous child.

She smoked, despite a chronically weak chest, and died, still hacking, of pleurisy (the same thing which, I suspect, will kill me). 'Coughing ['corfin'] well,' she would say complacently, after some racking fit. Her conversation was limited to days drawing in or out, what was on the 'placards', what was in the evening papers and — mysteriously — 'rabbits, rabbits, rabbits!' on the first of every month.

My mother, 'Lol', was, by contrast, blonde and spirited. Coming third, she may well have been somewhat overlooked and given fewer chores (such as minding younger siblings like herself). One of the advantages of coming late in the family queue was that one was left alone. The principal disadvantage was hand-me-downs.

Lol was clever — as I have said, sufficiently so to be offered a scholarship. But the blue coats were deemed to cost too much, and she was a girl. Nor did the family want members who got above themselves. Colchester, even in later days, had an ingrained, feudal fear of social mobility. Rising in life brought danger. Safer to keep one's place and be respectable.

It was cruel on my mother to be denied even the couple of extra years' schooling which would have brought her to sixteen. Despite the Smilesian mythology, it is impossible by self-help to keep up with the trained packs of scholars in school. She left school at fourteen, in 1930.

It was a bad year to enter the labour market. The Wall Street crash had brought slump to Britain. My grandfather was unemployed. At one point, he was recruited to sweep leaves in the Castle Park behind his house for a farthing an hour (not for the money, but eligibility for the dole). The rent was paid by my grandmother's early morning cleaning. As a makework project for the unemployed, a bypass was built round the town, and I believe my grandfather laboured, unskilfully, on that.

'Service' was the only option for my mother. She induced my aunt Ivy to go with her to London. An agency had found them work, cleaning rooms in the student hostels of London University. 'I've seen both my girls at Bedford College,' I heard my grandmother boast in later life. She did not mention that her daughters were there to change the beds, empty the chamber pots, and sweep the students' rooms in their elite premises in Regent's Park. Liz and Ivy were crammed into some tiny dormer at the top of the building, or out-housed in a hostel, fiercely supervised by some dragon of a matron. Their role was to make life easier for those luckier women undergraduates.

Ivy soon returned to Colchester: the big world was not for her. She would look for a soldier husband in Colchester's garrison population. My mother, who always had more of the Dick Whittington in her than any of her family, stayed on to find her fortune.

★ ★ ★

How my mother met my father, I don't know. She was presumably still in service, mopping

29

and cleaning. Their meeting may have been at a Lyons Corner House, or some palais encounter. My mother had taught herself the intricacies of the Foxtrot and Quickstep long before. She (now 'Liz') had also, from watching movies, learned sophisticated styles of smoking. She had a brilliant way with cigarettes, holding them elegantly in her varnished fingers, and pulling the smoke in sexily. She had taken the habit up at thirteen. Sixty years later (combined with the chronically imperfect Salter chest) it would kill her. Emphysema, bronchitis, late-onset asthma.

Once they were in their relationship, my father took Liz in hand. He enrolled her in the Polytechnic, gave her books to read. It was he who encouraged her to spend what little she had managed to save on a Pitman course. Shorthand typist was a huge step up from chambermaid.

Liz was quick-witted, fast-fingered, an apt student and — with her blonde (strenuously peroxided) hair — petite and beautiful. Like other girls in the 1930s, she took her style — and hoped-for glamour — from the movies. The Veronica Lake frontal wave eventually came to be her preference. As would I in later life, she purged her accent of its Essex taint, retaining it only for comic effect (and for satirical comment on the lumpen-Colcestrians).

My parents must have married in early 1937. There was a miscarriage before me — or possibly after, I never got the event straight. They set up home in Brixton, perhaps through a police housing scheme (although A-Division were headquartered in the West End). They were to have three years of marriage. Had they had more, I was always told (to my only-child horror), they would have had a large family. That was what my father wanted: a clan.

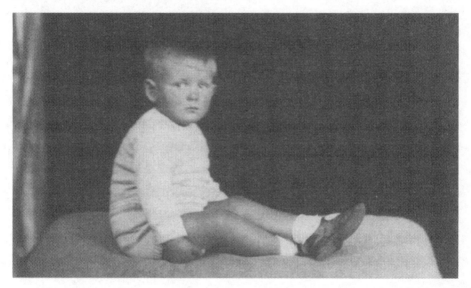

Glum and one

I was the firstborn (or first to survive) — John Andrew: the bearer of a paternal, grandpaternal and Scottish name. It was intended, I suspect, that I would golf for my country. Or the other country. Or whatever.

I began life on 9 October 1938. The date — it would haunt me ever after — is awkwardly pre-war. It coincided not with the first of the bombs — which would have been historically grand — but the last of the bananas. Mashed, the fruit was the first solid food I ate, so my mother later told me. I would not eat another for six years.

Half Orphan

Of the death of my father I know little, other than that it happened in 1942, far away from Brixton. He did not have to join up. In 1940, after Dunkirk, there were more men in uniform than battles for them to fight or equipment to fight with.

My father, I was told by a relative who happened to be with him, had been walking through Hyde Park, past Speakers' Corner, when one of the soap-box windbags — clearly thinking it was 1917 when white feathers were fluttering everywhere — stopped his harangue to inquire pointedly why a strapping young fellow like my father (towering over the other listeners) wasn't in uniform when civilization was in peril. I hope that speaker, whoever he was, has been blown for eternity to windbag hell.

The police uniform he wore while working certified that Jack was in a reserved occupation and, aged twenty-nine or thirty, he was in a late call-up group anyway. But the accusation stung. The Scots, ever since 1745, had a tradition of fighting for the English monarch as enthusiastically as for their native chiefs. Given his educational background he was able to volunteer for the Royal Air Force and qualify for cadet pilot training immediately after his basic training. (This must have taken place in or around Blackpool, judging by my parting memory.)

Jack in South Africa,
a few days before his death

It was a gallant thing to do, but foolish. No Salter would have done it. He was posted, after passing out from square bashing, to South Africa, where the RAF did much of its training in the open spaces. For a few months he must have had a good life. White South Africans were fiercely patriotic and hospitable. The finest picture I have of him dates from that period.

He was, as I gathered from his letters to my mother (which I furtively read one afternoon, before she burned them), a good trainee, one of the stars of his intake. But it was wartime, when the authorities permit a five per cent casualty rate in training (more than currently die in action among British armed forces in Afghanistan). Training fatalities are necessary to bring men to the necessary pitch of military efficiency, but to die with white chevrons still on your lapels is an inglorious exit. There are no medals, and a hugger-mugger tribunal of inquiry at which blame may attach to some wretched miscarriage of efficiency.

I like to think he was piloting a Wellington, a firetrap made of wood, designed by Barnes Wallis (he of the bouncing bomb). I would hate to think that he might have been training on the less glamorous Anson. The long and short of it (as my mother learned) was navigational error, cloud, a mountain and a fiery, horrifically painful, death. His charred remains were only identified by a bridge in his teeth (boxing had rearranged his jaw rather drastically). What they could scrape together was buried, with the other five per cent, in South Africa.

I remember nothing of the actual telegram ('the War Department regrets to inform you'); nor did my mother keep it (she was always good at moving on — or away). She was in London at the time. The only story she told of that period is that she was visited by her father who, as he went, left a shilling on the mantelpiece. She was so enraged she threw it after him. She would resolutely refuse to be devastated.

My mother returned to Colchester, where her family could provide child-minding. There was lots of property available, and she took a large ramshackle flat over a shoe shop, Lennards, in Long Wyre Street opposite what was grandly called The Arcade. Anything less like Walter Benjamin's image of the ideal shopping parade than that shabby row of retail outlets is hard to imagine.

The girls in the shoe shop were kind, allowed me to play with the X-ray machine, through whose green glow I would examine that fifty per cent of the human body's bone structure that exists below the ankle. I am amazed I have a single spermatozoon left. Some new shoes every now and again would have been useful, but those I did not get. My

WPC Sutherland, diminutive

Liz's favourite studio photograph of herself

plates are today as disfigured by outgrown footwear as those of any Chinese princess. Cobbling was always a better deal than new shoes.

Despite being a five-foot-nothing woman, Liz found work as a wartime police constable. It was pure Rosie the Riveter. She would bring home truncheons and handcuffs. She could fill in forms, thanks to quick wits and 120wpm, more efficiently than any of her superannuated, or spavined, male colleagues (all the able-bodied were by now enlisted). The station was just at the other end of the Arcade. There was convivial after-hours drinking at the Cross Keys, just downstairs alongside Lennards. (If she were worried, which she never was, she could nip back up and make sure I was all right.)

And, of course, there were the Americans.

Yankville

The town of Colchester has, over the millennia, absorbed many invaders — with as little ruffling of its surface as Grimpen Mire. But the important invasion, as far as my childhood was concerned, did not happen on that 'longest day', 6 June 1944. It happened in early 1942 when our American allies (since Pearl Harbor bounced them, reluctantly, into the war) began streaming from their transatlantic troop carriers into hastily thrown up bases on the flatlands of East Anglia.

God knows what all those bleak fields, pinched towns, ill-fed and worse-clothed natives looked like to them. But for me, Hollywood had come to Colchester at last. It was as if the Regal's walls, in Crouch Street, had turned crystalline, and the picture palace projectors played, like Ack-Ack searchlights, over the whole township, bathing it in glorious Technicolor, from East to North Hill, the High Woods to the banks of the watery Hythe.

The Eighth Air Force ('The Mighty Eighth') would be the biggest thrill for Colcestrian womanhood since the Roman legions marched in. The nearest USAF base in Colchester was Boxted — walking distance from town. Not that any airman ever walked: fleets of 'passion wagons' ferried them to and from the High Street or — at weekends — to London.

Prudent locals, unless they had access to 'red' petrol, had put their cars up on blocks for the duration. It was bikes or Shanks's pony till victory — or, should the worst happen, never. Colchester's taxis, clapped out Wolseley bangers, did a roaring trade and declined to stop for natives for whom the word 'tip' primarily denoted the municipal rubbish heap. There was the added nervousness, on the cabbies' part, that they were routinely robbed if they were foolish enough to pick up British soldiery after closing time.

For a culture addicted to the flicks it was the big rock candy mountain. The Yanks were classy. They spoke like Americans — unembarrassingly so, unlike the wannabe homegrown youth, with their Alan Ladd quiffs, Bogartian shoulder pads and feeble attempts at Errol Flynn moustaches; they could 'play it real', as rappers say. They were magnificently nourished. And they had access to branded liquor (something only available to the home population 'under the counter'), cigarettes, and generous overseas allowances with which to buy good things (not least women — some of them bad things).

They were husky and (for a while, at least, before the watery Essex sun bleached their skin to local pallor) tanned and well washed. Tanned but not tawny: Negroes were generally restricted to service activity, and to base — the dangers of 'buck n-words' (no bowdlerization then) consorting with Essex maidens didn't bear thinking about. The maidens, however — given the opportunity — were more adventurous than their guardians. There was at least one girl on my grandmother's street who bore a black ('as the ace of spades!') baby; and was enshrined in local legend for a generation. The baby itself was quickly disposed of and doubtless grew up in some godforsaken Barnardo's.

Children quickly learned the cute phrase, 'Got any gum, chum?' With luck, the Americans would dispense not just strips of Wrigley's Spearmint, but Hershey bars, Babe Ruths and loose coins. They were good-natured and shrewdly calculated that the way to a population's heart was kindness to its children.

A shorter way, where women were concerned, was fully fashioned stockings — garments that reached organs more interesting to men at war than hearts. 'Rayon' and 'utility' underwear was a constant humiliation. Any supplier of luxury intimate garments (spivs, failing others) had an inside track. Hence the ubiquitous joke about English women's knickers, 'One yank and they're off.'

Americans, as I observed with a child's moral neutrality, found the wives of West Street and Wellington Street (my grandmother's patch) much to their taste. One of my West Street pals found himself with a new family member he was instructed to call 'Daddy Tex'. The supply of candy ended promptly, when Matthew's un-Texan dad — alerted by some nosy neighbour (not impossibly my grandmother) — got 'compassionate' leave to come home and sort out his domestic problems: uncompassionately, one gathered. We regretted the sweets; no neutrality about them.

Such marital discipline could be brutal. Along the road, in Wellington Street, lived the Paxons. I was friendly for a year or two with the son of the house, Brian, immediately after the war. His mother was a slow-witted cow-like woman, with a snarlingly nasty husband whom the children avoided. I hung out with Brian, for no particular reason other than that he was there.

The family history was known around the streets, and muttered about for years after.

While fighting in Italy, Paxon Sr was informed, by the usual poison-penmanship (or womanship), that his wife had moved a Yank in. His American cuckolder had wisely decamped by the time he stormed back to beat his wife into pulp, and kick her downstairs. As my grandmother said, with grim relish, 'he thought he was still fighting them Eyeties'. She was manifestly brain-damaged, but effectively Stepfordized — a virtuous wife for a hero to return to after he'd done slaughtering Italians.

Widows like my mother had nothing to fear. There was no compassionate leave from wherever Jack was now stationed.

★ ★ ★

Whatever the occasional violence, the Americans' arrival filled a vacuum, as British forces fought overseas or were confined to faraway camps and barracks — their genitals tamed, khaki paranoia was convinced, by secretive doses of potassium in their tea. When they got back on a weekend pass, clumpily booted, in ill-fitting, unpressed battledress, tieless (only officers enjoyed that luxury), shapeless berets, gasmask boxes bouncing on their scrawny haunches, their appearance and accoutrements only served the more to glamorize their

43

American rivals, who looked as if they'd just walked off the movie screen. The War Cabinet might call them allies. For British other ranks, the Americans were another foe — along with the Germans, the Japs, the spivs, the trade union stewards, and the soft-faced men who got rich while others laid down their lives — for what? The right of profiteers to profit and Yanks to lay their wives. What a war!

In the 1944 film, *Waterloo Road*, diminutive John Mills, garbed as above, is shown coming back to find his wife being diddled by a burly spiv (Stewart Granger). Mills does battle to win her back. But anyone watching that film would be more impressed by Granger — soon to become Gainsborough's top matinée idol. The lounge-lizard, brothel-creeper-shod, brilliantined, smooth-talking, shoulder-padded Americanized spiv was the role model the watching male youth emulated in the privacy of their bedroom mirrors. Not Private Splod of the Latrine Corps.

At least the Americans fought — despite the consoling (and perennial) myth among the British armed services that their allies were cowards without massive firepower to support them in battle. The Mighty Eighth sustained fearful daylight bombing losses over Europe until the arrival, late in the war, of long-range escort fighters — the P51

Mustang. Boys like me were, before they had mastered polysyllables, accomplished spotters. I was particularly accomplished. No mystery why: somewhere, deep down, I was waiting for a Wellington to come winging back. One of my aircraft was missing.

For me — formative human putty that I was — the American invasion instilled an indelible sense that the greener grass would always be across the Atlantic. Green, though, is the wrong colour. In very early childhood, I was convinced (thanks to film noir) that the apples in America were smooth and black, rather than the wormy things I scrumped in late summer. Forbidden fruit really ought to be black.

I was also fascinated by spaghetti — what D. H. Lawrence would call spaghetti in the head, that is. There were lots of pasta comedy routines on the cinema screen. One from a Three Stooges short is still etched into my mind. I can see Curly sucking in a single strand elastically. It speeds up as it reaches his puckered mouth, then — snap, and ragu is splattered into Mo's irate eye. With British soldiers dying in Italy, pasta was off the patriotic menu, along with sauerkraut and bratwurst. Tinned spaghetti, when it arrived in the late 1940s, was a challenge. Some ingenious housewives clamped it between bread, and called the grotesque sandwich Mussolini's Revenge. It was also served on toast, like Welsh rabbit (the 'rare-bit' never survived translation into Essex). I love *echt* pasta now, and never eat it without a faint tang of 1940s relish.

Over the last quarter of a century, I have spent more than half my life in America — never, however, with the sense that it is home. The American Immigration people label me, with accurate paradox, a 'resident alien'. But it is, and always now will be for me, Jordan — the land of milk, honey, black apples and elasticated pasta, glimpsed from that Colcestrian Pisgah in the 1940s. I have always felt kinship with Irina (the Mo of the trio), at the end of *Three Sisters*, declaiming Moscow, Moscow, Moscow. For me, had I known the place, it would have been Pasadena, Pasadena, Pasadena ('where', as the song puts it, 'the grass is greener'). Unlike her (or Moses, or most of my Yank-struck generation), I finally got there.

I am aware that my wholly uncritical emotions about America and Americans are a weakness — 'romantic' would be the kind word. Less kindly, it's a version of what Australians call the 'cringe' — voluntary subservience to an imperial power. But for me in my directionless 1940s, America supplied necessary bearings. And the idea of America set like concrete around my little, impoverished, Colchester world. It would be my life-lie.

★　★　★

It was as USAF residue that I came into possession of my first V-discs — 12-inch records, the performances donated free by American swing bands ('V' stood for 'Victory'). These included *Sing, Sing, Sing,* the virtuoso Goodman, Krupa, Harry James double-sided jam session. (That many of Goodman's hits were the arrangements of a barely credited black genius, Fletcher Henderson, rather than the Jewish clarinettist, I did not discover until decades later.)

Even luckier was my mother, who heard Glenn Miller's airforce band playing Boxted, as she did other swing and entertainment stars — Bob Hope, the Andrews Sisters ('Don't sit under the apple tree', etc). I was never taken along to these events: indeed, I suspect that my existence was unknown by whoever enjoyed her company. Not for me any 'Daddy Tex'.

There were, none the less, rich crumbs from the American table. The Long Wyre Street flat was littered with ASEs — American

47

Service Editions. My mother was still on her self-improving trajectory and received them gratefully. The ASE volumes were paperbacks in landscape format, designed to slip into a combat-trouser side pocket. Nathaniel Hawthorne in the foxhole, along with US-issue Zippo lighters which my mother now always used to light her cigarettes.

I ploughed through as much of the ASE *Moby Dick* as I could master (waiting with growing impatience for the whale depicted on the cover), Saroyan and Hemingway. Saroyan (an Armenian-American writer now virtually forgotten) worked well for me; for my mother as well.

As a policewoman, PC Sutherland liaised with American officers to control overt prostitution and, more sensitively, prevent under-age, or otherwise vulnerable, 'good-time girls' from being carried off to the base, or plied with too good a time at the semi-legal houses and flats (with dubiously acquired 'hotel' licences and convenient bedrooms) which catered to the Americans and that much-resented minority of native Colcestrians with ill-gotten money to burn. Identity card raids were common. Often after the inspection, my mother told me, it would be drinks all round. It was a morally relaxed time.

Under-age girls — any age girls — were only too willing to escape the quotidian drabness of their lives. They would happily pile into any passion wagon on its way back to Boxted, booze, Benny Goodman, and whatever good times came after by way of repayment.

It was galling to British manhood, particularly those in uniform, that their girls didn't put up a better fight in these bad times for their men. Anthony Burgess, in his memoir *Little Wilson and Big God*, scornfully describes one young scrubber shrieking to another scrubber across the street, in the northern garrison town where he was stationed, 'I'm off to get shagged by the Yanks. See ya later.'

Burgess was embittered against Americans even more than most British servicemen by an assault on his wife Lynne, by GI deserters in London. She never recovered and later drank herself to death. It was rarely that brutal, I suspect, in Colchester. The snowdrops and redcaps, along with my mother's bluebottles, kept order. Not that the Americans always behaved like Galahads. Whenever one impregnated a girl, he was given the option of posting to a remote station, where — wartime regulations being what they were — he could rarely be tracked down. Many girls were left with only one option — the Good Shepherd Hostel on East Hill, where no girl with her belly of shame would be turned away.

I have a distant relative my age whose father, dying of cancer forty years later, wrote to her from somewhere in America, begging forgiveness for having abandoned her, unborn. She indignantly refused the offered conscience money. Her mother, bravely, had 'kept' her, but it meant foregoing any hope of marriage thereafter. What self-respecting man would take on such iniquitously used goods? My mother always kept a portrait photograph of my father in her bedroom, to establish her widow's credentials. Neglected I might be; bastard never.

When I got up in the morning, I would find Lucky Strike or Chesterfield butts in the ashtrays — lipstick crescents on half of them. I remember once being woken up late at night, dozily, to meet an American called 'Russell'. He had spectacles, a mild quizzical expression and a senior officer's dress uniform. Major Milquetoast. I bless Russell, and remember him specifically, because he left books (signed 'R. Maxwell') behind him after his visits. Among others was the delightful Max Shulman satire on war, *The Feather Merchants* — a book which holds its place as one of the funniest I've ever read.

Of course she slept with these night visitors. I would bet my life Russell went back to Boxted next morning tired but happy. I suspect too that I was dragged from my sleep because he too had a young child back in America and it suited the two of them to be sentimental about it before getting sentimental about each other. Did I, in some recess of my juvenile mind, know the life my mother was living? I must surely, during some night terrors or warning siren, have blundered, bleary eyed, into her bedroom. If so, my mind has done her work for her: any flagrante delicto memory of whatever looseness she allowed herself is erased. There was always plenty of circumstantial evidence.

There is a line in *Kipps* which has always recalled my mother to me. One of H. G. Wells's counter jumpers says to another: 'We're all in a blessed drainpipe, and we've got to crawl along it till we die.' My mother was never going to be that kind of Kippsian rat. Not for her the Colcestrian drainpipe leading, downhill all the way, to the Mersea Road cemetery.

I remember her taking me to a post-war 'fair' run by the garrison on the Abbey Fields — their in-town training area. For them it was public relations, bridge-building. For me it was 'what larks!' For my mother it was a chore. In one of the khaki marquees there was a display of a very early wire voice recorder. 'Can you sing?' asked the RASC man with the microphone, roguishly. He had been taken by my mother's Lana Turnerish looks. 'If I could sing', she returned, with a dry throaty irony I always loved, and a scornful look at the Colcestrians milling around us, 'do you think I'd be here?'

At the time, I didn't understand what my mother was doing — or, most hurtfully, the minimal part I seemed to be playing in her life. Now I can admire her pluck. But part of me has always resented it as unmaternally selfish. Like other first-borns, I tend towards the fable of the mother pelican who tears her breast to suckle her young — with her life's blood, if needs be. That's maternal. Filial is to drink up, grow strong, and remember the flowers on Mother's Day.

Liz's philosophy was that of the resourceful survivor — sod pelicans! I've seen it occasionally (and always memorably) in other widows, who have decided that merry has it over suttee every time. Not for my mother widow's weeds, or surrender to the first man back from winning a war who proposed, only to sentence her to life in the kitchen. Or so she told me in later life, and vehemently, when I ventured to complain about our rackety home life, and how other children of my acquaintance actually had a home life. Where were my ginger nuts and milk on the kitchen table when I came home from school? That iconic image had struck me as summing up all that was missing in my upbringing.

My mother did not just want to live; anyone could do that. She wanted a life. Widowhood was freedom — and, more importantly, if she played her cards right, the chance to 'make something' of herself. She would not have shot down that Wellington herself. She wished it hadn't fallen out of the sky. She grieved for Jack. But freed from the burden of wifedom and motherhood (more than the once, that is) she would accept the gift. And use it.

John, of course, was an inconvenience — baggage to be stowed, kindly but firmly. If I wanted ginger nuts and milk she would give me five bob or whatever to buy them. That too was a kind of liberation.

Wartime Motherhood

Unlike the riff-raff she monitored in her capacity as policewoman/social worker, my mother was careful with her body. Contraception was universally available in wartime: doubtless whole factories went into overtime production to keep the nation's warriors, if not morally pure, then at least disease free and 100 per cent fit to die for home and country.

I would find condoms, still packeted and easily mistaken for American gum, in the street and at school share them round as balloons — which, like other mythological pre-war goodies (bananas, whatever they might taste like), were 'off' for the duration. And perhaps for ever. My mother I discovered, on one of my rummages through the Long Wyre Street cupboards, had among other intimate paraphernalia (the enema I recognized, alas, from personal experience) a large object that only decades later would I identify as a diaphragm. Doubtless many would-be siblings had beaten their tadpole heads against its impermeable wall. Good thing too.

The aircraft based at Boxted were Liberators. The name was, in point of aeronautical fact, better than the aircraft deserved: lumbering, underpowered vessels, far inferior to the svelte Flying Fortresses whose aluminium glistened silvery in the high sun. Their name as well, with its overtones of battlements, was equally ill-chosen: 'Flying Barracuda' would have been more appropriate for the high-finned, deadly B17.

One was sometimes aware of ('bloody!') Liberators all day. There was such a rash of nerves (understandable, given the horrific in-air casualty figures) that the American authorities instructed that any plane reporting, on take-off, 'engine malfunction — permission to land' would have to circle the area until its fuel tanks were depleted or two of the four engines visibly conked out (they could maintain safe altitude on three). In the process, the crew would be seen for the yellow-bellies they were. Those Liberators, circling like lazy wasps in September, remain in my mind more clearly than the first thousand-bomber raid, which I may have seen. I have what is probably another screen memory of the sky black with streaming aircraft (but didn't that armada fly at night?). It could have been an overlay from a Pathé news item. My mother took a jubilant, frankly bloodthirsty pleasure in seeing the bombers go out — sweet revenge, I suppose, for what the Germans had taken from her.

However inappropriate for the B24, 'Liberator' was an apt name for the planes' air and ground crews. The war and its shakeups were hugely liberating; their presence broke up the old class barriers, the inherited cages of Colchester life. Those who flew the coop most thoughtlessly — the 'GI Brides' — were destined, in many cases, to be sadly disappointed. Glamorously uniformed heroes faded in civilian wardrobe and workaday employment. Home on the prairie would turn out to be a dirt-road shack; the city apartment a couple of rooms in a coldwater tenement looking out on an airshaft. America was not Hollywood (nor, as thousands of hopefuls would find who arrived at the downtown Greyhound depot, was Hollywood Hollywood).

I remember the amazed horror with which one GI Bride wrote to her mother, living up the street from my grandmother, that the American family actually broke wind while eating dinner — *and laughed at it*. The news shot up and down the street as over-the-fence gossip. It was deglamorizing in the extreme. It was fifty years (in Mel Brooks's *Blazing Saddles*) before Hollywood would get round to fart jokes.

My mother had her American lovers, but not for her any waste of time in shellac or celluloid fantasies. Her Americans, in the flesh, were chosen wisely, discreetly and sparingly for what they could yield. Not money — she was no more a whore than she was a bobbysoxer or swooning film-fan: but for lessons in life. Class was what she wanted; and escape from the class into which she had been born.

Her final choice was not a north but a south American, 'Ham' Hamilton. He was, in civilian life, the editor of Argentina's leading English-language newspaper. 'Hamilton' (as she always called him — a 1930s affectation) was cultivated, smart and very rich. His family, Scottish and lairdly by origin, had blended with the Hispanic aristocracy and had huge ranch holdings in the pre-Perón pampas. He had a round face, round glasses, and a softish-looking body. He exuded privilege.

Ham treated me well, often reading me stories in bed. (He was particularly good on the many-voiced *Wind in the Willows*. I realize now, of course, he was keen to lull me to sleep so they could get on to the real business of the evening.) His civilized, slightly drawling voice was one I could usefully mimic. Oddly, he was curious about my vocabulary as well: I remember explaining to him at length, as he nodded, taking it in for future use, what an 'Aunt Sally' was. He rolled the phrase round his tongue. Cosmopolitan as he was, there were little pockets of foreignness in his personal culture.

On the outbreak of war he had volunteered and on arrival in his 'home' country he was commissioned with field rank and assigned to one of the intelligence units attached to the elite parachute forces. He was dropped into Arnhem in 1944, doubtless expected to report vividly from the front line on the military coup that Montgomery fondly believed would shorten the war by six months. He came back (one of the lucky ones) from that misconceived bloodbath deafened and traumatized. Two-inch mortars had done for his eardrums; the carnage had shocked him into perpetual tremulousness. Major Hamilton was an invalid in uniform when he and my mother got together.

His shell shock took strange forms. I remember one night they got hold of a chicken, roasted it, and feasted at Long Wyre Street. Charles Laughton's *The Private Life of Henry VIII* had been a popular film from the 1930s, and Hamilton amused the company by throwing the gnawed drumsticks over his shoulder, like the merry monarch in the movie. Suddenly he turned chalk white, and declared, in (genuine) panic, that he had gone blind. Chicken fat had splashed and congealed, opaquely, on to his specs. He honestly thought something awful had happened to his eyeballs. The man was a bag of nerves.

Ham (like me) was madly in love with my mother. That was borne out by later events and the fact that he could not take his eyes off her in company. She was not, I suspect, madly in love with him; but she clearly found him a superior bill of goods. She liked educated men of Scottish background, and he was a useful ladder on which to rise; and malleable. Rise she would: using her wits, her body, her native intelligence and the openings which the huge shake-up of war had fortuitously offered her.

Family Life

While my mother was on shift at the nearby police station (or more interestingly engaged) I was left alone a lot, or parked with my grandmother. My aunt Ivy — always, since their Bedford College days, less adventurous than her younger sister — worked her own, more drudging shifts making 'bushes' (something to do with tanks) on a construction line at the Britannia works off Priory Street. Priory Street was a strange little row of cramped houses by Vineyard Street, where in centuries gone by, during that medieval global warming, monks at St Botolph's Priory had grown grapes to get godfearingly sideways on. The Merry Monarch did for them what Hitler was currently doing to the Jews.

Ivy had done something much despised in a garrison town, something barely above walking the streets. She married a regular soldier. Bill Reilly, her husband, was a Scot from Lanarkshire, who had served years in the cavalry in India (at least a couple of them waiting for a place on one of the two troop carriers plying, inadequately, between 'home'

60

and the subcontinent). Like my father, he was an enthusiastic boxer: light-middleweight; nimble, with fast feet and hands. The amateur's vest (only professionals, I was solemnly instructed, fought bare-chested) was still, when I first knew him, faintly etched by the distant Indian sun on his torso as, on his arms, were blurry tattoos of his military unit, together with the words 'Mother' and 'Betty', his sister who had died young.

Chronic lack of other employment had led Bill to join the 17th/21st Lancers — an elite cavalry regiment, nicknamed the 'death or glory' boys from their death's-head cap badge, strikingly like that of the SS. For the first five years of his service, he was a soldier on horseback. Now, after a spell in England, he was in tanks — specifically the American Sherman. A petrol-fuelled firetrap (he would have five burn out under him), the Sherman overcame the German Panzer by sheer force of numbers: we had more tanks than they had shells. Bill saw action in Italy and was gallant. He had been mentioned in dispatches, earning oak leaves around his Italian campaign medals. He was, none the less, the dullest man in my family group. So much for heroes. Life ran over him without leaving any interesting mark whatsoever, as far as I could see. How he met my aunt, while kicking his heels in Colchester, I don't know. Neither of them danced, she didn't drink, he had no line in chat. A mystery.

After the war was won, by men like him, Bill (formerly known as WO2 Reilly, 17/21st) was left standing forlornly in his demob suit, looking for something to do with the forty years that remained; something worth tattooing on his impressively muscular arms. 'British Road Services', the nationalized firm he went to work for after the war, would have been absurd. He had killed for Churchill; now he was changing spark plugs for Attlee. He was grimly hopeful, during the Korean conflict, that World War Three would break out. He foresaw recall to the colours; bigger and better tanks. And some meaning to it all.

I remember his last medals arriving years after the war: there was a years'-long backlog. With 'for export only' the absolute priority in post-war Britain, there were more urgent things to do with strategic metals. When my father's belatedly arrived, my mother threw them away — a gesture which now seems to me as gallant as Siegfried Sassoon hurling his Military Cross into the Mersey in 1917.

Back in 1943, when Ivy married Bill, the army did not run to married quarters for other ranks; married allowance was a few shillings. My aunt, for a guinea a week, got a vast, run-down, two-storey flat in a seventeenth-century house at the bottom of East Street. It had barely been renovated in three hundred years (it since has, and would cost over a million). It was furnished with sticks picked up for a song at Reeman & Dansie, the auction house on East Hill, whose proprietor sat in on seances with my grandmother. There was a thriving spiritualist underworld in Colchester, as there had been during the Great War. So many dead voices out there once again, trying to get through.

The East Street flat had a bath with taps marked hot, but no supply of heated water. The bath had to be supplied from a copper in the kitchen, which took hours to boil, usually on Saturday evening. I remember a teacher coming into a classroom, one hot Friday in the summer term, and wrinkling his nose in disgust, murmuring 'bathday tomorrow'. My mother and I would go to East Street for my weekly dunk (she could use the station's facilities). Usage was strictly hierarchical, women and children last. Depending who was around, I came in second, or scummy third, the tepid, opaque water feebly boosted by an infusion from the electric kettle. In adult life I have always, for preference, showered. No scum.

Ivy got the East Street place in expectation

of children which she desperately wanted and would never have. 'Fibroids', she eventually discovered; like 'bushes', I never quite worked out what they were. I was left with her during, and increasingly after, the war. She had an ambivalent attitude to me, the unwanted child of a sister who was getting so much more out of life than her. She was dutifully attentive and sometimes emotionally violent, in a self-lacerating way.

But under her care I felt no more important than the dog — 'Rusty', a half red-setter she had got for company, and because its flame-coloured fur was the same tint as her hair. Every afternoon she would lay the beast down and hunt for fleas on its fur, cracking them between her fingernails; there would follow a dusting with Bob Martins and, every few weeks, a bath in sheep dip. (Rusty came after me.) The dog was sensible and put up with it all. And so did I, as Ivy savagely brushed the shoulders of my school coat and my hair (same brush) as I left for the morning bus. Once I had gone, she would hoover the flat's tatty carpets madly, listening to *Housewives' Choice*.

When my mother was busy, I would be parked on her or my grandmother. Sometimes I was sent, for a week or two, to relatives whom I barely knew. I was never (except in Scotland, by my father's sister) treated unkindly. But I was always on the edge: unbelonging. I could only get approved of by being 'good': next to invisible and wholly inaudible. Books were an obvious way to be 'good'. If, as it was said, I 'always had my nose in one' I could be up to no mischief. Or so it was thought. In fact, every syllable I read put another inch between me and them.

The continuous suppression of self, in the interest of being 'good', laid down explosive deposits. Drink would be the detonator. The 'seen and not heard' imperative left me, for life, absurdly dependent on the approval of others (reviewers, nowadays); and, at the same time, angry at those who had this undeserved power over me. It was a recipe for psychic strain at the time and eventually ('add alcohol and shake well') catastrophe. Mischief, like murder, will out.

As the war dragged on, I was trailed around according to the timetable of the hour. I was 'parked' (I hated that word) wherever convenient; sometimes forgotten for whole half days. Once, I recall, I was left in Long Wyre Street for a terrible thirty-six hours. The friend at the station my mother had charged to 'look in' never turned up — some emergency greater than a lonely child, presumably. Meters hardly ever ran out where I was parked.

I was, I repeat, rarely abused and never cruelly. There was no coal hole, no torment. And apart from the occasional cuff or slap from males (mainly teachers) who happened to be around, I was never physically assaulted — and only once sexually. My mother, when I was twelve, injudiciously allowed me to be taken off blackcurrant picking by a neighbour: during the lunch hour, eating our sandwiches in the cab of his van, he dived at my genitals. I let him do what he wanted; which was not impressive. A couple of years later he was arrested and sent to prison. I said nothing about it to anyone.

There was much more kindness than abuse (and much more benign neglect than either). I recall my mother in London spending six shillings she could ill afford (or was not keen on parting with) on a book for me at the Marylebone W.H. Smith's. I must have been around eleven at the time. It was *They Died with their Boots Clean* by Gerald Kersh. I was at the station to be sent off to some relative in Nottingham, and nagged her for the book. It was, as she would see it, a sacrifice — but I was being discarded. And, now I think of it, the subject of Kersh's docunovel — patriotic guardsman undergoing basic training and preparing to be posted abroad — had a certain significance. He was not otherwise a writer I was interested in.

There were random, but relatively frequent, acts and gestures of generosity and kindness of that sort. Pocket money was rarely stinted. Above all, there was that privilege denied most children at most times: adult company and the opportunity, as a quiet and omnipresent observer, to see into adults' private lives — often more perceptively than they did themselves.

And, to keep me from free fall, there were the decaying vestiges of at least two extended kinship groups (mysterious uncles and aunts in places as far flung as Nottingham) to be called on for short stays or crises. In Long Wyre Street I had a pile of *Life* magazines, ASE volumes and other reading matter. I could work the living-room wireless. There was a goldfish called Chloe (named for the Spike Jones and his City Slickers novelty number) in the bowl over the set — a focal point of the room.

I remember on one occasion Alvar Liddell's fruity tones announcing on the six o'clock news, 'Hitler is dead.' Just that. My mother scooped me up and danced round the room with me. She was not given to physical emotionalism (I cannot remember her crying) and her embraces were normally reserved for

67

others. Chloe took the news calmly, and was right to do so. Hitler wasn't dead. It was a premature press release from the von Stauffenberg plotters, many of whom would soon be dangling from piano wire.

Salterism

My uncle Arthur, the youngest of the four Salter children, was conscripted shortly after the declaration of war. He had been, in civilian life, a sales assistant in Sainsbury's. Behind the counter he would slice rashers of bacon and cut cheese into the required weight with the same kind of wire that did for the von Stauffenberg crew.

Arthur was one of H. G. Wells's little men (like my mother, he was five foot nothing). When I was an adolescent, and such conversations were in order between men of the world, he told me a good Sainsbury's joke, relished all those years ago over their breaktime tea and Woodbines. 'There's this Sainsbury employee goes to his doctor and says 'I can't help myself, I have to put my dick in the bacon slicer.' 'Good God!' says the doctor, 'fight it, my boy.' [The joke is subsequently padded out, for as long as time is available.] Finally he goes to the doctor and says — 'It's no good, I've done it. I've gone and stuck my dick in the bacon slicer.' 'What happened?' asks the appalled doctor. 'She got the sack as well' ' was the laconic punchline. Fall about.

Until he was assigned to whatever unit might need his skills with the bacon slicer, Private Salter was allowed to continue living at home on a billeting allowance. Camps were being hastily thrown up all over the country. My grandparents, at this period, had moved from the Maidenburgh Street warren to a small artisan's cottage in West Street, one of a terraced cluster near the town centre. It fronted the street, with only a doorstep (religiously scrubbed and red-leaded every day) between house and pavement. The doorstep was the only thing in the house which was often scrubbed: no passer-by could accuse 12 West Street of lacking sanitary decencies. Inside was somewhat different. There was no bath, not even of the primitive East Street variety. Most days it was the morning cat's lick, with bowl, kettleful of hot water and flannel. Like the towel, the flannel was a collective item.

When absolutely necessary, my grandparents and Arthur used the public bath-house in Culver Street. It occupied a steaming storey over the town's palatial public convenience whose tiled halls and ceramic Shanks's urinals, stretching as far as the eye could see, could have accommodated most of Colchester's male population simultaneously.

'Please Adjust Your Dress' instructed a large sign at the exit. Like the 'No Spitting' on the top, smoking, deck of the buses, it was a reassuring indication that Big Brother had things in hand. (There were lots of jests on that theme.)

West Street had an outside lavatory. For peeing, during the night, there were chamber pots (although the idea of 'bedchamber' was as inappropriate as 'warming pan' in that tiny house). I rather loved that 'lav', with its furry lagged pipes and strong, Harpic-and-human smells (particularly as it baked, under its creosoted planks, in summer). There was no liftable seat, cesspit disposal, no light, but enough gap at the top of the hasped wooden door to spend as long as one wanted reading the squares of the *Mirror* or *News of the World* which my grandmother would frugally cut up for toilet paper (the Sunday paper, with its coded 'intimacy then occurred' reports, could be particularly exciting — although it was a Dead Sea Scroll task to join the articles together). My uncle Arthur once saw me taking a sandwich along with me into the lav, and cuffed me ear-ringingly hard. No one ever washed their hands afterwards, or cuffed me for not doing that. It is, I suppose, the one authentically medieval experience of my childhood.

My grandfather had come down in the world. But he still had shoulders and a back. For all that came out of it, he might as well not have had a mouth. He and Arthur irritated each other mightily and reacted with seething silence in each other's company. The house was not large enough for two grown males — more so when the elder suspected the younger of being someone else's offspring. Kenneth, shaven headed and rusty suited, found employment clearing bomb rubble or carting away railings (the metal, allegedly, to be metamorphosed into Spitfires). He was, not to mince words, a heavy duty dustman. Later in life, I would picture him as Magwitch to my Pip — without the Great Expectations.

Arthur could have given lessons to Schweik. He whimpered uncontrollably at the blisters raised by the first few days' square bashing (my grandmother dutifully bathed and elastoplasted his suffering feet, cursing the army and their boots all the while). There was to be no death or glory for Arthur Salter; and as little square bashing as a wide-awake conscript could get away with. While billeted at West Street he showed me, with scorn, the vast and useless Webley pistol which he'd been issued. You could not, he said, hit the side of a barn with the thing, even if you were inside the barn at the time. (He was right. Despite all the Roy Rogers virtuosic gunplay I saw on screen, I came to the same rueful conclusion years later. The army was still, in 1959, using Webleys.)

After training, Arthur was assigned to a tank regiment. He later described his D-Day to me. Unlike Bill, and as unheroic in his soldiering as his brother-in-law was inarticulately heroic, he was a side-splittingly good raconteur. Once landed on French soil, he took cover under his tank for twenty-four hours, he recalled with self-mocking irony. It was, he confirmed, a very long day.

I remember asking him, in my plane-spotting days, if he'd ever seen an ME262, the years-ahead-of-its-time German jet fighter. Yes, he said, once. Or, at least he'd heard the terrifying whine of its twin BMW engines, and dived again for the trusty undercart of his Churchill. One of the few things about that two-ton mass of iron, with its puny two-pounder peashooters, was its protection against shrapnel and the dreaded Spandau machine gun — if you were underneath it. In battle, German panzers, with their massive 88mm cannon, could swat British armour like flies.

On another occasion, he described being instructed how to use the Boyes gun, the

British Army's infantry anti-tank weapon. Compared to the German Panzerfaust or the American bazooka, the weapon was useless: firing merely served to signal to the enemy, as its rounds bounced harmlessly off their vehicle, where to send a well-aimed high-explosive shell in return. With Falstaffian sarcasm, Arthur mimed the Sergeant Instructor airily explaining to the trainees that, like a Bren, the Boyes could, despite its hefty recoil, also be fired from the waist — and, in demonstrating this versatility, dislocating his hip, to be carried screaming from the range on a field stretcher.

Such events persuaded Arthur that discretion was the better part of tank battle. With the weaponry odds so stacked against Tommy Atkins, the command to charge into the valley of death was always wisely sidestepped. In his last years, as his brain softened, he would hint he had been in the SAS. It recalled George IV who honestly believed on his death bed that he had led the fray at Waterloo. Probably I shall die deluded that I personally pulled down the Berlin Wall, shouting 'Freiheit und Demokratie!' as I did so.

Lance Corporal Arthur Salter was, in fact, almost killed in the war, but — like his father (and mine) — ingloriously. In transit camp

74

one winter, one of his comrades idiotically threw a jerry can of scavenged petrol on the camp-house fire to generate some warmth. The explosion which ensued seared off all Arthur's skin and body hair (that on his head never regrew) and had him on the critical list for weeks. The pain of first-degree burns must have been appalling: he would in afterlife go pale when the coal fire exploded with some fragment of miner's detonator left in it (or so we liked to think, when it crackled or blazed up). His father lost an eyeball: Arthur lost his luxuriant head of flaming-red hair. Dulce et decorum est, be buggered.

After the war Arthur fiddled his way into the Control Commission — the provisional occupation administration for Germany. For a couple of years, he lived a life of luxury: skiing in winter, good food and wine, a staff car and a driver. He met an Englishwoman in Berlin, also in the Commission, who introduced him to good books and culture. She persuaded him to join the local Anglican communion and get himself confirmed. Like my mother, he picked up such things fast and used them intelligently.

He did not want to marry her (or anyone) and tried emigration to Australia when the Commission job wound down. It did not serve. Hard physical work (he tried mining in the outback) was not to his taste. And he was disgusted, he said, by the Australian habit of filling up their beer mugs from a bowser during the late afternoon 'swill hour' and drinking themselves into more than antipodean stupidity. Like my mother, he inherited enough of the Victorian evangelical distrust of alcohol not to be at risk from that temptation. A further generation down the line, I had no such inhibition: I would have been all in favour of bowser boozing.

Arthur followed the same path as my mother into self-improvement and social promotion. But it was done in a less dashing and ultimately rather dubious way — at least as I saw it. His mature years had an aroma of sell-out about them. After a wretched period on the dole, and a comically botched suicide attempt, he married the good woman who had taken an interest in him in Berlin, and handed over the conduct of his future career to her.

By native wit, and some hastily acquired certification, he became a schoolteacher, and a good one — good raconteurs invariably do, in my experience. He retired a deputy head in west London and concentrated on cultivating roses and consolidating his middle-class credentials. For a boy who left school at fourteen, sliced bacon for fifteen shillings a week until he was eighteen, and had never made even sergeant rank in seven years' army service, it was a commendable social climb.

But he was not to the manner born. The tuned ear could always pick up the false notes in his cultivated accent. His voice never

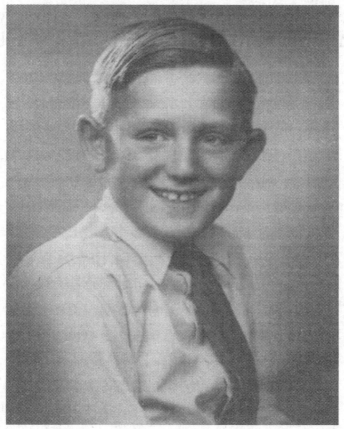

Aged 10 - note the teeth

modulated, or de-Essexized, itself as successfully as my mother's had done. (Or mine, I hope.) To my ear, he sounded a bit like Terry Thomas or Leslie Phillips (neither of whom belonged to the Hooray Henry class they made a career of mimicking). And the falseness carried with it a sense of kow-tow. Upper-class ears are as good as mine at detecting accents that do not ring true. Retaining saving shreds of authenticity while rising in the world of the British class system is fiendishly hard. The voice is always liable to betray you.

Cuts

Most children of my era had their tonsils and adenoids out. It was an era which had blind faith in prophylactic surgery. The lower orders it was felt, like a well-tended herbaceous border, could be slashed into health.

Tonsilectomy often involved high order deception. Henry Miller, in one of his *Tropics*, describes being taken off, as he thought, for a jaunt to a Brooklyn boatyard, only ('let's just drop in here for a minute') to be drugged on the way and wake up, less a considerable quantity of flesh, with the worst sore throat of his life, and a lifelong distrust of anything parents might henceforth say or promise. My own experience was roughly similar, if less traumatic. Or perhaps I had less New York spunk.

I particularly resented the spoonful of 'jam' (in fact some ghastly-tasting medicine) that was stuffed in my mouth before the mask was put over my terrified face. My back molars were also removed (another gas mask, more terror, no jam) in order to give the other twenty-eight teeth room to 'breathe'. The extraction left a gap between the front two gravestones wide enough to slip a half-crown through. It meant I would travel far in life, I was told consolingly. That did not help with the girls, and in adolescence I smiled as little as a Victorian patriarch.

I was circumcised at birth (like the royal family, one was again consolingly informed). I have never been sure whether foreskinlessness helped with the girls or not; there seem to be two schools of thought on the matter. What was left of my juvenile anatomy, all appendixes (excluding the one in my abdomen) surgically excised, was presumed to be immune by virtue of target removal — a kind of scorched earth policy.

But I was not, despite the prophylaxis, entirely healthy in early childhood. Few of my generation were, although I escaped the absolute horrors of diphtheria, scarlet fever and infantile paralysis. The last of these created regular summer panics in which, as the word spread, the municipal swimming pool would empty and cinemas would suddenly lose their Friday night queue. Poe's red masque had come to Colchester. Salk's vaccine ended all that.

My worst affliction was abscesses in the ear. I suspect it was the result of poor diet: although I took my cod liver oil and malt daily, it was chronically deficient in fresh fruit or vegetables. Concentrated orange juice, I seem to remember, was restricted to pregnant and nursing mothers — a lot of it, doubtless, dribbled illicitly into glasses of mother's ruin. Peroxide (always bottles of that around, my mother not being naturally as blonde as Hollywood dictated) was the home remedy prescribed for my agonizing head pains. A milk-jug full of the stuff would be heated and decanted down my ears. I can still hear the fizz as it gurgled down into some far chamber of my ENT system, hunting out and soothing the abscessed spot. Or so it was hoped.

My grandmother, given to still homelier remedies, fried a small onion and bound it into my afflicted ear ('Clark Gable' ears, at that jutting-out time of my life) with an old stocking. The warmth the oily vegetable pulsed down into my Eustachian tubes was presumed to be medicinal; it was probably as good as anything else available in that pre-antibiotic time. I lost the finer edges of my hearing in the process — either the abscesses or the peroxide were to blame. I exonerate the onion.

Otherwise, I was fairly healthy. Sweet rationing spared my teeth from premature decay, as did abrasive toothpowder. (We favoured a chalky brand, called Eucryl, which my mother used to scrape tartar away.) Once a year my mouth was hacked into, without anaesthetic, by a school-visitor dentist who had a foot-treadle drill and would snarl 'shut up, you little donkey!' as he did something that closely resembled Laurence Olivier in *Marathon Man*. My jaws were early on loaded with metal. I suspect the school dentists subscribed to the prophylactic doctrine on the grounds that alloy decayed slower than bone.

A survey, much commented on in the US press in May 2006, reported that Britons of my age were healthier than Americans. Various reasons were adduced. The NHS was one — although the socialized medicine-hating American press was disinclined to go too far along that route. Another, more favoured, explanation was the calorie restriction and fairer distribution of nutritious foods imposed by wartime and austerity period rationing.

The post-war 8d (3p) meat ration, which would (forget supermarket trolleys) fit inside a lady's handbag and still leave room for the purse, ration book, vanity case, two weekly eggs and 4oz of butter, was, after all, good for us. As were the exotic snoek, whale, kangaroo tails and other offal that were served up in lieu of proper (pre-war) food. Like Octavius in *Antony and Cleopatra*, we feasted (or turned our noses up) on things 'which beasts would cough at'. But, if you believe the papers (I don't entirely), we didn't sicken. It was the steak-eating Yanks who did.

My favourite food was toast, fork-browned by my grandmother at her coal-fired range, and so saturated in butter (she knew someone at Sainsbury's, unsurprisingly) that it had to be held in cupped hands, like a damp face flannel. The blazing warmth of the fire on one's cheeks added to the treat.

Treats were few. One was always hungry, often cold, and stoically unaware of the fact unless the pangs became overwhelming. There was, for me, another difficulty. I have never had a delicate palate, but I do have one which is abnormally responsive to verbal stimuli. I still have a range of food aversions which I can trace back to the irreverences of the school lunch table, over the fifteen years I ate there. There was, for example, a suet and meat concoction which, in recognition of its alarmingly glazed surface, was called snot pie. I have never been able to look at even an innocent veal-and-ham since, without a faint spasm of nausea.

Sago was 'frog spawn' (which one could just about swallow). Semolina pudding was 'headmaster's spunk' (unswallowable). Jam roll — nicknamed 'period piece' — invariably prompted the same gag reflex. Corned beef, which was the only meat served us during the war, I could never face: the white lard, crystallized into small globules, was firmly believed to be flies' eggs. There was actually a mutiny on the subject in my primary school dining room. I have never enjoyed bully beef since.

The Family Racehorse

My mother liked to claim, usually in passing and to defray any fleeting sense of guilt, that she had made 'sacrifices' for my school education: Colcestrians have a tendency to gild the truth. My long-time colleague Stephen Fender, who came across several in his university teaching career, liked to say that the Colchester Royal Grammar School (where I would later end up) was the only institution in the country to offer its pupils A-levels in treachery. That is hard. But there is, if (against nature) I'm being honest, an element of truth in it. Like the Highlanders who exasperated Dr Johnson on his jaunt to the Hebrides, Colcestrians firmly hold that lies are more beautiful, and always more convenient. If they thought otherwise they'd never put up with the place, or their place in it. Willed self-delusion makes things bearable.

My mother, although less afflicted with the town's self-delusiveness than most, saw herself, I think, as a kind of Sorrell Sr, whenever any anxiety as to her maternal duty crossed her mind (not that it often did). In

Warwick Deeping's 1925 best-seller, a self-sacrificing parent (born a gent, and a decorated Great War officer) plunges into the social abyss to become a hotel porter in order that his son, Kit, shall have a better life. Thanks to his pater's more than pelicanish self-sacrifice Kit eventually becomes a surgeon; a real gent. Members of my family, infected by Deepingism, would vaguely conjecture that I too would rise to that godlike profession. I suspect my mother was, at some period, entranced by passages like the following (Kit has just passed his exams with flying colours):

Tucked under his porridge plate, Kit discovered an envelope addressed to him in his father's handwriting, and on opening he found that it contained a ten-pound note.
'I say, — pater! — '
Sorrell had been pretending to read the morning paper, and he glanced up at his son's serious face.
'Well, — old man?'
'You know — you oughtn't — to be so jolly good to me — '
'Why not? Something to celebrate with. You have worked hard.'
Kit got up and, going round the table,

bent down and kissed his father on the forehead.

'You are a sport, pater.'

So, in her different way, was mater. But this scenario about Surgeon John was classic Colcestrian fantasy — a lie conveniently stuffing the hole where an uncomfortable truth should have lain. I was idly bet on, with family money, as they might have placed a wager — with whatever spare cash jingled in their pocket — on an outsider in the Grand National. I was the family flutter. In their hearts was the thought that I might 'better myself'. But I was given that opportunity only because they had no other immediate use for me, or were confused about what uses were appropriate. Had there been no war to distract them from age-old family ways, I would have been thrown into the same mix as they had been, never to rise above decent working-class existence. If I was lucky.

As it was, I had freedoms. History gave them to me by destroying the ruts that had made them what they were. There was no obvious rut for me to trudge along, as they had done, no family precedent, nothing to hitch my future to — no role models, no targets (I never, for a moment, went along with the surgeon nonsense).

What I did have was constant upheaval, in the interstices of which I was supposed to get an education. I attended five schools between the ages of five and twelve. As far as early schooling was concerned, I was like those animals raised in captivity then 'released into the wild' and fondly expected by their former captors to thrive (have they not been lovingly cared for?)

I wandered aimlessly — literally. A report from the first school I attended — St Mary's, a private institution — records 37 late arrivals and 12 absences in my first term. The report also notes that my vocabulary was excellent, but there was a tendency to 'over-excitement' (particularly with the tambourine) in music classes. The headmistress was driven to protest at the unpunctuality:

Dear Mrs Sutherland,
    Your son, John, has arrived late at school every morning this week, on one occasion two hours late. When asked where he has been, he offers a charming smile and says 'walking'. Could you please arrange for him to get to school on time.
    Yours faithfully,
    Jane Woodhead

I was five and a bit, and had to tramp both

ways — some three miles — by myself, the breadth of a garrison town in wartime (often, in winter, in the dark). It was, as it happens, fascinating. There were soldiers marching around, holes in the road, martial bustle. In the streets there would be packets of discarded chips from the night before. Horrible to say, I would sometimes pick them up and eat them. The taste is not, I recall, unpleasant. I shall not be checking out that recollection, but I still feel a tingle of curiosity every time I pass discarded fries in the street.

If you turn neglect and childhood loneliness on their head, and call them 'space', they can be seen as something enviable. I was given all the space a young human animal could want. Others the neglect might have made feral or autistic. Me it made a bad timekeeper, a bookworm and stale chip eater.

There are, Samuel Butler once complained, orphanages for those unfortunates who have no family — but where, he plaintively asked, are those even more necessary asylums for those who do have families? My upbringing, fatherless, largely motherless, would have tested the witty Victorian's thesis perfectly. Who knows, it might even have confirmed it. Familylessness works. Mysteriously.

Under Fire

Towards the end of the war — long after most of the 14,000 London evacuees shipped in 1939 to Colchester had returned contentedly to their East End slums — I was 'evacuated' to Edinburgh. The pretext for this Siberian exile was a raid on Colchester by the Luftwaffe, in February 1944. It was, in strategic terms, surprising. The tide, as the politicians insisted, had turned. No more Blitz. Blackout discipline had relaxed. The Long Wyre Street flat got by with its pre-war curtains. We were, as every news bulletin confirmed, now bombing German cities to buggery. Let them look to their windows.

But the Luftwaffe had a few kicks left in it. I recall being scooped up from bed during this selfsame air raid on Colchester. In the history books it is called one of the last-throw 'nuisance raids' that the enemy's manned aircraft undertook before handing the 'straf England' mission over to their rockets.

It may have been a nuisance for the mandarins in their Whitehall bunkers, but it was bloody disturbing in Colchester. I was woken up, not by sirens, but by bangs and ear-shattering aircraft engine noise. The nominal targets (wholly missed) were the tank works where my aunt Ivy worked (she might have been 'on' that night) and Davey Paxman's engineering factory. But so inexpert were Goering's bomb-aimers, so imprecise their technology (compared, for example, to the American Norden bombsight), that they scattered their load anywhere built up and inhabited-looking. After the war I spoke to Franz, the pilot of a Heinkel 111, who confessed he didn't care where the bombs dropped so long as he could pick up a few extra knots of speed and escape the British fighters.

The Heinkels were nearer their nominal target that night in 1944. At least they hit Colchester. As my mother dragged and half-carried me through the streets I saw three Spitfires (from Hornchurch, perhaps) roaring at roof-top level overhead. By St Nicholas Church there was an elderly, trilby-hatted gentleman poking angrily at a fizzing incendiary bomb in the gutter with, of all things, an umbrella. England fights back. Spits and brollies.

My mother and I ran the couple of hundred yards, hand in hand, to the vaults of Colchester Castle, a designated public shelter. It was well chosen. The structure is of massive Roman foundation; was fortified by the Normans, besieged by the Roundheads, and suffered its major damage from a demented nineteenth-century speculator, hoping to enrich himself from its saleable rubble. He went bankrupt: no one ever had an easy victory over Colchester Castle. It is an ugly pile — with, oddly, a stunted tree growing on its surviving tower, allegedly planted to celebrate the Battle of Waterloo — but it must have offered refuge to generations of frightened women and children, perhaps even as far back as Boadicea's ravages.

In 1944 the air raid shelter was in the castle vaults, where the medieval dungeons had once been. I can sniff in my mind's nostrils the clammy, cold, stony smell and see the crimson red sand buckets. Anderson shelters, by contrast, smelled of dirt: and worse, since people inevitably used them as privies. We had one, in the wild garden behind the flat. But such refuges were avoided; they inspired a Poe-like horror of being buried alive with dried heaps of human sewage for company on the way to eternity.

While we waited in the depths of the castle for the all-clear, I slept on one of the bunks. Next morning we discovered Long Wyre Street had escaped but the area around West

Street, where my grandmother lived, had been hit, with more damage to add to the two huge bomb sites within a hundred yards of her house.

It's all very vivid, more so than what happened to me three days ago. But, most of all, I remember the fact that when the bombs fell I was, all of a sudden, important. I mattered; I was worth saving. What, it is asked, is the one thing you would pick up as you ran from a burning house? In Long Wyre Street it was not the family photograph album, not Chloe, not the jewellery, but me: John. Psychologically I was affected, lifelong, by that night's bombings. Not traumatically: just the opposite. It gave me a dangerous, and potentially self-destructive sense that it was only in dire emergencies ('where's the boy?') that anyone took any notice of me. Otherwise I was such a 'good child' that I was neither seen nor heard; self-suppressed into non-existence. Extreme danger, by an Orwellian paradox, was safety.

When, fifty years later, I wrote Stephen Spender's biography I was struck by a poem he wrote. It was 1917. He was six years old (as was I, in February 1944). A mine (he calls it a bomb) had drifted ashore at Sheringham, where his family was living, in a large house on the Bluffs, during the Great War. It was night. The Home Guard was instructed to get all the women and children into shelter.

> Then a bomb exploded —
> The night went up
> In flame that shook
> The shrubbery leaves,
> And soldiers came
> Out of the dark speared with flame,
> And carried us children
> Into their dugout
> Below the earth
> Ear pressed against
> The khaki uniform
> Of mine, in his arms,
> I could hear his heart beat —
> With the blood of all England.

Spender wrote the poem for his last collection, when he was in his mid-eighties. For him it was, he suggests, the moment when his sexual orientation was given its crucial twist. The world suddenly formed itself, in a moment of crisis, around him as its nucleus. He was embraced; cuddled — as he never was by his sternly Edwardian parents.

It was, for me as for him, a formative moment, and he puts it better — or more poetically — than I can. Except it was not, for me, some hairy-vested, working-class soldier, but my mother: a woman whom I loved and who was so hard to hold or be held by. In later life I would court crisis, or the total incapacities of drunkenness, in order to be noticed and cared for. Come, friendly bombs, as another poet put it. If that's what it took to bring us together, let them fall.

Evacuation

After the bombings, and with the first V1s landing a few weeks later in June, the decision was taken to send me to relatives in Scotland. The pretext was my safety — that, at least, was what I was given to understand.

But doodlebugs didn't come into it. The real reason was more that my mother's relationship with Hamilton had reached the stage of discreet cohabitation: I was in the way. She did not want to marry him (he was willing enough); or anyone (she did not want to be tied down again). But neither did she want me to witness her intimacy with a man to whom she was not married. She might keep it from outside eyes, but how could I not know who shared her bed? — more so as I was getting older all the time, staying up later and growing to look 'the picture' of Jack (as relatives would say who, unlike me, had known what my father looked like in life).

By the simple calculus of childhood I knew, although I could not admit it to myself — still can't — that I was less important in her life than whatever man she happened to have taken up with and be using at the time. But I was important enough to her not to be wholly ignored or wantonly disposed of. An acceptable arrangement was necessary. A period with my Scottish relatives would be acceptable (to my mother, at least; my feelings were not a factor).

I seem to remember being put on the overnight Flying Scotsman whose streamlined engine (can this be true?) left from North Street Station on its way north. Perhaps my memory is glamorizing what was a wrenching moment of separation: the last of Colchester. I was carrying a little blue suitcase, which I still have — that I am sure about — and some sandwiches. My mother asked a woman in the carriage to keep an eye on me: which she did.

The train didn't fly; no trains did in the 1940s. I was met at Waverley Station, a long night later, by my father's sister Jean — unsmilingly. A handsome, tall, hard-faced woman, she lived half a mile down the hill in Dalmeny Street, with her husband and a daughter, Mary, my age (another child, Thomas, would be born shortly after the war). How she recognized me, I don't know. I wasn't labelled. Perhaps what they said was true, I had the look of my father.

The Rankins' tenement was on the third floor. The street was one of the rows of

Craigleith granite tenement blocks running at right angles to Leith Walk. The flats had been built alongside the majestic New Town development of the early nineteenth century, to house the servant and worker armies who made the gentry's life in their grand Georgian squares grand. A few miles further down Leith Walk was the abyss: the dock area (later immortalized in *Trainspotters*). Where my aunt and uncle lived are regarded as handsome properties nowadays. Lawyers live in them.

It was clear to me that I was there principally for the money I brought to the household. Jean's husband, Walter, was a dental technician. He must have had some useful disqualification that kept him out of uniform: from what one saw during the course of an average week, alcoholism was a likely candidate. He made casts for false teeth, working from home in what would have been the spare bedroom. One could trespass into it and look at tray upon tray of wonderful-smelling pink mouth putty, some with gleaming teeth in them.

I learned how the things were made. An impression of the gums would be taken with the aromatic pink wax. Porcelain teeth would be inserted. Then, in a nifty vacuum chamber, the wax would be heated and washed away, to be replaced by fast-setting and durable vulcanite, or acrylic. A little polishing, and it was dazzling smiles all round.

Most were destined for young mouths. This was a period when everyone in my parents' class glumly expected to have false teeth by their mid-thirties — more so in Scotland, whose population craved sweeties and biscuits as junkies do their fix. Girls would be given a set of snappers for their eighteenth birthday, the more brilliantly to shine on their great day.

Being fitted for dentures meant having all the natural teeth extracted, in one or two painful sessions, and going round toothless for several weeks while the gums hardened. Orwell has a passage in *Coming up for Air* on one's dentures marking a threshold in life: the point at which self-delusion evaporates. The novel opens with the middle-aged, lower-class hero, George Bowling, regarding himself in his bathroom mirror:

I was trying to shave with a bluntish razor-blade while the water ran into the bath. My face looked back at me out of the mirror, and underneath, in a tumbler of water on the little shelf over the washbasin, the teeth that belonged in the face. It was the temporary set that Warner, my dentist, had given me to wear while the new ones were being made . . . say what you will, false teeth are a landmark. When your last natural tooth goes, the time when you can kid yourself that you're a Hollywood sheik is definitely at an end.

(Not entirely true, George. *Coming up for Air* was published the same year that *Gone with the Wind* hit the movie screen. Clark Gable — Rhett ('frankly, my dear, I don't give a damn') Butler — had false teeth. Vivien Leigh disliked kissing him for that reason. But millions of women of my mother's class and age found him desperately sheikly.)

My mother was unusual in holding on to her natural teeth. They were a fine set, preserved in their intact whiteness by her 'Lady Jane' finickiness. Even on her death bed they still managed a faint gleam — not that one could see them behind the oxygen mask. Would that she had protected her lungs as carefully from tobacco smoke as her teeth from nicotine stains. But then, no South American lost his heart to a Colchester girl because of the pinkness of her lungs.

Ivy and my grandmother had theirs out early on. One of my earliest memories is my aunt sending me out (I must have been five-ish) to buy Steradent fixture from the chemist. There was a regular panic when someone came to the door. Teeth were routinely removed at home, along with the hat and overcoat. It was always wise to check any glass of water that happened to be around before taking a swig.

Anything to do with dentures was a steady line of work and Walter Rankin was adept at his chosen line of oral sculpture. His hand must, however, have shaken sometimes as he shaped his wax. He was habitually drunken, as, less often, was my aunt. Indeed, I remember riotous hogmanays when the whole of Edinburgh was drunk, and it was pointless to send the children to bed.

There was a large contingent of Polish airmen in Scotland, banished there by Churchill to protect the virtue of English maidenhood. The Poles carved through the lassies (and any douce matrons who happened to be available) with inexhaustible energy, charm and good humour. They were dashing fellows, and bibulous. I would, a little later, have a young cousin who, it pleased my mother to hint (maliciously), was probably half Slav (he wasn't). The Poles loved children; many had been obliged to leave families behind them. They would have given a child all the gum in their possession — had they had any.

At night I slept on the living-room sofabed, with my cousin Mary. We would sometimes suck pennies before going to sleep. They were gobstopper large in those days, and could be up to fifty years old. Used coinage has an odd, sharp taste, and the pennies gleamed the next morning as if newly minted; I consumed my statutory peck of dirt fairly early in life. I very soon developed so thick a Scottish accent that when, eighteen months later, I returned to Colchester, I could no more be understood than a child with a dozen pennies in his mouth.

Luxuries and sweetmeats were few. When you went, basket in hand, for the 'messages' (all on tick) from the Co-op at the end of Dalmeny Street, an Oxo cube or cinnamon stick would be added for the boy. At the fish and chip shop across the way they would sprinkle sweetened cocoa on the threepenny pokes of chips for children. Adults preferred astringent salt and vinegar. White haggis (less peppery than the blood-soaked black variety) was also a favourite delicacy. The Scots fry everything (even, famously, Mars bars); it is a diet which shortens life. But life should be sweet, while it lasts.

There were hardships. For the first time in

my life, I was routinely beaten. I was strapped horribly once by my aunt who found a sixpenny piece in my trousers. I couldn't account for how I'd come by it; honestly couldn't (I must have stolen it and repressed any consciousness of the offence). I remember the pain of the beating, and the humiliation of being able to offer no excuse other than the worse-than-useless 'Don't know, Auntie'.

Even worse than the strap were the disgusting, canary-yellow Gregory powders which one would be given whenever one complained of illness. They were regarded as cure-all tonics, efficacious in proportion to the awfulness of their taste. For me, they were Edinburgh in tabloid form. Most illnesses were far preferable.

There must have been kindnesses and indulgences as well. I can remember only one — a request that I be excused wearing underwear, which I found itchy. It was granted. The right sleeve of my blue cardigan (buttoned to the neck with a high collar) was constantly glazed with nose wiping. And, over a fortnight or so between washing, socks would be as leathery as the shoes that covered them.

The life of the tenements was, for a child in the 1940s, rich and primitive. There were wholly untended parks whose vegetation had run wild and a vivid street life. I formed a friendship with a German prisoner of war, whose daily task was to unload and unroll coconut mats for the Territorial Army to exercise on, in the large dusty hall across the street from where we lived. (The event was strikingly like what Bill Douglas records in his autobiographical film, *My Ain Folk*.)

The German prisoners were well treated and some even stayed on after the war (famously Bert Trautman, Manchester City goalkeeper). There was little hatred for them (except among the Poles). There was, by contrast, a visceral hatred of the Japanese, who would — as one boy whispered to me in the dark stairwell at Dalmeny Street — cut off women's breasts and sit their prisoners on bamboo shoots which, in that dark and manured plot of the body, would grow a foot in twenty-four hours. I slept squirmingly for nights afterwards. It was not, of course, something I could share with my bedmate, who affected her mother's severity with me and manifestly wished I were gone, so she could have her bed to herself again.

Compared to Long Wyre Street, Leith Walk was dangerous by night. It is so no longer; last time I was there, I was astonished at how gentrified it had become — bistros and boutiques everywhere. In the 1940s, it had barely changed since Scott's day (he lived in a grand town house between Princes and George streets). I can remember being given a lift by a dray horse and cart up the hill to Register House and Waverley Station, with its notorious cold and ankle-freezing hundred steps up to Princes Street. In Colchester (with its lingering rural habits) the passing coal carts would provoke a stampede of housewives to pick up the horse droppings 'for the roses' or whatever plants were struggling for existence in the back garden. In tenemented Edinburgh they lay, further aromatizing the polluted air of Auld Reekie.

Smells were omnipresent and one's infant nostrils were sharper. My cousin and I would stand for whole afternoons on a bridge in the Princes Street Gardens looking over the rails as the trains pulled in and out of Waverley, breathing in the smoke and steam from the trains as they passed underneath, enjoying the rush. The gardens themselves lay on the soil of the drained Nor Loch, where the Old Town's unwanted babies and other garbage had been thrown two hundred years before. The famous floral clock, I seem to remember, was stopped during hostilities.

Hogmanay was a riotous, colourful revel. The mood of the other 364 days of the year

105

was unrelenting grey. It was compounded by the East Coast weather. Occasionally there would be a winter snowfall, when the wind blew in from Scandinavia; there would be the excitement of slabs of snow falling sixty feet from the roofs, crashing to the pavement.

But generally the climate of Edinburgh is not harsh. What makes it depressing are two things. One is the 'haar' — a dank sea fog, which can set in for days (Mary Queen of Scots got two weeks of it, when she arrived, triumphantly, in her capital). Even more depressing is the fact that there is so little difference between winter and summer. You look at the weather page in the *Scotsman* in February and it's Edinburgh 47°F, London 50°. In summer it's London 75°, Edinburgh 54°. It gets you down.

The city's overpowering grey has (or had, in those days) another origin. The moral climate was cold and stony — or, at least, it was for me. My Scottish relatives were con-vinced that my mother, as they sarcastically put it — sometimes in my hearing — was earning her living on her back in Piccadilly Circus. They charged her, as she thought, an outrageous amount for my bed and board (a shared sofa, bread and dripping, and Oxo cubes for treats): fifteen shillings a week. Since her pension from the War Office was about half that, and the police pay less than munificent, she was paying through the nose.

She may have had some income on the side, but it was not earned on her back. And God knows, she needed anything she could get. Forty years later she remembered bitterly going for a drink with her in-laws and being stiffed for a round in some godawful Edinburgh public bar smelling of disinfectant, which cost her 12s 6d. The then outrageous sum stuck in her mind and has stuck in mine. The fact was her Scottish relatives were jealous of her making a life for herself. And, irrationally, my aunt blamed her for wonderful Jack Sutherland's death. John Sutherland was no recompense — too much of the 'English woman' in him.

On arrival at Edinburgh, in summer 1944, I was now between five and six, and obliged by law to attend school. I learned the advanced skills of reading at a primary in Leith Walk, by the choral method: the teacher would write a word or phrase on the blackboard, the class would chant it back. The school was still using slates for writing, dictation and copying exercises. If my experience is anything to go by, it works as well as Apple computers.

Despite the Stone Age educational technology, I was lucky in that Scottish education

— even at that low level of life and social class — was the best in the UK. Literacy and penmanship were valued; so was the discipline which kept classes of forty-plus in order (we were ranked in what would now be called stadium seating). I, like most pupils, suffered the tawse. My offence I cannot remember — probably some mild cheekiness — but I recall the ceremony with a condemned prisoner's distinctness: the box being sent for, some goody-goody fetching it from the head's office (an entry would have to be made in the punishment book), the tessellated thongs (kitten of nine tails), the sudden stinging, and breathtakingly painful, impact on the palm; the punishment being observed — for their good as well as one's own — by the whole, hushed, class. One cried.

Back Home

Eventually the Scottish arrangement fell through. Why it did, I was never clearly told — no one ever consulted me about the decisions which were taken about me, however life-changing they might be. Nor did anyone ever feel obliged to justify or explain those decisions once taken.

But this is what happened. With victory and demobilization in late 1946, Hamilton pressed my mother to return to the Argentine with him. He could not live without this woman, God knows why; he could have bought a Colchester harem with the money he had. He would not insist on marriage but he hoped that — wowed by the South American land of plenty — she would in time relent. Any man who loved her (including me) was forever plucking the petals off an imaginary dandelion: 'loves me, loves me not'.

For over a year now, they had been (discreetly) together. She had finally agreed to go to the Argentine ('loves me'): but she made no promises ('loves me not'). No Kippsian drainpipes — not even silver ones.

He was hers if she wanted him. But marriage to him would have meant ownership — his ownership of her. Also, I suspect, she did not want more children; they too owned a woman. (I was always safe from rivals on that front.)

She dearly wanted, however, what Ham offered, other than himself and little Hamiltons. Travel was one: to this point in her life, she had never been farther afield than Scotland. She wanted the 'good things' previously denied her class, and currently denied the English people en masse. Hot water, for example, and the opportunity to keep clean without the humiliation of a kitchen kettle or public bathhouse. Clothes that were not Utility, shoes that were not cobbled, and underwear that was soft to the skin and beguiling to the male eye. Fashionable garments, while she was still beautiful enough to set them off. Civilized company and clean dry sheets.

Ham would find her an honorary job on the paper: set her up in an apartment. Or perhaps they cohabited under an assumed married name — I would never know. A child was not carry-on baggage in the trips she was contemplating, nor did she ever feel obliged to account for her decisions in life.

No one used the word, but I was to be

fostered. Some relative(s) would be generously paid (Hamilton's generosity, obviously) to look after me. There would be regular comfort parcels — sweets, American comics — and an affectionate, conscience-clearing letter every now and then. But fostering it was.

A permanent continuation of the Scottish arrangement must have been considered, and floated with them; Dalmeny Street was eager enough to make an honest penny (or peso) from me. But I suspect — and I heard enough acid comment to confirm the suspicion — that the remnants of Calvinist rectitude in their Lowland Scots make-up (despite the lure of thirty shillings a week) obliged them to take a moral stand.

They disapproved (Scottishly) of my mother's nail varnish, lipstick, blonde hair, and her stylish way with cigarettes and Ronson lighters (Zippos had long gone). The Tango was the last straw for the Calvinist spine. They could already see the Carmen Miranda bananas on my mother's head, and the 'paint' on her face. I was spawn of Jezebel. They could not bring themselves to look after her child, in order that she, having abandoned all motherly responsibility, should be free to live in sin in Argentina, a region associated with racing car drivers and 'playboys'.

111

Jealousy, of course, came into it. As it was, after a year and a half, I was shipped back to Colchester as no longer wanted — even by Dalmeny Street. I suspect that my mother had originally told them that she was going abroad for a holiday only. When it became clear that she was living in shameless Argentinian sin, and had always intended to, the Scottish conscience could bear it no longer.

Thank God for nail varnish and Carmen Miranda. Had I remained another three years in Scotland I would have ended up, like my cousins, in a world of Edinburgh grey until my soul (like my underwear, when I wore it) turned the same colour.

It was my long-suffering aunt Ivy (with backup from my grandmother) who took me on. I don't imagine she was entirely keen. But the money talked and she admired her younger sister uncritically. I was, as children go, 'no trouble'. And there were vacancies in Ivy's life which my presence might fill, in addition to that perennial hole in the family purse. (My mother, now I think of it, was doing her bit for the post-war export drive, sending harder currencies than sterling back to the homeland.)

Bill, now demobilized, had settled into his job with the newly nationalized British Road

112

Services as a fitter. Ivy (like her American counterpart, Rosie the Riveter) had no job prospects in the post-war world. She was a housemaid who knew how to make obscure parts for obsolete tanks. Neither skill was in any demand in 1946.

Her inner resources were few. She could write and number, but I never saw her read a book, nor spend more than a few laborious minutes with the *Daily Mirror* (at my grandmother's, when she dropped by in the afternoon after the shopping). As a cook, she was functional. There would be joint and roast potatoes on Sunday. This was a highpoint, eaten to the accompaniment of *Family Favourites*. I never, even now, eat roast potatoes without hearing an echo of Cliff Michelmore's and Jean Metcalfe's mellifluous voices — they eventually married, over the banal musical choices of their programme.

Thereafter lunch (called 'dinner') was downhill all the way to the following weekend: cold meat Monday (with pickle), mince and mash on Wednesday, sausages on Thursday, pot luck till Sunday.

My aunt cleaned the house furiously every morning, between *Housewives' Choice* and *A Story, a Hymn, and a Prayer*. That was the only touch of spirituality in the household.

There was nothing in the East Street flat to stimulate any life of the mind — the all-day blaring Light Programme acted like a low-level narcotic, suppressing rather than stimulating brain activity. She and Bill intended to have children when things settled down. I would keep the berth warm.

For me it was the better of two poor options. But I was not party to the arrangement — merely a piece of family furniture to be moved as the family felt convenient. This, by luck, was moderately convenient to me.

My War

John Boorman's autobiographical film, *Hope and Glory*, roughly parallels my own experience during World War Two. The director celebrates — with more romanticism than they really warrant — the delicious freedoms and sexual excitements that war and Americans brought for children and women. The men were away, their dependants could play. The ending of the film has Boorman's young hero turning up to school only to find it destroyed by a doodlebug — a V1, that most random of weapons (unless, like Graham Greene in *The End of the Affair*, you believe God was directing them down on sinners He was particularly interested in).

'Thank you, Adolf,' the kids whoop as they dance, like redskins, around the debris. Second World War children (unlike their First War predecessors) had little enmity towards the Hun (partly because half of them had to play Germans in the fighting games, as half played Indians). Unlike the Hitler Jugend, there was no attempt to indoctrinate the young with Churchillian ferocities. Ideology was just another of the inexplicables of the adult world.

One schoolyard chant in Scotland (the accent is required for the rhyme) went:

> V for Victory dot dot dash
> Hitler's got a wee mustache
> If you find it never mind it
> V for Victory dot dot dash

Hitler was comic — Chaplinesque. As propaganda it was probably more effective than the children's edition of *Mein Kampf* which the Hitler Youth had forced down them. Churchill, with his cigar, tommy gun, rude V-sign and baggy boiler suit, was also a figure of fun — less Chaplin than Oliver Hardy.

Like Boorman's tyke, I can feel a certain warmth for the Austrian tyrant with the wee mustache. Bomb sites (once cleared of explosives) were playgrounds more interesting than any modern council can provide, strewn as they were with treasure trove, handy missiles and interesting debris. (I remember spending one morning with a dog's skeleton, some householder's luckless pet.) They were places where juvenile outlawry could happen. It was on one such bomb site, by Wellington Street, that I had my

116

wholly mystifying sexual initiation, aged nine. Some older kid was sharing a bedroom with a cousin, incestuously and gleefully. He was prepared, brute that he was, to share the poor girl around. What followed was, for me, as incomprehensibly ritualistic and pointless as the serving of communion wafer and wine would have been. I did not have the slightest idea what a 'do' (Essex dialect is hopelessly unimaginative) meant. A rubbery contact, no penetration (she was not so lucky by night, I suspect), and some great business of life was mysteriously sealed. But what, exactly? I did not know, but tried to look knowing.

A couple of years later a farmer's son (such things could not be kept from them) explained the facts of life, in crude and unmistakable detail, one summer afternoon on the top deck of a No. 5 bus trundling down Lexden Road after school. At that period, one would have waited until middle age for one's parents, guardians or teachers to fill one in; sexual instruction was as scarce as Sanskrit. My informant's name was French: nicknamed Frenchie — after the condom, about whose precise use I also learned on the No. 5 bus. A few years later he blew his head off with a shotgun, accidentally, crossing a stile on his father's land.

Had Hitler's war not killed my father, I

would have been surrounded by siblings in a caged world of age-old class barriers with a mother released from 'domestic service' into the same (but unpaid) servitude in the home. I am grateful for that, if not quite to the Boormanish degree. World War Two was not all bliss to be alive and heaven to be young, but it was better than the alternatives — death, or pre-war England.

I am one of a shrinking minority of Britons who have eaten Woolton Pie, been bombed on and lived. For me that opening sentence of Orwell's *England Your England* still raises hairs (also shrinking, year by year) on the back of my neck: 'As I write, highly civilized human beings are flying overhead, trying to kill me.' I don't know whether they were highly civilized or not, but those *Kampflieger* in 1944 would have burned me up as crisply as my father, and gone back to their *Wurst und Wein* at Cherbourg, or wherever, and felt good about having survived to bomb another day.

I too survived and, on the whole, had a good war. My father had a very bad war in that he never got further than that part of a foreign field that is forever England. And my mother, I suspect, had the best war of all. She survived to enjoy some very interesting foreign fields.

118

Home and Away

By the time I returned, speaking my incomprehensible Scottish, my mother had long since decamped to the Argentine, and would be gone three years. She was bound for the land of the gaucho. For me, I was saddled with Colchester.

I have never quite been able to come to terms with the town where the pieces of my broken childhood largely landed. Colchester, where most of my childhood was unspent (Larkin's word, of course) was, in terms of its standing among the towns of England, about where its football team, 'the United', normally hovered at that period: middlingly high in the Third Division. Or in a bad season, battling it out in the Southern League in front of a crowd of tens.

Nowadays Colchester, still a no-hoper on the national soccer pitch, does outstandingly well in the 'crap town' league invented by some wit in the 1990s. The town is demolished by an atomic bomb in Orwell's *Nineteen Eighty-Four* (thank you, George), starting World War Three — though why Eastasia, or Eurasia, should bother to target an urban nothing in East Anglia, with the Great Wen temptingly nearby, is not clear. I suspect Orwell didn't like the place.

Colchester was, within living memory (mine almost), a handsome market town with a distinguished Civil War record and a central place in English history going back to the Romans and the Iceni. Like Mexico and America, proximity to London has been its curse; as has what, to adapt Larkin, one could call town unplanning.

In my childhood, the town's population was some 60,000: which meant that a lot of Colcestrians, most of whom had been born there, knew each other. The High Street still had a Saturday market. I worked on one of the fruit and vegetable stalls in my later, wilder school years, spending the day's money that night on drink and what was left the next week at Doncaster's secondhand bookshop.

In my film-going years Colchester boasted five cinemas. They ranked hierarchically, from the Regal (a custom-built picture palace, with restaurant, portraits of stars, pile carpet), the Playhouse, the Hippodrome (the last two converted music halls, the latter with some fine interior decor), the Headgate (a converted chapel) to the Empire, the town fleapit — still gaslit in the 1950s. And I seem to recall the usherettes going up and down in the intervals with Flit guns. Perhaps there really were fleas.

My very earliest film memory is seeing a Tarzan film at the Hippodrome (from the detail of some nightmare-inducing snakes); it must have been *Tarzan's Great Adventure* and the date 1943. The effect on me may be gauged from my first (preserved) exercise in prose, written a year or so later. It is evidence of no prodigious precocity: by this infantine time of life Thomas Macaulay was reciting the whole of *Paradise Lost* and, doubtless, composing hexameters. But my little essay expresses a desire to fly the coop, escape. It also has, I like to think, an exuberance of vocabulary which is a credit to its author.

Colchester also had a repertory theatre. Every week's production was a miracle of improvisation by a small squad of underpaid assistant stage managers and volunteers. In my late, self-improving and socially aspiring teens, I would see an actor called David Baron on stage — doing whatever part the weekly lottery turned up, learning his lines over half pints in the Wagon and Horses, and pigging it in some wretched boarding house. He later renamed himself Harold Pinter and, rep legend still has it, his career was revolutionized, and his genius kindled, by performing in *Waiting for Godot* (was he Lucky? I saw the production but can't remember). It was his first encounter with Beckett, I have been told. England's theatrical revival began at the Albert Hall, High Street, Colchester, in May 1955.

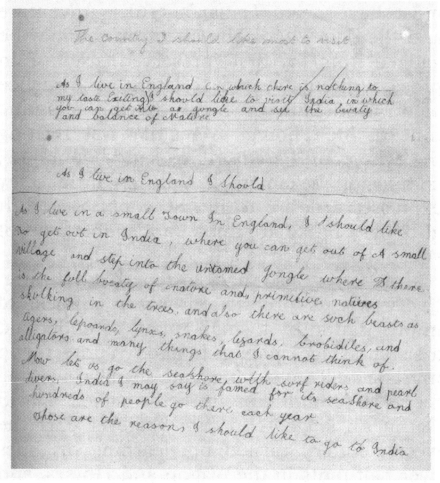

Juvenilia

The former Corn Exchange, a few yards down the High Street, had been converted (clumsily) into a palais de danse at the weekends and a roller-skating rink on weekdays. Neither was done with metropolitan style; too much agricultural chaff in the floorboards perhaps. I can remember seeing a modern-dress version of *The Merchant of Venice* one evening at the Rep (what was Baron that evening — melancholic Antonio, perhaps?) and going along afterwards to catch the second set of Johnny Dankworth, his 'Seven', and the delectable Cleo Laine (she was not yet Cleo Dankworth, and he was not yet 'John'). The life.

For me the cinema dominated — that and Colchester's surprisingly good public library (since precinctified into a bleak Waterstone's and ghastly coffee house). I was marinaded in celluloid. For a couple of years, after he returned from his peculiarly unsuccessful stab at Australian emigration (£10 out, £200 back), my uncle Arthur would go five times a week to cheap matinées, and would persuade me, too often, to skip afternoon school. (I was at that period going back to my grandmother's for lunch — a dreary repast. I made the mistake of telling her once I loved her mince, and that was what it would be, five times a week. The meal was a pretext for my mother giving her money without injuring her pride.)

Arthur returned, tail between the legs, from

Australia, unemployed and at the loosest of ends. He was still in two minds whether to marry the well-educated woman who had taken him in hand in Germany. He haughtily refused the menial jobs offered him by the Labour Exchange and forfeited his dole pittance: something that infuriated and depressed him. He got by on handouts from his mother and sister. He made at least one suicide attempt (with 40 aspirins). Looking back, I can see that in tempting me to truant it wasn't just company he wanted. He was — irrepressibly good-natured as he was — jealous of me; more particularly of the life promises held out to me and denied, equally deserving, to him.

On my part I was glad to be led into temptation. The velvety, cigarette-laden atmosphere of the picture house was magical to me. The only unpleasant thing was walking out, dazed, into daylight. Sometimes I would catch another film that same evening, with whatever adult was kind enough to take me. It was only on the Saturday morning matinée that I would go by myself. That was somewhat less magical.

The films one saw at the time were overwhelmingly American. They were, if one had the crystal ball to see it, Colchester's future: the direction in which the town was slowly and uncomprehendingly drifting. On the rare occasions I go back there nowadays and walk through the town's vandalized centre (more devastated by urban renewal than even Franz and his Heinkel could have hoped for), I see massed Colcestrians uniformed in Levis, baseball caps, sneakers and T-shirts — some grotesquely marked 'Harvard', 'Princeton' or 'Lakers'. America, like some alien stain, has seeped into the Colcestrian fibre. I shall doubtless live to see the A12 renamed the London Freeway.

There remained, in the late 1940s, remnants of an older natural way of life, going back (as the local jest had it) to times immoral. For me it was to be found on the banks of the rivers Stour and Colne.

The Fishing Year

In the late summer of 1948 I became infatuated with angling. The rod forged a temporary, but while it lasted intimate, bond between me and my grandfather. He was now working as a council labourer, doing whatever odd jobs came up. I would see him sometimes as I walked back from school, jammed three abreast in the cab of his three-tonner. We would not acknowledge each other.

The rivers, ponds and mill races around the town had, thanks to the war, hardly changed since he himself was a boy. He had, in his youth, been a devoted angler: for sport and for the table. His expertise was in coarse fishing — something which none the less has some fine points of art. He had stored in his mind the whereabouts of broken-down wooden bridges, probably standing in Constable's day, which teemed with roach and rudd. He knew the sluggish eddying curves along the Colne where bottom-feeding gudgeon could be scooped out — thirty an hour if you could be bothered with the pointless things. There were mill races,

126

favoured by the darting and beautifully silvered dace, which were harder to entice on to the hook.

More important prey than these tiddlers were eels, pike, tench and the inedible (but beautifully rainbowed) perch. For my grandfather the craft had not changed since Izaak Walton. Until my juvenile passion revived his own interest, his angling gear (all by now as antique as my father's golf clubs) had lain in store for years. He had a quiver of tarred rods in his creosoted back-garden shed that no one else had the key to, reels full of waxed line, round tins of split lead weights (you nipped them over the cat gut with your teeth), feather and bobbin floats, and scores of different-sized hooks, some of which had to have the rust rubbed off them, livebait cans, keep nets and gaffs. There were lumps of indestructible but now crumbling beeswax (for coating the line), which gave the whole collection an old-honeyish smell.

Smells were an inseparable element: the instantly stale stench of eel, for example, and the slime that caked, flaked and fell as one watched it from the hands, almost before the beheaded eel had stopped its maddened wriggling. (The real battle began once one had got the evil things out of the water; they could tangle ten yards of line in as many seconds.) Quite different was the cold, muddy tang of newly caught pike (and the furiously glaring eyes and bared teeth — many fish can look hungry, perch for example; pike can look downright angry). My grandfather didn't much value maggots as bait, preferring earthworms, but sometimes he would leave out some meat for the flies and keep a few, still redolent of rotting flesh, in a tobacco tin (which had its own original aroma).

For eighteen months fishing brought me close to my grandfather, although we never talked about anything except matters in hand — the weather, what float to use, why were (or were not) the fish biting. Every Saturday I would report to his house in Colchester's West Street, early (roused from my bed by the excitement of the day to come). We would pack the equipment: rods, in their cloth jackets, the tackle bag, the livebait can. For refreshment there would be sandwiches (usually Heinz sandwich spread, for me) and Corona bottles filled with cold, unsweetened tea. Then we would get the lumbering Southern Counties red double-decker to Stratford St Mary, the first stop past the notorious Gun Hill where innumerable carts, coaches and horseless carriages had come to grief over the centuries. On some occasions he would get an ancient, lovingly oiled bike and we would cycle to some out of the way pond which was home to the mysterious chub or carp. I once caught a grayling — the coarse fisherman's trout — in a stream near Wormingford.

The millpond, Stratford St Mary

If it were early summer and eels we were going for, it was mainly Stratford we started from, a village divided between Essex and Suffolk by the river. The Constable 'Great Landscapes' exhibition of 2006 at Tate Britain featured, as one of its centrepieces, an oil painting of the Stratford Mill and Pond, in the early nineteenth century. Other than the Mill's being now a ruin, the water and its

129

banks were unchanged, a century and a bit on, when I fished there.

In winter the catch would be pike, and the water between Dedham and Flatford (whose mills are similarly immortalized by Constable, himself a grain merchant's son). My grandfather knew spots, in tributary streams, where one could load the livebait can in a brisk hour and then go to the main river to hunt the larger prey. He also, by some kind of instinct, knew where pike lurked. Voracious and savage as the fish are, they keep out of each other's way, patrolling their territories. They snap at anything live, slow and edible, even their own young — the delightfully named pickerel. But (unlike perch) they are not stupid. They do get rather reckless in thunderstorms, I discovered: but not so violently as eels which practically leap out of the water when lightning strikes.

I don't know which was the crueller in this engagement, the fish or the fisherman. With live bait, the huge hook had to be inserted firmly below the dorsal of the luckless roach one was using. It had to go deep in the flesh, otherwise the pike would not swallow the hook into its gullet. But it had to be not so deep that it killed the bait. The smaller fish had to wriggle (in agony). Pike were not interested in dead fishmeat; they left that to bottom feeders, like carp — and fishermen. I pray that God is not a small roach — or, if He is, that He is a very merciful roach. Otherwise I shall spend many eternities with a sodding great hook in my back, avoiding the snapping jaws of some infernal crocodile.

The Stour (unlovely name for the loveliest of rivers) where my grandfather and I fished in those years is now primly crisscrossed with maintained footpaths, signposts and velvety lawn. It resembles nothing so much as a Disneyfied 'Constable Land'. Tourists teem along its banks, after lunch at a gastropub, as numerously as once the roach did in its waters. The angling rights are owned by clubs who have filled the water with alien 'sporting' fish. Anglers line up (to my nostalgic eye) like soldiers in a rape line along the beaten-down banks. They are allowed their statutory 'catch', and throw any surplus back. Some luckless fish must have jaws like pincushions. There are competitions for best angler of the day — as if it were a fishathon. Fishing with hand grenades would be, to my mind, more natural. But I am biased and sentimental on the subject.

My passion for fishing ended as suddenly as it had begun. Angling was, as I look back, my last emotionally sustaining connection with a historical past stretching back to the time when the first Colcestrain broke off a willow branch and attached a thread and bent pin to it.

George Orwell, who pen-named himself after a Suffolk river, has a riff on the subject, in the novel quoted earlier, *Coming up for Air*. I read it at school, and it must have seeped into my mind, since I have unintentionally echoed it: or perhaps it's just minds thinking alike (the mind below ostensibly belongs to the other George, 'George Bowling', the hero-narrator):

I *am* sentimental about my childhood — not my own particular childhood, but the civilization which is now, I suppose, just about at its last kick. And fishing is somehow typical of that civilization. As soon as you think of fishing you think of things that don't belong to the modern world. The very idea of sitting all day under a willow tree beside a quiet pool — and being able to find a quiet pool to sit beside — belongs to the time before the war, before the radio, before aeroplanes, before Hitler. There's a kind of peacefulness even in the names of English coarse fish. Roach, rudd, dace, bleak, barbel, bream, gudgeon, pick, chub, carp, tench. The people who made them up hadn't heard of machine guns, they didn't live in terror of the sack or spend their time eating aspirins, going to the pictures and wondering how to keep out of the concentration camp.

The novel was published in the year of my birth. The 'civilization' Orwell laments, and the fishing ethos that went with it, still had a little kick left in it, ten years on. No longer. He was right there.

A few shards of natural life stay with me, like unhealed scars. I still know a bit more about the country than my son, or current school leavers who are of the belief that cows lay eggs and chickens (voices supplied by Eddie Murphy and Mel Gibson) exist only to march along a conveyor belt to the grilled flames of Colonel Sanders. I feel a subdued sense of relief when it rains ('good for the farmers') and have an irresistible yearning to knuckle my forehead in the presence of anyone squirearchical looking, in case they pull down my hovel and exercise their seigneurial rights on my womenfolk. I know that nettles grow over ground where human beings once lived and that dock leaves will always be found nearby to soothe the nettles' sting. I know the ash comes into leaf later than the horse chestnut and you scarify the trunk of a walnut to get better crops from it. But to make anything of these faint echoes of an earlier time is sheer sentimentality. Any real links between me and 'natural England' were broken at least a generation before I came on the scene. And not all the Green parties, folk singers and Fleet Street giveaway wall charts ('Today: the coarse fish of Essex!') can put them back together again.

Preparatory

It was a period of broken links. On my return from Scotland, my mother having departed, I had been enrolled mid-term, aged eight, in yet another school: my third so far; two still to come. There was an initial problem: my thick, working-class Scottish accent made me as incomprehensible as a Hottentot. It was a month or two, and after much painful jeering, before I could recover my native Essex and pass for local.

My new school was a good one, but dying. It was the grammar school preparatory department (the 'Pre'), a fast-melting fragment of the pre-war education system. With the 1944 reforms and the introduction of entrance by eleven-plus, it was an anomaly, and had been given five years' grace to wind down, as the kids already enrolled passed through. I would be there for its last eighteen months, along with a dwindling band of pupils, privileged — against the tide of the time — to receive a pre-war education. My status was that of a first-class stowaway on a sinking vessel; and the last aboard. No one joined the school after me.

Nor should I have been there. How I was inserted into this school, after the doors had firmly closed to others better qualified, I do not know. My mother, I suspect, must have 'known' someone. Throughout life she was good at identifying men of local power and patronage. To my knowledge, she had flings with a couple of councillors over the years, and there were probably more. It was their committee pull which got her a seat on the bench in her later years.

Seated on ground, far right,
less happy than I look

The school place, however she got it (there was no mystery where the money for the fees and uniform came from), was a pay-off to me — a 'sacrifice' thrown over her shoulder as she headed off down South American way. I could not complain (not that I ever dared to).

The Pre was an annexe to the 'Big School'. Its thirty-odd and yearly shrinking band of pupils were taught in a converted private house, with fine dilapidated gardens. The earth, where it had been turned over for Anderson shelters, was speckled with Roman earthenware; there must have been a large midden there fifteen hundred years before.

The adjoining grammar school is a pompous, red-brick, Victorian-Elizabethan structure. 'One kindly mother we salute, that she may stand for ever' ran the (since decommissioned) school song. It has stood for four centuries and more.

The school's interior walls were emblazoned with honours boards glorifying those who fell in the Great War, school captains and first-class degree winners (at Oxbridge, exclusively). There were no such boards in the Pre. CRGS, unusually, owned outright its own ground and property, which has given it an uncommon independence over its destiny since the 1960s: the place may well stand for ever. It gets outstanding results in current league tables, though the honours boards have gone — they're now electronic on *The*

Times, Guardian and *Independent* websites.

Pupils (including those in the Pre) wore the hideous purple jacket and cap which made 'grammar bugs' figures of contemptuous fun, and not uncommonly assault, to their less privileged peers as they walked the streets to and from school.

The Pre was staffed by a couple of fearsome spinsters, Misses Stanyon ('Nagbag') and Wagstaff ('Wagbag'). Stanyon, particularly, was an intelligent woman — one of those whose abilities had ended up under-utilized in primary schoolteaching because all other avenues were blocked to her sex, however able. It gave an edge of razorish impatience to her instruction. She merited better than childminding: she knew it, and made us feel it. Nagbag could teach across the field and ran her school as efficiently as Albert Speer. I remember looking, with strange stirrings, at her plumpish, stockinged legs, as they splayed beneath her desk. Wagbag's did nothing for me. Both were strict disciplinarians, not afraid to strike children. Kindly mothers be damned.

The teachers never went into the boys' bog. All the years I was there it had on its wall a prominent graffiti instruction redolent of the 1940s: 'Please do not drop fag ends in the urinal as it makes them soggy and almost impossible to smoke'. The male janitor left it defiantly unerased, as a kind of gesture of solidarity with the boys against the humiliating gynocracy under which he, like they, groaned.

Apart from the two dragon ladies, boys in the Pre were taught by the most expendable teachers from the Big School, particularly one lugubrious oaf, Mr Daniels, whose nickname, 'Hairy Dan', followed him over the way. 'Lazy Dan' would have been as appropriate: he prepared nothing by way of classwork. He once punched me so hard in the stomach I collapsed, winded, and had to be taken off to lie down. He intended, I think, a kind of manly camaraderie, and miscalculated the blow. 'The boy fainted' was the version given out (given the poor food, fainting was common).

I am hugely grateful to HD. In order to fill in time, during what for him must have been a humiliating confirmation of how little his headmaster and colleagues thought of him, he read virtually the whole of Harrison Ainsworth's *Old Saint Paul's* to us. I thrilled, and still do, at the hack Victorian gothicist's description of the Plague, the Fire, the murderous nurse, Judith, and the undertaker, Chowles, with their booty stolen from the dead, drowned by molten lead in the climax to that novel.

Retreating to either side of the cell, they glared at each other like wild beasts. Suddenly, Judith casting her eyes to the entrance of the vault, uttered a yell of terror, that caused her companion to look in that direction, and he perceived that the stream of molten lead had gained it, and was descending the steps. He made a rush towards the door at the same time with Judith, and another struggle ensued, in which he succeeded in dashing her upon the floor. He again opened the door, but was again driven backwards by the terrific flame, and perceived that the fiery current had reached Judith, who was writhing and shrieking in its embrace. Before Chowles could again stir, it was upon him. With a yell of anguish, he fell forward, and was instantly stifled in the glowing torrent, which in a short time flooded the whole chamber, burying the two partners in iniquity, and the whole of their ill-gotten gains, in its burning waves.

For a child who had been bombed that stilted Victorian prose rubbed against the nerves like emery paper. One says 'Victorian', but large sections of Ainsworth's novel are lifted, verbatim, from Defoe's *Journal of the Plague*

Year. That too chimed horribly with what one had witnessed in one's short life.

Hairy Dan's other favourite novel — or at least the one with which he chose to while away our mutual hours of confinement — was *Lorna Doone*. For children who had endured the apocalyptic winters and fuel cuts of 1946 and (particularly) 1947, Blackmore's description of the 'Great Winter' of 1683 struck a chilly chord. 'That night', recalls Jan, of the coldest night:

> such a frost ensued as we had never dreamed of, neither read in ancient books, or histories of Frobisher. The kettle by the fire froze, and the crock upon the hearth-cheeks; many men were killed, and cattle rigid in their head-ropes. Then I heard that fearful sound, which never I had heard before, neither since have heard (except during that same winter), the sharp yet solemn sound of trees, burst open by the frost blow. Our great walnut lost three branches, and has been dying ever since.

Jan, with his sixty-inch chest and his sixty-two-inch otterskin weskit, feels the cold no more than a Devonshire polar bear would. It was different for me — Smike Sutherland.

Malnourished, half-orphaned, wretchedly shy and sorry for myself, in the winter of 1947 I — like most of the country — was colder than I have been in the whole of my life since. There is part of me which, like the trapper Sam McGee in Robert Service's poem, is chilled to the soul and will never be warm.

Victorian fiction has always spoken to me more eloquently than any other literature. It was a country to which I had a visa, my Argentine. The Victorian Novel was part refuge, but also interesting to explore and, more significantly, a place where one could find the wherewithal to explain things, put them in order. It also put me in touch with a world before world war. It was not then all that historical. In the 1940s the late Victorian England of, say, *Jude the Obscure* was historically closer than — say — Bill Haley's *Rock Around the Clock* is now. One knew Victorians — my grandparents, for example. My grandmother drank tea from her saucer, with the slurping justification: 'Queen Victoria did it.' She would know.

Hairy Dan, without intending to do anything other than skive, planted in me a love of Victorian fiction which has shaped my professional life and made sense (for me) of that life. It was a strange Open Sesame, but one of the more important in my life. Bad teachers are not always bad for their pupils.

I was chronically bullied in my time at the Pre. The bullying was ritualistic. The last boy in (and I was *fin de ligne*, after me came nothing) was, by tradition, nominated 'stinker'. Colchester, as in everything, was depressingly unimaginative — and, as the upside, not particularly nasty. There was no Flashman, no roasting. There was no one in the Pre like Graham Greene's diabolic classmate with the dividers, who incarnated evil.

I was pushed, jostled, humiliated, routinely insulted. Noses would be held, as the stinker passed by. There was an unpleasant baptismal ritual relating to a deity called Bog God (head down the pan, stinker to the stink, farewell, etc). I humbly accepted my role as He-who-shall-be-bullied. There was a kind of security in having a role, however lowly, in this intricate society. At the top were the 'toughs', kings of the castle. I was at the bottom. Belonging was all. I suspect the teachers knew about these practices but, like warders and the brutal pecking order in prisons, the two Misses turned a blind eye in the interest of maintaining order. Bullying is, as Foucauldians know, delegated power, not anarchy.

One of the complaints my teachers

routinely made about me at the Pre was 'vagueness'. One reason that I didn't make a strong impression was absence. In one term, in 1947, I was absent for 36 of the 62 teaching days — illness, truancy, forgetfulness. Ostracism, when I did turn up, diverted me still more strongly to the one thing for which I needed no assistance: reading. I began to consume books voraciously at this period. It was the one thing I could do well — not least because it was a retreat into oneself. Given the huge teaching burden placed on the Pre's spinster workforce, 'reading hours' (i.e. benign educational neglect) could be sprung on us at any time of the day.

There were perennial problems to do with class. I was, as regards 'manners', as alien as a Craig Raine Martian. The other children there were solidly middle class, sons of farmers, solicitors and prosperous High Street shopkeepers. Their families had cars, took holidays, drank tea on lawns and had women of my aunt Ivy's and grandmother's class who 'did' for them.

I was the child of a fast woman, with a family little better than urban peasantry. I was once invited to a fellow pupil's large house in Lexden, Colchester's west end. We were told, airily, by his mother to go and wash our hands before tea (in the garden!). I found myself alone, wholly bemused, in the bathroom, doing desperate things with a nail brush that spattered dirty spots all over the mirror. The towel, after I used it was as filthy as a coalminer's gusset. Doubtless the Bog God smiled, as he looked up from the WC. After a few such experiences I mastered the art.

Another Year, Another School

The pre finally closed down a year before I was eligible to try for the Big School. In the year before taking the elevenplus I was removed (by my mother's remote instruction and subsidy) to a private school, Endsleigh House, which had been recently set up as a speculative venture in a mansion with huge grounds on the edge of town. This was my fourth school in five years. The fees were, by the standards of the time, exorbitant.

I performed miserably in the entrance test and was downstreamed into Upper 3B. Upper 3A was where the ten year olds expected to pass the eleven-plus were put: they got the better teachers. I was certainly intelligent enough for the other class but I was invariably confused by tests. Constant domestic and educational disruption had rendered me chronically unable to acquire skills, or to come to terms with anything unfamiliar — I was always too nervous about a sudden change of scene. It was like finding some shape in a kaleidoscope another hand was forever shaking. I was slow to learn to cycle, to swim, to pass exams. I was never quite sure what was wanted of me, and too frightened of disapproval to be myself.

As it was, the year at Endsleigh, perversely, was a pleasant interlude. The low pressures and low expectations of the Upper 3B environment, coming when they did, freed me to do the two things I most enjoyed: read and wait for Saturday's (and on some glorious weekends, Sunday's) fishing.

The school did not invest heavily in reading materials (there was no library). As a snip, the school bursar had picked up a pre-war classroom supply of (Captain) Frederick Marryat's 1840 bestseller *Masterman Ready*. This was prescribed for Upper 3B. Upper 3A got the more demanding *Oliver Twist*.

Marryat was one of the nautical novelists who, a few decades after Trafalgar (a period when past victories are most golden and sentimentalized), penned a series of improving tales for children, stiffened with his own experiences before the mast. He was a Victorian household name, now forgotten even in the classic reprint series.

Masterman Ready (like *The Coral Island*) is a corrective to that most fanciful and ridiculous Robinsoniad, *The Swiss Family Robinson*. A marooned middle-class family are given lessons in survival (*Lost* style) and — the children particularly — moral duty and civility by the seaman who is cast ashore with them, Masterman Ready. Above all, they learn from this lower-class person the imperative of humbly accepting and doing one's best in whatever station in life it has pleased God to place one. It is a lesson he has magnificently absorbed. Who is the master, and who the man?

Ready (as his name suggests) is, like Black Beauty, a good servant. Ever Ready. The point of his existence is to make middle-class lives comfortably middle class. Whether it's creating delicious stews out of jungle materials or fending off cannibals, that's his role in life. His reward is a warm glow of duty done and, when the time comes, a warm welcome from St Peter. He dies, having been pierced through some vital but unidentified organ by a savage's spear, with these last words to his mistress: 'Don't weep for me, dear madam. I'm only sorry that I cannot be any more useful to you.' There follows the death rattle.

Most of Upper 3B found the book unspeakably boring. I loved it. Marryat's improving tale spoke to me. I too wanted to serve. If only some family could have found their apprentice boy 'ready' indeed. During this slack year I also came across an omnibus volume of George Du Maurier's trio of author-illustrated novels. A *Punch* cartoonist of genius, Du Maurier turned to fiction when his eyes began to fail. He duly turned out the late Victorian superseller, *Trilby*: the novel which inspired the hat, the name of at least one American town, much anti-Semitism (in the depiction of Svengali) and David Lodge's fine novel *Author, Author*.

Trilby was not, as it happened, the Du Maurier novel which most entranced me. My favourite was *Peter Ibbetson*. I was particularly attracted by the magical technique developed by the hero, 'dreaming true'. Imprisoned for life for a crime of passion, Ibbetson discovers that if he goes to sleep with his arms placed in a special way above his head, dreaming becomes time travel by which he can, at will, revisit his own past. Night after night I would lie in bed and attempt to dream true — invariably waking up disappointed with agonizingly stiff arms.

For those who are interested (few are in Du Maurier nowadays) there is a dry summary of the novel in the encyclopaedia on Victorian Fiction which I published in 1990. Of the thousand novel summaries contained in that laborious tome, which took up ten years of my working life, I had, I reckon, read over seventy before the age of eighteen.

Du Maurier was, like Trollope, a 'lesser Thackeray'. That was a route I would track later to its source: the great English Horatian. In the meanwhile, I read, as young people do, with the indiscriminate appetite and inexhaustible energy of a garbage grinder. Biggles, Just William, Pearl S. Buck's (interestingly adult) The Good Earth, Stevenson — not Treasure Island (overrated) but Kidnapped: the lost child in Scotland theme appealed to me. Alas, I had no Alan Breck willing to cut his silver buttons off for me; but the wicked uncle Ebenezer was not a hard part to cast from my family. One of the more reread of my books was Ernest Thompson Seton's anthropomorphic animal fables. I also picked up, at a young age, from the twopenny library in the nearby newsagent, a copy of Robert Heinlein's The Puppet Masters — the source text (via Jack Finney) for the classic sci-fi fable, Invasion of the Body Snatchers.

The reading was random but manic in its intensity. And there were, of course, comics. I yearned for Friday and the new Wizard, Hotspur and Rover and the series heroes: Morgan the Mighty, Johnny Fleetfoot, Baldy Hogan, and the great amateur athlete Wilson — a modest, working-class looking fellow, who would suddenly irrupt on a humble roadster, wearing cycling clips, and win the

Tour de France: or take on a galloping horse over a hundred yards, and win.

Alas, in the 1948 and 1952 Olympiads, there were no Wilsonish golds for Britain. And the Baldy Hogans proved no match for Moscow Dynamo or (of all teams) the Hungarians. The little man might have won the war: the peace would be a harder battle.

Even more eagerly awaited than the week's crop of British comics were the monthly packages of American comics ('Yankmags', as they were called) which my mother sent me, along with the conscience candies. On my precise instruction, she bought mainly Fawcett Comics. Captain Marvel was my favourite, and his unending battle against the evil scientist, Dr Sivana. As with dreaming true, Marvel's Shazam spell fed my fantasies of escape and omnipotence (the word is an acronym of the seven gods of power). Batman and Superman, as I told my mother, meant nothing to me. Only Mr Shazam.

These comics were unavailable in Britain. It was almost worth being a motherless child to get hold of them, still erotic with the fresh smell of paper and ink.

Reunited, in a Sense

My mother stayed in the Argentine three years. I can put together a rough outline of her life there; she never told me directly. I would, laboriously, write immensely long letters every Saturday night, telling her everything I had done, turning impressive phrases for her admiration. She replied seldom, cursorily and always fondly. She had, she would say, shown my letters around and they had been admired: which would inspire me to still more voluminous and eloquent feats of unrequited penmanship next Saturday.

She was in the country during the first, revolutionary, Perón era. Juan Perón had come to power in early 1946, borne up on a surge of support from the shirtless ones (*los descamisados*) and the army, a month or two before my mother arrived. The Peronist presidency would eventually reduce the country from its status as the richest of the South American states — truly argentine — to a basket case, and thence the ugly dictatorship that Mrs Thatcher (the anti-Evita) toppled.

For the moment, the lives of the rich landowners, ranchers and property owners (to whom Hamilton belonged) was unaffected. They could still move money around, they still had a lot of it, and the currency was still hard enough to be exchangeable (the first five pound notes I ever saw — white serviette-sized things in those days — were flashed around by relatives of Ham's at the Trocadero Hotel in Piccadilly; there seemed to be more of them than serviettes). The money which she sent back to Ivy for my 'keep' must have come from her protector, partner or whatever he was, via legitimate currency channels. She was also, as I later realized, squirrelling some of it away as an emergency fund — should she, for example, wish to take the expensive journey home. She had no intention of being trapped, at any point in her life.

My mother's blonde hair and petite beauty led to her being routinely mistaken for Eva Perón. I was sent a newspaper cutting (from Hamilton's own paper) recording one such event. To my biased eye, she looked more like 'Evita' at the height of her co-presidential glamour than Madonna ever did — although, as she told the soldier, singing was not her talent ('don't cry for me, Abbey Fields').

Rusty, the household red-setter, had a litter

of puppies: I was allowed one, a bitch, and called it, inevitably, Evita. I didn't house-train it properly. One day I came back from school and was told it had been run over. I more than half suspect the beast was given the five-shilling humane treatment in the Butt Road vets. It was a troublesome dog and never (unlike me and Rusty) mastered the seen and not heard principle.

In my innocence, I would boast about my mother and show around a photograph of her I had. I was mystified by the strangely sympathetic looks I sometimes got. Others raised questions I did not. What, precisely, did she supply in return for the money which was, manifestly, rolling in and trickling back to East Street, and the private schools I was attending? She may have had some secretarial sinecure at the paper. Her shorthand — thanks to Jack — was good, if idiosyncratic, and her typing fast; and, by now, she could write fluently and accurately. But secretarial wages — even in the land of silver — do not run to fur coats and the jewellery, costume watches with limply lustrous 18-carat chainmail bracelets, and the two steamer trunks full of shoes, handbags and silken things which she later brought back with her to England (together with a 17-jewel Swiss watch for me). She was living a rich person's life, among the very rich, in a country which the war that had impoverished us had passed by.

One was told that, when ships came up the River Plate into Buenos Aires, the smell of sizzling steak was so overpowering it could be detected, salivatingly, five miles off. We made do with Bisto. Argentina is a warm country, but my mother returned to England with a chinchilla fur coat which had to be kept during summer in a commercially refrigerated store. Even if affordable, such luxuries were unavailable to all but the criminally rich in Attlee's England.

She had always affected varnished nails. Three years' exposure to Latin beauty resulted in nails of Nosferatu length. She picked up during these years a certain foreignness of manner, a half-toss of the head to stress whatever point she was making. Her vocabulary had enlarged to that of a woman with tertiary education. She could make conversation — not merely talk. She could make conversation in Spanish, if need be.

I never found out why the Argentine arrangement fell through. It wasn't because Hamilton lost interest: he travelled to England three times after she left him, to persuade her to think again. The offer was always there. She was, at one point, tempted and told me (I was fifteen at the time) that we were both going to the Argentine. I was vaguely excited at the prospect, but she eventually decided against it. I never knew what swung her one way or the other. But I would have liked some of that luxury.

My guess is that she perceived that the country was going to the dogs fast in Perón's disastrous second term. She had seen it happen before, as a young girl in the 1930s. She may have gone off Ham physically. Like GI Brides, she missed her mum. She was still in her mid-thirties and, with her new layer of cosmopolitan chic, she may have wanted to try again for the life-prizes she had always sought. Independence was high among them. One thing I am sure of: she did not come back to England to be reunited with her son, any more than she had left the country to be separated from him.

I was not standing on the quayside at Southampton with a bouquet when she docked. I was not at Waterloo when the boat train steamed in. Truth was, I did not know precisely when she was coming back. A telegram could have told us, to the minute: but none was sent. I came back from school, one September afternoon, expecting nothing special, and she was there. She had stopped off in London, where arrangements were made for her luggage, then travelled light to Colchester.

There was a kiss, an embrace, a waft of scent, and I fell in love with her, again, on the spot. She had been out of my life for long enough — five years — for me to see her not as a mother, but a woman. Any incest taboo had evaporated. I could (at that moment, at least) feel a guiltless sexual pang. She was in travelling clothes, modestly bejewelled, impeccably varnished and glowing with expensive make-up and three years' sunshine.

The first thing she did, after a visual inspection and the statutory 'How you've grown', was to pounce on the Essexisms I had picked up, overlaying my Lallans Scots (thank God her ears were never offended by that monstrosity). I can remember the scene exactly: it was my job to go down and fill the coal bucket (there would be a big fire that night). 'Oi've left a bitter dust, sorry,' I said. 'I've trailed some dust in,' she echoed, quietly. I would, over the next few months, be her mynah bird, picking up the inflections and accentuations of my new class identity: son of Elizabeth Sutherland.

She moved in, pro tem, with my aunt and uncle, assuming, by right of glamour, No. 1 slot on the bath rota. She also took over my bedroom; I was moved upstairs to the attic.

157

(Bizarrely, ten years later, I would have a life-changing affair, and nights of love, with a woman who rented that attic: it was where I had pumped away, working off my first sexual fantasies. Life's circuits are strange sometimes.)

My mother got a job as a welfare officer on the vast council estates (houses for heroes) built in the post-war period on the outskirts of Colchester — Shrub End, Mersea Road and Monkwick. She was now that most hated thing in English life, as Orwell observes, a 'nosey parker'. More important to her, it was 'professional' nosey-parkerism, bringing with it NALGO (National Association of Local Government Officers) affiliation, a monthly salary, not a weekly pay packet, and (in time) a car allowance.

It was white collar work. How did she get it? — a trollop (as some doubtless said behind her back), without any training other than basic school education. I never asked the question at the time, though as the years passed I knew of her 'connections'. Doubtless, it was through one of the councillors she befriended, in whose gift jobs like hers were.

A couple of years later, when one of these local grandees became besotted with her and recklessly bombarded her with letters, she contemptuously tore them up and threw them in the bin. I extracted them and pasted the pieces together (years of practice in my grandparents' lavatory had given me the skills and patience for such tasks). It was incredibly frank and sexual stuff. It would, as the love-mad official confessed, have landed him in the divorce court, and possibly the criminal court, if it got out.

It might well have done. To my shame, I photographed the letters (it was during my brief camera-mad phase: I had converted the coal cellar into a primitive dark room). I did not intend to do anything with them. Reprehensible as the act was, it was a symptom of the bafflement I always felt with her — my inability to 'read' her. Instead, I would read her private correspondence. It was part of a lifelong attempt to assemble her into some meaningful shape. About the same period I found the letters from my father in South Africa (soon to be burned). They had passed under the censor's eyes and were bland: but seeing his fine handwriting, and the officerly endearments ('darling', 'poppet', 'I love you'), was achingly disturbing. It was as if I, not he, were the ghost in the triangle, unable to be heard by them.

She did her job well, rising up the rungs over the next ten years until, dizzily, she

159

graduated into management and, on retirement, was rewarded by being made a JP. No longer inspecting the class in which she had originated, she was sitting in judgement over them. Her nickname in later years, she was amused to boast, was 'rich bitch'.

She also cultivated a long relationship with a man who, like her, had made something of himself — rising by almost Nietzschean will (over the rubble of a disastrous marriage) to wealth in the motor trade. It is not, I can warrant, something you achieve by being a nice guy.

The two of them, rich bitch and rich bastard, ended up on a yacht in the South of France. Mars could not have been further from the Colchester in which they had been brought up. He never much liked, or understood, or wanted to understand, me and eventually cuckooed me out of her life. It was done without malice, as a squash player might barge his opponent out of the centre of the court, the better to dominate the game. He dominated better than most people. It was the key to his business success.

They married in 1961, in her (biologically safe) late forties. I saw relatively little of her after that. For many years, they were abroad. She told me, very late in life, that she regretted giving up the freedoms of being single. But adaptation to anything came naturally to her. She could, as the proverb had it, have fallen into a cesspit and come up smelling of roses. I am certain that waiting until I was in my twenties and launched in life before remarrying was not done out of consideration for me. She wanted to ensure that her intended was well-off enough for her never to have to worry about money again. Which, by ruthless entrepreneurship, he was.

The smoking caught up with her in her seventies. She died, after a week's unconsciousness on life-support apparatus. It was supporting nothing she would have called life. Her widowed husband suggested that I pay for the funeral and cremation, 'she would have liked it'. We drove to the ceremony in his Aston Martin. If she had made a will, I never knew about it. She left me nothing, and he passed nothing of hers on. Ten years later, after his own health had deteriorated, I got a message that he had some clothes and personal effects of hers he wanted me to have (he had remarried). I didn't reply. If there was one thing she taught me, it was not to be sentimental about the past. Or her. That doesn't mean I didn't love her. Or she me.

Scholarship Boy

In 1949, on her return from Argentina, Liz had lifeforce enough to run a power station. One of the first things she did in her new job was to take her hapless sister's life in hand. She got Bill and Ivy a council house (one of the nicer ones); for the first time in their lives, they had a fridge and running hot water. She also smoothed their way to adopting the children which Ivy's fibroids had denied them. They turned out to be good parents. My mother was also instrumental in getting her brother out of his slough of despond and aspirin nonsense, and into a teacher training college. She slipped money to my grandmother, who received payment that would not have been out of place at the Red Lion Hotel for my predictably unpalatable lunches (mince, mince, mince). About, or for, her father, she could do nothing. But, incredibly, she was able to jolly a smile out of him now and then.

My affairs were harder to sort out. My mother had come back at a critical moment: the eleven-plus year. This was the major fork in a child's life. I was aware of its significance:

'the scholarship' was what had been denied my mother and Arthur. I was to be luckier — if I could prove myself.

After I had been sent to bed, I would sometimes, aged ten-plus, sit on the stairs going up to my attic bedroom, under a plastercast Venus de Milo, whose jutting breasts were beginning to interest me as I trudged up the wooden road to Bedford. If I stamped up, with over-the-shoulder good-nights, and then crept clandestinely back down, I could eavesdrop on what was said; which (especially in summer when it was warm and still light) I sometimes did.

On one such occasion I overheard my aunt Ivy complaining, in her horrible Essex whine, about my inaudible 'mumbling'. She didn't realize that I didn't want to speak like her, and that I didn't want to hurt her feelings by speaking like someone better than her. Result? Verbal paralysis. Every time she commanded Rusty to 'Lay down' for the afternoon flea-hunt, I shuddered. And, rather than resolve the issue, I mumbled.

More worryingly, I overheard — it must have been in early 1949, before my aunt and uncle were shipped out — a debate about what to do with me, should I fail the 'scholarship' (as they still called it, with reference to their own missed chances).

Present at the discussion were my mother, two uncles, and my aunt. I should be apprenticed as a bricklayer, the aristocrat of workers in these house-building times, Arthur suggested — jealousy of me getting the better of him, although, on the face of it, the idea was sensible. It seemed to get general assent — although not from my mother, I was glad to (over)hear. She, I understood, would keep me on at Endsleigh, with the other duds. But could she afford to? And what would I do at sixteen?

The prospect of the trowel, hod, and the hard outdoor life struck horror into my heart, even if brickies were earning handsomely (as much as £20 a week — much more than my schoolteachers) with all the post-war construction and reconstruction. Manual work, even skilled manual work, was not to my taste. Since I could remember, I had been bought Christmas and birthday presents designed to encourage a practical bent in me. It was not a direction in which I was inclined to bend.

I was happy to have model aeroplane kits, Meccano, steam engines fuelled by meths, ingenious little dynamos, John Bull printing pads, fretsaws, chemistry sets. They were pretty and represented property. Like the boxing gloves hanging on the hook behind my door, they symbolized adult interest in me: I mattered sufficiently to be 'spoiled' with things that cost money. I valued them as an absentee landlord might value his acres, but I was buggered if I was going to be enthralled by them.

The dog, Rusty, would probably
be a better mechanic

What these mechanical things signalled to me was a one-way ticket to a life in oil-stained overalls; or, if I was lucky, a Montague Burton ('the 50 shilling tailors') suit supervising men in oil-stained overalls. When my uncle Bill instructed me in woodwork, or dismantling the oilier parts of my bicycle, I was cack-handed. Subconsciously, the maladroitness was deliberate. Books, something in me had decided, were the door through which my future lay (I had to ask for them by title: they never came unsolicited). But to get to the richer stores of books, I would have first to pass the eleven-plus barrier. Bricks awaited, if I failed.

When I joined UCL in the 1970s, at thirty-plus, I never knew whether to spit or genuflect at the psychology department which I passed daily on my way to the college's wretched refectory (bad catering was a part of its defiant rebellion against Oxbridge sumptuousness). It was at UCL that Cyril Burt did his pioneering work which led to the introduction of the eleven-plus exam — the main tool by which Butler's 1944 Education Act was implemented. Essentially the Butler reform reversed the old Marxist slogan 'From each according to his abilities, to each according to his needs'. The eleven-plus rewarded those determined already to have superior abilities. Those that had, got more.

The root problem was resources. Only about 20 per cent of the school population at large could be provided with a 'good' education. 'Good' meant the kind of teachers, plant, uniforms, equipment, books, playing fields that the misnamed public schools had enjoyed for generations.

Grammar schools would be public schools for the public. But how to select the favoured 20 per cent? Burt's IQ test provided the required diagnostic machinery. By examination of twins separated at birth Burt and his assistants had discovered that — whatever the social variables (class, location, access to education) — children possessed an innate and measurable 'intelligence': brain power, IQ, Intelligence Quotient. The right questions could penetrate through any overlays of class or educational advantage to that raw stuff, intelligence. The eleven-plus was less an exam than a tool designed to measure IQ on a percentile scale. The results, if you went along with Cyril, were scientifically 'fair'. Nothing could be fairer. Aristocracy out, meritocracy in.

There was, as it emerged in the 1970s, only one flaw in Burt's research. It had been faked. The man was a charlatan. In fact Old Mother Riley, looking at the successful intakes and their backgrounds, could have told the politicians that 'intelligence', as Burt measured it, was as much culturally specific as it was native or genetic. Moreover, young children (quite capable of picking up a complex language in three years) could learn the techniques required to score above median on intelligence tests — provided, that is, they were taught the techniques (Upper 3B wasn't; Upper 3A was).

None the less, straight as the gate was (and somewhat crooked the path leading up to it), the gate was, in the late 1940s, slightly ajar. The burden placed on a working-class child whose family had a candidate for the exam could be immense. The traditional reward for 'passing' was a bicycle — a Hercules or a Raleigh. The penalties for failing were harder.

Recently I looked at the hands of a friend I have been close to for forty years, since I was a teenager. He and a couple of others in his school, highly intelligent and well taught, had deliberately failed their eleven-plus because they did not want to be split up — deracinated, declassed. It was a noble decision and not uncommon; a child capable of passing the exam was also intelligent enough to choose not to. My friend's hands, after a lifetime's 'real' work (including a lot of bricklaying), are knuckly, horribly bent and give him constant pain; they are long worn out. Mine are as soft, straight, supple and 'useless' as they ever were: I'll go to the grave with the hands of a young man. He, I should add, will go to his grave leaving over a million pounds.

Who knows, I might have been a half-decent bricklayer, if never a millionaire. Once I have mastered something mechanical (such as driving, five-finger typing or computer programming) I do it averagely well. But I have never been good at exams. A lifetime's teaching has confirmed my belief that not only is intelligence unmeasurable, so do patterns of learning ability vary from child to child. I, personally, always had difficulties in the early stages of learning any skill or technique. It's physical as well as mental. It took me ages (with a kindly uncle panting behind me, steadying hand on the saddle) before I could ride a bike, or let go of the side-rail and swim, or understand how equations work. Once over that stile I learned competently enough; but I needed help (not always there) to get over it.

It was not a recipe for success post-1944. I got mediocre O-levels, downright awful A-levels (amphetamines didn't help) and entrance only to a third division university — as such things were judged then. I don't know whether my impediment is a feature of mental wiring, like stuttering, or acquired. It could be a nervous fear of leaving the known for the unknown — terror born of long years of insecurity. Whatever the case, it's a fact.

Take-off is difficult for me: that is the point at which I needed good teachers — or, failing that, good luck.

In a system as nakedly competitive, and as unidimensional, as the Burtian I was disadvantaged. The eleven-plus could be prepared for, but I got no preparation. The exam flummoxed me. There were three sections: English, Maths and General. The exam was sat in the classrooms of the mock-Elizabethan grammar school which a lucky one-in-five of the examinees could expect to call home over the next seven years. The exams were, like the school, sexually segregated.

I can remember the classroom exactly — first floor, by the window looking down on the headmaster's house and gardens. One image sticks in my mind. As the papers were being distributed a boy in front of me took out a then new-fangled ballpoint pen: a 'biro' as they were called, after the Hungarian inventor. 'If you use that,' the invigilating Squelch said, 'you will fail the examination.' Dip and blot with the exam-issue pens and inkwells was mandatory. Ballpoints made writing too easy. I hope the man is burning, on a pyre of discarded exam scripts, somewhere in teachers' hell (Hairy Dan's sentence I'll commute, on grounds of

Harrison Ainsworth).

I did well on the English verbal, badly on the others and was called for 'interview' — which I waltzed through. Face to face with adults, I could gauge exactly what they wanted. There was a passage to read out — about a Mrs Beauchamp (which I pronounced correctly, 'Beecham') who was said to be 'captivated' by a stranger she met. What did the word mean, I was asked? 'Entranced,' I shot back, adding 'enraptured' for good measure. I knew all about captivation. With the one word I was in. I chose a Hercules.

I would be downstreamed again — all interviewees (given their lower IQ point score) had to be. But I would be put as high up as possible — in the middle of the three incoming streams. If I was smart, I could trail the top pack and join them at the end of a first-year reshuffle.

Dunroamin

After my mother had put her sister's life in order we stayed a while in the now cavernously empty East Street flat before she took on a small apartment in the centre of town.

The new place had geysered hot water (which meant baths on days other than Saturday), two corridor-connected bedsits, no living room, paraffin-mantled heaters (surprisingly efficient) and a scullery, barely the size of a telephone box, in which it was tactful not to linger if the other person were using the adjoining toilet. No matter. My mother would no more have thought of cooking a meal than bottling jam for the Women's Institute. What hot dinners I had were provided by my grandmother in West Street: mince with everything. Her menu instilled in me a lifetime conviction that there is very little food of which the eating merits the trouble of cooking it.

The apartment in Wellington Street was a machine to live in — and all the machine I wanted, if she were living there. In the first couple of what would be eight years' cohabitation I would hang around by my mother's workplace, the housing department offices in Stanwell Street, from five o'clock on, like a swain outside the stage door. 'He's here!' I would sometimes hear colleagues shouting up the stairs to her office. When she came out (always late, usually waving, sometimes kissing colleagues) we would catch a movie. In those days you just walked in at whatever point either of the two films on the double bill had reached, and walked out likewise. It could be puzzling to see the denouement — of, say, *From Here to Eternity* — before the exposition, or central complication, and with a second feature intervening. But it pleases me to think that it was good training for my later explorations of narrative. Bricolage.

After we came out of the dreamhouse, the walls of my stomach kept from pleating by a sixpenny bag of KP nuts, it would be fish and chips, or pork pie, or — if she were minded to 'cook' — scrambled egg sandwiches, her speciality, and very quickly rustled up. As likely as not, she would then (it still being an hour or two before closing time) go out 'for a drink', or whatever. And I would be alone with the radio, my book, or just myself. Lights out was entirely up to me. Reveille as well, most days.

By the time I was fifteen, my mother and I had drifted into amicably separate lives. When I came back from whatever I had been doing after school (a lot of hanging out on bicycles up to the age of fifteen) there would be, if I was lucky, a ten-shilling note, or a couple of half-crowns, on the scullery table. If unlucky, a cheese and pickle sandwich or a tin of beans. Or — if it was a bad day — the scrawled instruction to 'get something at Gran's — love, M'.

After the age of sixteen, when I was mad about jazz, I would wear out my vinyl on the record player in my room, bought at huge expense (another 'sacrifice'), until Willis Conover's two-hour, short-wave jazz programme on the Voice of America. 'The most listened-to jazz disc jockey in the world', Conover's mission was to bring down the evil empire, corroding it culturally. There was collateral corrosion in Colchester every night, round about midnight (a Thelonius Monk number I loved).

'Rock me, rock me, in your great brass bed,' Ma Rainey or some other mother of the blues would croon, 'eagle rock me till my face turns red', and, under the blankets, I would think of my own timid explorations beneath gingham and finger-defying navy blue serge. Eagle rocking was many years away, perhaps for ever — whatever it was. Jelly rolls were another area of interest. And black men digging each other's potatoes.

The radio — a vast multi-valved, mahogany-cased thing, brought back by my uncle Arthur from Berlin, that took five minutes to warm up — would be perched on a chair, to the right of my bed. On the left, I had a tasselled bedside lamp (its central column feebly imitating a dripping candle) on the bedside bookcase. I would read and listen. Conover's programme went out until midnight and sometimes I would wake up in the small hours, to the sound of short-wave static, like the little girl in *Poltergeist*. I have, in later years, a chronically weakened left eye and right ear. I trace the disabilities back to those five years, glued on one side to the amplifier, the book angled sharply on the other, to get the page into the brightest light. Heaven, the French wit said, would be a sofa and an endless supply of novels. For me it was a single bed, a two-week loan library book, a 2-amp radio and a 40-watt bulb.

In the morning, we kept out of each other's way in our separate rooms and ablutions. By the time the latter included shaving (a 'Blue Gillette', frugally reused for a fortnight), I affected toast (sliced Mother's Pride, singularly misnamed) and Fry's chocolate spread

175

for breakfast. From the age of seventeen, I added the Gallic chic of green-tinned Nescafé 37. Milk, in the fridgeless scullery, was always a gamble in summer. Sometimes I would double the spoonful, lob in sugar, and conceive it espresso. Coffee bars and Gaggia machines were all the rage, as Attlee's austerity mellowed into Macmillan's You've-never-had-it-so-Good (almost as good as his class had always had it, the old grouse-shooting Whig meant).

At the weekend, my mother would have procured from Gunton's (Colchester's nearest approach to a delicatessen) a tin of ravioli. Spaghetti sarnies were long gone — with the snoek. By the time I was wearing suede chukka boots and cavalry twill, there was even a bottle of Dimple Haig to be found somewhere in her room. Another, empty, bottle was a saving receptacle for sixpences — which would go in, but could not be shaken out: you had to shatter the bottle to get at them.

It was a civilized life, if less cosmopolitan than I fantasized it to be. I had all I wanted. I was living with the woman I loved, in a condition of domestic equality. I had solitude and a warm place to read. We had our occasional lunches or suppers together — usually 'out', always convivial. For the whole of my life, I have always felt a warm sensation of security when women (nowadays publishers, agents and editors, mainly) buy me lunch or dinner. Sometimes at night we would chat. She would recount things from work, with a caricaturist's eye: the manager Forbes, who was upper class and a womanizer; 'La Fotheringham', the typist with phenomenal speeds on the typewriter whom any man could womanize; patrician Snape, who kept a small, much-nipped brandy bottle in her bag, and might — if you barged in without knocking — be found splayed out on the Forbes desk, 'taking dictation'. She had a minor public school son who looked down on me, and whom I hated. My mother's view was consistently unshockable and amused; she expected very little from human beings.

It was enough for me that we were under the same roof. TV came late, when I was around seventeen. It never meant much in the flat. There was no reason, other than my mother, to hang around 18 Wellington Street. Certainly not the BBC, which, at that time, closed down at ten after a diet of indigestible Reithian piety with the implication that all God-fearing people by now should be in bed. Porridge (unsweetened) for the mind.

The man she was (mostly) with had a huge

American car, a pre-war Hudson Terraplane. I would see it cruising around like a great black pike. Sometimes she would be in it — sometimes, even, fur-coated; he in his black Crombie overcoat or overemphatic houndstooth. Although he had been ground crew, RAF, during the war, he sported a Battle-of-Britain handlebar and looked the part. His accent, and what I thought of as Aunt Ivy-isms, betrayed him — to my spitefully attuned ear, at least. He was making his way, using discarded partners and exploited employees, as his stepping stones to 'real' money. With the inexorable growth of car-ownership, it was there to be had. There was a new sucker taking to the road every minute; they were easily parted from their cash.

Obscurely, she 'did his books' (something very different from the books illuminated by my nocturnal faux candle) — her explanation for being out most nights. Sometimes I would come home after school and find the door to her room locked. She was doing rather more than his books on those occasions, I deduce.

I would feel what change I had in my pocket, make myself scarce (perhaps a milkshake down at the St John's Street bus station), and wander back later when the afternoon's doings were done. Sometimes, as

178

I could detect, she was doing other men's books. But, always, she was discreet and private. She never intruded into my life, and absolved any pangs of conscience she might have had with the fiction that I was brilliant and doing wonderfully at school, thanks to the sacrifices she had made for me. Like the ten bob on the table, she was generous, but never deeply involved in lives other than her own.

Grammar Bug

My life, meanwhile, was turbulent, in a dull kind of way. Nineteen forty-nine marked my entry into secondary school. The Burtian revolution, five years since launch, was running at its most madly utopian. A state experiment was being carried out on the British school population, as scientifically fallacious as Lysenko's on the sprouting grain fields of the Ukraine.

Following the Burtian rulebook, the 1949 intake at Colchester Royal Grammar School was streamed. There were three first-form classes: 1S (top scorers in the eleven-plus), 1C (ho-hum), 1G ('well, give the buggers a second chance — not that it'll do any good'). Notionally there was constant fluidity between the streams as they flowed, year by year, form by form. Variations in IQ (a fixed entity, as it had been conclusively proved) would emerge with ever more calibrated precision. The suffix letters, S, C and G, were chosen for their alphabetic neutrality, unlike Endsleigh's judgemental Upper 3A and Upper 3B, in which one was categorized like Hollywood movies.

But, as common sense would predict, the

top stream, with its more demanding standards and top teachers, flowed faster. The system handicapped the slower streams with a less demanding curriculum and less able teachers. The lowest stream of all was, most of it, destined to be disgorged, like so much juvenile sewage, at sixteen. An exception might be made if some outstanding sporting ability were discerned; something, for example, that might give CRGS victory over the two minor public schools who deigned to grace a grammar school's rugby fixture list: Felsted and Framlingham.

The scars for those thus extruded would be lifelong. Yet those scars might well be lovingly stroked, with Aguecheek ('I was loved once') pride. They had been contenders. A mechanic, who slaved in an unheated, clanging workshop for the ogre destined one day to be my stepfather (a figure with whom, thank God, I would never have to share a home or, horrible thought, a workplace), his head forever dug into the entrails of some spavined car, was one such CRGS reject.

Ernie contrived to insert into any pub conversation, as his oily hands cradled the pint mug, the proud fact that he had attended 'the grammar' — until the chop at sixteen, that is. It was like the fabled Indian degree: 'BA (failed)'. German mechanics I have since met take pride in their tradesman's expertise, not in their educational failures.

Looking at the sixth form it was clear as day that those initial, first-form settings might as well have been set in concrete. But no more than a field marshal at Passchendaele did the architects of Burtopia let casualty figures (80 per cent losses on entry, 30 per cent losses at exit) trouble them. Their scheme was right — for the country and for the future of the human race. Cyril had told them so.

And, anyway, there were more where we came from. As a Colcestrian Napoleon might have put it, a night of (sadly unParisian) love in the town's catchment area could replace all the lives the school annually tossed on the national scrapheap. There had, as it happened, been epic copulation with the returning of the nation's heroes in 1945. Bumper harvests of bright young boys were assured. Wastage was nothing to worry about — unless you were one of the millions wasted.

The middling class I was placed in, 1C, was a handicap, but not necessarily a one-way ticket to scrapheapville. There was even an up side. Downstream, one could be oneself while all the top fish swam, furiously and uniformly, in their shoal. But the sense of inferiority niggled. One was graded second class: official. And in subjects like maths, ground was never to be made up. Hence, in my case, the drift to the soft option, English.

Theory predicated a system which should be both socially classless and above political ideology: as distilled of impurities as the statistical tables on which Burt had erected his educational Laputa. It may have looked good in the UCL lab, where the mad scientist methodically cooked his figures to make them fit. It sure as hell didn't work on the ground.

'Colchester Royal' was an institution of sixteenth-century foundation and, like the grammar school Shakespeare went to in Stratford, had been founded to serve burghers (if that doesn't sound too Big Mac). You were a prosperous glovemaker or merchant, like John Shakespeare, and bright young Will got the education which would allow him to rise in life, without necessarily uprooting him from his community.

For over two centuries before 1944, its grammar school had been municipal Colchester property, as much as the Castle or the Moot Hall, the mayoral chain or the oyster feast (an annual 'tradition' allegedly going back to Roman times, in fact invented in the nineteenth century). After 1944, the CRGS catchment net was cast far beyond the town into the county hinterland. Smart kids were bussed in from miles around. It was no longer Colchester, but Educational District 17, East Anglia, which the school served. Among its small boarding contingent, there were kids poached from as far afield as London. As far as Burtism was concerned, the school had no more connection with the town than an aircraft carrier has with a port where it happens to be refuelling.

Internally, CRGS obstinately adhered to traditions of local service that — after 1944 — were officially and irreparably severed. It was irrational because the school, its 'masters' and governors were no longer choosing pupils for the good of Colchester, however their municipal minds might conceive that aim. The system was doing the selecting now. And the system didn't give a pinstriped Whitehall fuck about the town; its brief was national.

Ideology — what was called 'school spirit' — presented other intractable problems, at least for a few more years (my years, alas). Value systems and codes of conduct (manliness, pluck, play up and play the game) were deeply rooted. And they were radically un-Burtian. The system scorned such ancient historical baggage: it obstructed educational achievement. Metrics were what mattered. There was safety in numbers: grades, statistics, IQ percentiles. They were the facts on which the future could be planned.

But CRGS was still permeated, anachronistically, with fictions — specifically, the public-school ethos pioneered by Dr Arnold at Rugby a century earlier. Rugby, of course, was *the* CRGS game: soccer was for oicks. It may have been the people's game and — in the 1940s, with no TV — even more fanatically popular than today. But there was no place for round leather on the playing fields of Colchester Royal.

The school had, like the institutions it forlornly aped, a 'house' system (meaningless without all the pupils and masters boarded), and an annual 'cock house' competition, based on sporting performance — rugby, pre-eminently. The 'houses', which, unlike Eton or Harrow, were wholly imaginary structures, were named after historical heroes of Colchester and the school: Harsnett, Shaw Jeffrey, Parrs and Dugard. They might as well have added Tommy Handley and Two Ton Tessie O'Shea, for all the names meant to me.

There was a school song, composed by the above Jeffrey, in the patriotic period around World War One, which articulated what was fondly hoped to be the lofty idealisms of CRGS — and England itself. It was composed at the same time as the new

185

'Elizabethan' main building was constructed, in 1910 (hence the reference to 'Tudor banners'):

> Now hands about for Colchester
> And sound a rousing chorus;
> In praise of all our comrades here
> And those who went before us.
>
> Tradition gives us pride of birth
> Brave hearts and gentle manners
> For we are sons of men who marched
> Beneath the Tudor banners.
>
> So as we pass the torch along
> Aglow with high endeavour
> One kindly mother we salute
> That she may stand for ever.
>
> Sing, boys, sing
> Floreat sodalitas
> Sentiment is more than skill
> So sing together with a will
>
> Floreat sodalitas
> Tas Colcestriensis

This school song was bellowed out, uncomprehendingly, on break-up and other big days, under the school honour boards, in the dust-and-unwashed-boy-smelling assembly hall. In a Pavlovian way I liked it: but only because it was associated with holidays and the great summer release. If that was all it took to get out of the place, sing, boys, sing — with a will.

Honour, like IQ, was 'streamed' on these gilded plaques, to which the eyes wandered during the morning lesson or while listening to the wholly dishonourable detention list read out on Friday morning (on which, cautious fellow that I was, the name Sutherland rarely figured). The boards listed the 'fallen' (*pro patria mori*) and the 'risen' — those who had won scholarships to Oxbridge. The names were inscribed in gilt: they would live forever more. Most pupils would pass between the pillars ungilded, *los olvidados de Colchester*. No gilded board for them.

The school, for all the theoretic egalitarianism of its newfangled entrance exam, was riddled with obsolete codes which went against the grain of its new, Burtian, ethos. Who, with the eleven-plus razor at their throat, could believe that sentiment was more than skill? Was it sentiment that got you into the grammar school? What was 'sodalitas'? — it sounded like the kind of thing naughty priests do to altar boys.

The school was littered with no longer legible totemic symbols, which none the less radiated actively. Tudor banners were no longer in style, but the venerable 'Royal' in CRGS was commemorated by the uniform of purple jackets, ties and hats. Walking through the urban dinginess of the clothes-rationed late 1940s, the newly admitted pupil, throbbingly chromatic (his purple purchased, expensively, from the school outfitter in the High Street, Owen Ward, who had fiddled a monopoly), was, as the local phrase went, 'a sight'. One might as well have worn a boater down a coal mine.

We were mocked by the soccer-playing, eleven-plus-failing, drably clad townees with a rhyme of archetypal Essex literary poverty:

> Grammar bugs
> Eat slugs
> Dirty little hummerbugs

What that last word meant I never knew. But one heard the jeer wearyingly often as, bug-like, one crept home.

The very stupid, or wholly degraded, need never bother with exam results, any more than the beasts of the field. The upper classes in their public schools respect and use intelligence to consolidate their place in

188

society, but would never let themselves be tyrannized by the idiocies of social status by IQ score. Blood, family, money, connections, yes: but data points on a graph, devised by a mad scientist in a university that wasn't even Oxford? Be serious. If Prince Harry gets mediocre GCSE results, Eton has not failed. If CRGS failed to get its quota into Oxbridge, it was blanks on the honour board and dishonour all round.

The long and the short of it was: CRGS was an educational hothouse, and socially a madhouse. Aged eleven to eighteen, I was incapable of articulating any rational response to the institutionalized irrationality — certainly not rebellion. But I felt, intuitively, there was something wrong with the place — or, more precisely, with that searing sense of inferiority the place instilled in one, that there must be something very wrong with me. It was never the shoe, but the foot which was to blame. There must, I was convinced, be something misshapen in myself, in my chronic inability to fit in. Or later on, not being able to win a prefect's striped tie, star in the first fifteen or cruise, effortlessly, through the scholarship sixth-form class.

The school's confusingness was compounded by genetic confusion — my pride of birth, as 'our' song termed it. But which strand of the DNA that made John 'me' was dominant? I was never sure whether to march under the banner of Dashing Jack or the Schweikian Arthur.

Unlike my trophied father, I was not much good at sports — but with the haunting sense that I ought to have been and, indeed, could have been, if I was truly his son. I was big for the stunted era (blame ration books) and reasonably well-coordinated. It wasn't that I was afraid of physical contact: the bruising ('go for the legs') rugby tackle, the hard cricket ball that could break bones or stun you. I liked the mud and blood running down my shins, rather. I enjoyed the masochistic exhaustion, walking back (by myself) after a cold(ish) shower, feeling 'wounded'.

But on the pitch, in the fray, I was afraid, obscurely, of letting myself go. I could not, somehow, join in. I was terrified of the explosiveness of my temper, and the conse-quences, were I to lose it. Another part of me (Schweik Sutherland) refused to be a team player: it was a reflex, not a resolve — and, like other reflexes, ineradicable. When the Me262s flew over, and the 88s boomed, I was under the tank. In short, I was not a good sportsman, but never so bad as to be stigmatized as 'useless'.

Similarly, even in the bookish subjects I

loved, I was incapable of joining in or doing what I was told. I was derelict — not out of laziness, but on some bizarre principle. At O-level, for example, the prescribed novel for study was H. M. Tomlinson's *Gallions Reach*. I studiously avoided reading the thing, and actually went into the exam having not done more than skim the pages and read the Penguin blurb.

Why? Because it was prescribed and not to read it was a gesture of intellectual independence. I was like swaggering Zorba in the 1964 film — or, at least, so I would have liked to think. He will only dance for himself, not his master. I had, as a matter of record, not yet read Kazantzakis, and didn't like him when I did. But I distinctly recall reading *Rasselas* during the week of the exam, and could have chuntered on about the famous tenth chapter ('streaks of the tulip', etc). And I had, by this point, got through a creditable bunch of Trollope's Barsetshire novels, acquired from Doncaster's Castle bookshop. I had sniggered over Mrs Proudie's 'unhand it, sir!'

I could have inhaled Tomlinson as effortlessly as second-hand smoke. But I didn't; wouldn't. Why? Because someone else (the school, the board), not me, had chosen it. This curricular truancy was not a recipe for exam success. In fact, in an arena as competitive as CRGS, it was educational hemlock. Bluff, and quick footwork, could get one over the stile: but it won no prizes. And prizes were what CRGS was about.

On the other hand, perpetually vexed with myself as I was then, I cannot, decades later, criticize myself for that feeble *non serviam*. I have recently read Tomlinson's wretched composition: a sub-Conradian nautical work, shot through with Deepingesque philistinism, which richly deserves the oblivion into which it has fallen. It is not worth even two hours of a sixteen year old's time. I despise whatever prig imposed it on the O-level class of 1954.

Oddly enough, the reflex ('anything but the thing prescribed') persists. I always find it easier to read books I am not being currently paid to review than those that I am. I suspect it's fairly common with book-lovers generally. Browsing in bookshops or along library shelves is, in its mild way, a declaration of independence: 'I'll make my own choice, thank you.'

My school years were shadowed by feelings of guilt, demonstrable (measurable even) intellectual inferiority, frustrated desire, and not belonging. Looking back, I can flatter myself that there was, underneath it, a now discernible strategy, as there is in most defection. I was preserving what little (my reading) was mine. In the school, as in East/West Street, when I read I was in charge of myself. I have always been struck by a line in Trollope's *Eustace Diamonds*, after the governess Lucy Morris has been jilted by her MP lover: 'There remained to her the dreary possession of herself.'

At the time, my self-possession ('is you all you have?') felt like failure, confirmed every day in every way — by middling marks, by loss of caste, by a microclimate of low esteem and respect, which followed one like the cloud over some Jonah in a graphic comic book. But, mysteriously, I got through and was uncrushed. Many were less lucky in that educational bottling factory.

Most adults who became adults in the 1950s will look back 'in anger' at their childhoods and adolescence — that being the Osbornian flavour of their rebellious generation. They will go to their grave (having lived, most of them, decades longer and in hugely greater comfort than their predecessors) convinced that they were ill-used, misused or abused in their youth. And (unlike those unangry predecessors), they're not going to take it any more.

I was, I think, un-used rather than in any way abused in the places I passed through that I could never quite call home — since they never lasted long enough for me to get my roots down. It was all rather limboish. More could have been done for me: I could have done more for myself. It was a thin, unsettled environment I was brought up in, domestically. But, when you think of worse alternatives, limbo is not that bad.

I was misused at school — not by CRGS or its staff, who were, I think, as confused as I was by the system which had been arbitrarily wished on them by a political party very few of them voted for, implementing policies that even fewer of them believed in and none of them could make work. I, and many others, were abused by a huge experiment which nosedived abysmally, taking millions of children and the one life they had with it. Some of the Attlee government's grand projects worked (the NHS, for example). Some (British Rail, for example) were mixed successes. Some (the nationalization of the steel industry) failed. But none failed so catastrophically, or wasted so many young people, as the eleven-plus grammar school system. It was to education what the collective farm was to Soviet agriculture.

That, when I look back, I can still feel a Porterish anger about. But then, I survived and, ultimately, did well enough. What do I have to complain about? The waste.

By one of the odder circuits of my life, I was invited in summer 2006 to give the speech day address at CRGS. The honour boards have gone and the school anthem is wholly forgotten. ('Song? Didn't know we had one,' said the head, airily.) The ethos of the school is now wholly pragmatic and relaxed. It tops league tables annually. They even play soccer.

One Kindly Mother

By far the most impressive figure at the school was the headmaster. One knew his CV, as one did all the teachers' (except the two gays, JK and 'Harry', who like Holmes and Watson shared 'digs' and were very discreet about what went on between them — both were suspiciously affectionate to prettier pupils). The headmaster had got a scholarship to Oxford (Oriel, one was told); but some family, or financial, catastrophe prevented him taking it up. He went to Leeds. No honour board for Jack Elam. He got a first in history — but redbrick scholarship, however distinguished, held a person back, if they hoped to make it in the university world. Their jobs were lower down the scale. He was a sportsman, always likely to score high in the annual masters versus boys cricket match, a talented pianist, widely cultivated and — although not a Colchester man — active in preserving those structures of architectural distinction which could be salvaged from the council's indefatigable wrecking ball. His beautiful wife methodically restored the school's gardens to their pre-war magnificence.

He was brilliant, but remote and forbidding; of few words, but with a savage line in contemptuous sarcasm when impatient. He had little time, one felt, for any but the brilliant boys at the school. Unbrilliant me was beneath his notice or, thank God, the sharper edge of his tongue. He once praised an elegant antithesis of mine in an essay I wrote; I remember the praise, but not the phrase. He should obviously have been a don, but that option had been denied him: the higher childminding was his destiny. He commanded a corps of teachers, many of whom were returned, decorated, from the wars. He, I think, had not served — or, at least, not as 'actively' as those who had commanded ships, flown aircraft, or directed artillery fire at the enemy front line. There may have been resentment, and occasional insubordination, on that score.

Lytton Strachey says of Dr Arnold that he was, to the boys of Rugby, as grandly remote as a Greek god. So too was Elam (a name of forbidding, biblical resonance — 'Jewish', my mother wrongly informed me) remotely grand. Other teachers had nicknames, loaded with affectionate familiarity, scorn or fear: loony 'Algie' Platt, 'Dirty Bill', 'Ted' Cunningham, Basher Bond, Cosher Kime, Hairy Dan, Gob Fancourt, who showered the first three rows in his class ('poor fish', as the school joke went) with saliva, and the brutal 'Baron', 'Sammy' Hughes, who looked like a clergyman, had once been a speedway rider and never rolled his sleeves up in summer because he had tattooed arms. The headmaster was simply 'the head'. Like Jehovah, He was the not-to-be-nicknamed.

The 'staff' were not Stracheyan deities; they were, the most interesting of them, exhausted heroes. Warriors returned, their armour and their minds were rusting away in the oddly unsatisfactory peace which, with blood and the best years of their life, they had won for England — and its children. Two of the masters were veterans of World War One: both had been gassed and one wore tiny dark glasses to protect his war-ruined eyes — they gave him a Frankensteinian aspect. The other (a local archaeologist of distinction, forever digging up Roman remains) suffocated to death when I was in the fifth form: a belated victim of the Hun. Some poisonously fizzing canister, fired at random thirty years earlier, finally did for him.

Five of the masters, I calculated, had won MCs or equivalent decorations (they did not wear their ribbons, but discreetly let it be known they had them). In conversation with an Etonian ('Pip') I dropped the fact

— hoping, with that fatuous vanity boys sometimes have about their school — to impress him. I wanted some flash of comradely respect from him. We too served. In his house (not even the school), he replied, there were a couple of VCs. It was said vaguely, without unkindness. Competition for him was an irrelevance. His kind had won the game, generations ago. He later opened Colchester's first nightclub. I'm not sure he was telling the truth about the medals.

In the classroom, the quality of instruction was a lottery. Teaching was a profession, but yet to be professionalized. The factory production of 'qualified' teachers via Institutes of Education, certification, targets, benchmarks and ministry inspection was a decade off. I suspect that an MC is a better qualification than a DipEd, although it's a thesis not easily tested nowadays. The casual, out-of-class conversation one had with teachers was always more rewarding than any formal tuition. They had seen life — and death: quite a few had killed other human beings. I, who had spent my childhood mainly among adults, could get them talking — even about the killing, sometimes. (One described to me the moral dilemma of having a German in his sights, who was serenely taking his morning crap: did one wait until he was finished before ending his existence, or blast him into eternity unwiped? One for *The Moral Maze*. Oddly, Orwell records a similar experience, and sniper's inhibition, in *Homage to Catalonia*.)

Teachers at CRGS mainly winged it, or did this year what they did every year. There was no shame in what, to the modern quality assurance team parachuted in by the ministry, would look like bone idleness. And, to be honest, it was. There was an easy confidence in their laxity. Teaching was still a high-status line of work. Masters lived in the kinds of town houses that nowadays barristers stretch to afford. They wore gowns; mortar boards within living memory. *Master* was not an entirely empty title. Shortly after induction, my class was given a Colonel-to-the-troops-before-going-over-the-top address.

'There are', our new master told us, steely-eyed, 'two classes of people: sheep and leaders. You', thirty-five eleven year olds were then solemnly informed, after the statutory Churchillian pause, 'have been selected as leaders.' It was said with what I would later recognize as 'the tone of command'. We looked up, schoolboy mutton that we were, in our new purple togs, too overawed even to baa. We were, as Attlee's men liked to put it, 'the masters now'. Who told us? Our masters.

This teacher, Mr Nelson, nicknamed 'Horatio', was typical of the CRGS teaching force in the late 1940s and 50s. He had a pre-war lower second in French, from Nottingham. My guess is that he would have been lucky, had there been an Edwardian eleven-plus, to have made it even to 1G. My class, 1C, did not, of course, get the best teacher, 'DB' (Dirty Bill) — a demon with the vocab books and irregular verbs. But we were spared the entirely incapable Algie Platt, a polyglot and Esperantophile, with nails as yellow and clawlike as a badger's. This poor fellow was soon to go into gibbering nervous collapse when, disastrously, he married and discovered, in his virginal forties, that sex was even more difficult than preventing 1G going the way of St Trinians.

Even I, after the first lessons Nelson gave us, could see that his grasp of the French language could not have got him from the Gare du Nord to the Gare de Lyons without an interpreter. It did not count against him, in my eyes. 'Horatio' had been a pilot during the war, and had a distinguished service career. Moustached (not, alas, the famed handlebar), he had the 'wizard prang', sub-Wodehousian facetiousness (dentists, for example, when they came to the school were 'the fang farriers') and cool offhandedness cultivated by the Few. I idolized him. Frankly, I would have idolized the ex-pilot Hermann Goering if CRGS had recruited the Reichsmarschall to teach German (a subject patriotically dropped during the war, and not yet resumed). One needed no psychoanalyst to explain why airmen and, at the time, aircraft, infatuated me. Horatio had that self-deprecation which only enhanced the aura of heroism. Once, he recalled, piloting his Beaufighter and out of ammo, he had successfully distracted chasing enemy fighters by throwing toilet paper out of the cockpit. No Hun, Jap, Yank or Eyetie would have done that. Score another one for the RAF.

Part of Nelson, like other veterans on the CRGS payroll, was spiritually exhausted. What looked, superficially, like relaxed man-of-the-worldliness was, in fact, moral debilitation. William Golding, another warrior-schoolteacher to emerge from the Second World War, concluded that total war, and its genocidal horrors, had secreted evil, as bees secrete honey, and the post-war world was irredeemably corrupted. Civilization had died. It would never rise again, any more than sour milk can be made sweet. To register that was the best that those who survived could achieve. It was not post-traumatic stress: more a permanent state of whole body and mind detumescence.

The energy had gone, along with the point of it all. The Ralphs of the world, like William Brown and William Bunter, belonged to a wholly lost, pre-war era. From now on, it was Jack Merridew all the way. As the very last of the pre-war vintage, the last squeezing from before the fall, it is a pessimism which I've always found it easy to fall into myself.

For a year or two I studied Nelson with the devotion of a Carlylean hero-worshipper, and much more intensely than I studied French. Deep in his rigid personality, I came to see (and eventually dislike) seeds of prejudice, which pulsed radioactively, and would occasionally flare into bigotry. During Suez, we were mustered for a class in which Nelson (who had evidently served in North Africa) explained, vituperatively, the nature of the 'gyppo' foe. They were degenerates, one was given to understand, a species lower even than the Japs, who would happily sell their sisters for a couple of piastres. (The fact that, for the period of occupation of the Canal Zone, British soldiers had been eager to buy the commodity was overlooked.) The patriotic pro-Eden, virulently anti-Nasser ('Gyppo Hitler') tirade went on for forty-five ranting minutes.

Now eighteen, hero worship fast fading, I was more impressed by a Jaguar driver, who had parked his car at the side of the road by the town's Public Library as I was cycling along, the saddlebag of my (now ageing) Hercules loaded with the statutory half-dozen books. Mr Jaguar beckoned me over angrily. Expecting the usual bollocking for one of those mysterious offences unavoidable in youth I pedalled across, and stood, head obediently cocked, one foot on the ground, by his car window. 'That fucking fool of a PM of ours,' he said, 'that absolute fucking fool has bombed Cairo.' I was the nearest sentient thing he could say it to and it had to be said.

Even Jaguar drivers, the Conservative Party on wheels, couldn't stomach bombing Johnny Gyppo. Not because it was immoral: but because it was stupid.

Ich Bin Ein Berliner

There was an earlier critical event which had edged me into anti-Nelsonian attitudes. In 1953, I spent a summer in Berlin. I was now fourteen. It was the glorious season when Compton (knee-racked and long past his 1947 best, but still my Brylcreemed hero) swept the ball to the boundary to win the Ashes. I missed Arlott's subdued commentary on this victory (would anything have excited that man?), but thrilled when I read the small item in the German newspaper.

I was there on an exchange programme for British and German children who had had a father killed in the war. It was devised as a hatchet-burying exercise. Nowadays, flying over European borders is as easy as bus travel and less comfortable. But this trip to Berlin was my first trip abroad, and a threshold moment. It was also, at last, my first flight in an aeroplane — a BEA Viscount. The four-engined plane swooped in, as four-engined Lancasters must have done, low over Berlin. I looked down and saw a landscape of devastation. According to Evelyn Waugh, anyone over the age of thirty-five would need to go to the moon to recover the thrill of their first trip to Paris. Lunar craters could not have looked more chillingly unwelcome than what the passenger saw, descending to Tempelhof in June 1953. I knew about bomb sites: but what one saw in Colchester, and even in the East End of London, was urban acne by comparison. This was destruction. Bomb city.

Someone seated behind me said, as the awed passengers fell silent: 'You should have seen it in 1945.' The mind boggled at how anything could have been more pulverized. Of course, it wasn't entirely our explosives; the marauding Russians had laid the place waste, in the ferocious battle for Berlin. But, at that moment, 'bomber' acquired a new, sombre connotation: nothing could have justified that carpet of rubbled death. 'In ten years' time', Hitler had said before starting his war, 'you will not recognize Germany.' That was the one promise he kept.

Some things were indestructible. The family I lived with, the Schmidt-Fabians, were pure Berlin: they had that exhilarating, un-German quality (*Luft* — air) that citizens of the city pride themselves on, as Germans in Hamburg (a city where I would later have friends) pride themselves on Anglophilia. There were three boys in the family, all named according to the Nazi instruction booklet: Helmut (like me, 1938 vintage, very authoritarian), Otto (der Dicke, the witty clown) and Horst (a tearaway: later destined to drink and womanize himself into early invalidism). They, and two adults, were crammed into a tiny Charlottenburg flat (two of the boys were evicted to the living-room sofa to make room for me — they suffered it hospitably).

The mother, who had survived the bombs, the raping Russians (God knows how), the terrible winter of 1947 and the 1951 blockade, was a resourceful woman. And honest: 'Wir haben alles bejaht,' she said, when any discussion of the Hitler years came up. 'We all said yes.' And they paid for that assent. 'Mutti', as I was to call her, had survived, but using very different strategies from my mother (whom I would never call 'Mummy').

If the novelist Patrick Hamilton could have taken my mother as a model, Brecht could have done Mutti. She had married a couple of years before, out of motives of convenience, a former Luftwaffe pilot (a sergeant pilot — he had taken one look at the casualty figures and refused a commission). A Prussian, Franz 'Vati' Schmidt had flown Heinkels. Perhaps it was him, that night over Colchester as I scampered to the Castle. He had been imprisoned after the war by the Russians, and escaped. He was happily henpecked, and now a schoolteacher — a German Nelson. He told me all about Dresden — a war crime I learned about ten years before David Irving announced it to the British population at large. That too, I was astonished to learn, was 'worse' than what I could see around me in 1953. The word they used to describe the bombing of civilian centres, *schrecklich*, meant — I grasped — both 'awful' and 'terrorizing'.

In the boys' bedroom, where I occupied the bunk of honour, there was a portrait of the boys' biological father. He was a fine biological specimen, as his rank, regiment, insignia and aquiline good looks indicated. Many cuts above NCO Franz, he was a major. His uniform bore the distinctive lightning flashes and Totenkopf of the SS. He had died, I was told, on the Eastern Front: in a punishment battalion, for disobeying orders. It may have been a saving fiction. He must have done bad things for Himmler, like the other, black-clad, blond beasts. But then, my father — had he survived to get his wings — would have dropped high explosive for Bomber Harris on towns like Hamburg, and (late in the war, when the souped-up Lancasters could reach the city) Berlin or

Dresden. Beastliness was two-way.

I swam in the Olympic Stadium (seven years later, an officer in Berlin, I discovered that underneath that indestructible Nazi concrete was the vast ammunition store of the British garrison, who planned to fight to the last man, last round, when the Red hordes poured in their millions over the wire; no food was stored, I was told — the second battle for Berlin wouldn't last long enough for any meal). I ate Königsberger Klops (delicious meatballs), many kinds of sausage (the real thing, not Walls), and Berlin Brötchen for breakfast. I visited the 'sector' and (clandestinely) the 'zone' and witnessed the difference between East and West. The Kurfürstendamm had it over Stalin Allee — a vast, lavatory-tiled avenue — every time. History duly pissed on the Georgian tyrant's East Berlin monument. I drank the occasional glass of Schultheiss beer, and felt grown-up and German. It 'broadens the mind', one said of travel in those days. It un-narrowed mine.

I came back after six weeks, having gained a fluency (temporary, alas) in vernacular German and a political education. I also lost something during the summer. I had, to this point in life, thought of aeroplanes as weaponry as heroic as the shield of Achilles or Excalibur. My motives in 'spotting' them were sentimental, aesthetic and wholly patriotic. My father was in the mix somewhere. There was weekly excitement on Fridays, when *Flight* magazine would arrive with the papers, and I would get up early to pore over the new photographs and silhouettes. There was something beautiful about the Hawker Hunter, the Supermarine Swift, the Gloster Javelin, even the 'V' bombers — Victor, with its daringly high tail fin, the swept-wing Valiant, with its smooth engine nacelles, and the daringly deltoid Vulcan, which looked as if it had flown in from the pages of Dan Dare's *Eagle*.

By comparison, the American B47s were high-performance bombing platforms, no more beautiful than jet-propelled knobkerries. The North American F47 Sabres were black-smoke-belching engines, with cockpits and cannon attached as an aeronautical afterthought. No 'design'. The British planes, by contrast, were powered by Rolls-Royce engines — a brand associated with the limousine manufacturers who, legend recorded, had their afternoon char delivered on trolleys, with doilies and cucumber sandwiches. It was appropriate: these planes were masterworks of the air. A young Briton could be proud.

After Berlin, having seen what bombs did, rather than what bombers looked like, and every house in every street of a once-imperial city pocked with shell and bullet fire, it was different. I left spotting to others. The magic had gone. Looking back, the American air technology was more honest; it existed only to hurt.

I remained friends with Otto throughout life, and hooked up with him during my period of National Service in Berlin. Whoever devised that programme had done a good thing for me.

Cruising to Mediocrity

I scraped into Colchester Royal by the skin of my teeth, but I never, over the next seven years, really got *into* the school. The tests and exams came and went. Spots came suddenly, and took years to go, leaving lifelong craters behind them. I moved up a stream, but never moved up to the head of that stream — although I got a consolatory prize book or two over the years. I chose (with pompous self-regard) Ezra Pound's selected poems (with introduction by T. S. Eliot), Wyndham Lewis's *The Apes of God* (a signed, limited edition copy) and Robert Louis Stevenson's *Catriona*. The books were all gold stamped with the CRGS crest, so I did, after all, get a streak of gilt among the guilt.

Vocal chords thickened and voice broke. Puberty brought anatomical and libidinal testosterone storms. I got my first true sperm emission, and a strand or two of pubic hair a year or so later than happens now; about the same time as ration books and identity cards were discarded. I suffered morbidly, and privately, the moral pangs of self-abuse (about which the soon to be deceased

Frenchy had manually instructed me, in the Endsleigh lavatories). A pirated edition of *Fanny Hill* circulated at the school, which maddened its serial readers with lust. I got myself confirmed, at a late age, with the aim of setting things right with the Almighty and forestalling blindness. But, once confirmed, I never attended a single communion service, and still haven't taken the wafer and wine. If God is a Victorian patriarch, I shall pay.

Water pistols, conkers and stink bombs had their brief playground vogues. Then came Brylcreem, Windsor tie knots, yellow socks (considered madly dashing) and behind-the-cycle-sheds cigarettes. My smoking diary would be a virtuously short volume. I was brought up in a household as thick with fumes as a kippering shack in Arbroath. I was routinely woken up by a morning chorus of hacking, or phlegmy, or dry coughs, as distinctively identifiable as the voices of the coughers. I could, from my earliest years, distinguish 'Willy Woodbines' from Senior Service or Three Castles Virginia by their smell alone.

But why did I never get round to gasping myself? It would be nice to think that early exposure was a kind of aversion therapy. The reason was odder. I never felt grown-up enough, even at the height of my drinking days: still don't. I have, oddly, never smoked a whole cigarette in my life. My schoolmates puffed away like Thomas the Tank Engine. If I had taken up smoking in later life it would have been Three Castles — the only cigarette to be named in honour of my beloved Thackeray. Du Maurier was named after his principal disciple, the author of *Trilby*, and Woodbines carried a quotation from Shakespeare. Abdullah drew on the oriental romance of Robert Hichens. (One could have put together a half-decent literary syllabus from fag packets.)

There was a Coronation, and a tedious film to watch by way of collective celebration. We sang the school song afterwards. The two films to which the whole school was taken were Olivier's *Hamlet* (1948) and Mankiewicz's *Julius Caesar* (1953). I relished the sight of Jean Simmons's bare thigh in the mad scene and Brando's (surprisingly unmumbled) Mark Antony, with his before the event Beatles haircut. If those had been the only movies I saw over the years of my childhood and adolescence I would have expired from celluloid starvation.

Snot pie was served up, and not eaten. School milk was not drunk. (I was never angry at Mrs Thatcher on that score.) I went through six years, not once defecating in the wholly disgusting school lavatories; no communion with the Bog God, either. In the sixth form, I got a crew cut. It was, as Matthew Arnold would say, my criticism of life — and American. I was passed over for the first fifteen and offered the captaincy of the 'thirds'. The 'U's' meanwhile — Colchester United — had made it from the Southern League to the Third Division. Us both.

Aged sixteen, I got my first sports jacket. At the same period I tried, and gave up, old time dancing — a comic, prancing interlude. Somehow the Valeta, Gay Gordons and Viennese Waltz never matched my self-image. And the girls were more exciting at the Corn Exchange where the Creep (Ted Heath's mournful 1954 anthem) was displacing the Quickstep, to the indignation of dance-floor traditionalists. I outgrew roller skates. I acted — mumblingly (but, alas, without Brando's 'method') — in school plays. My Claudius was thought creditable. The sports jacket, in my last year, became Donegal tweed and my slacks drainpiped to fourteen inches round the ankles — narrowed by Marks the Tailor, in St John's Street (he must have made enough to retire to a mansion in Golders Green from the schoolboys bringing their trousers into his shop for alteration).

Colchester's Jazz Club was started: I was a

founder member — although its puritanically Ken Colyerish 'traditional' jazz was not to my taste. I mourned, ostentatiously (and mystifyingly to my schoolmates), when Charlie Parker died, on 12 March 1955. I fell in love with the Girls' High School beauty and made do with a less beautiful alternative. And she, of course, made do with me. I never saw her breasts, even down summertime blouse cleavage, or penetrated more than a finger's worth beneath the gingham. I would leave school a virgin: but I made exciting anatomical explorations in my apprentice drinking years. Pre-pill, even the Corn Exchange and Jazz Club tarts were careful; but one could go farther than with High School girls. By now the 'milkshake' had taken on a sniggering, bawdier connotation than when I used to while away the hours drinking them in St John's Street. One talked more sex than one got — groin-achingly more.

I made friends for life. They came and went every year. One, I now realize, was gay, but never, in that closeted environment, came out (even, I suspect, to himself). He went into the theatre and, last I read, had changed his name to Tony Marcel and was appearing in *Peter Pan* in Bournemouth.

Books came, stayed in the mind, or went. I

read far into the night, every night. I devoured H. Rider Haggard manically in my first year, Dennis Wheatley in my third, D. H. Lawrence, Wyndham Lewis and the Bloomsberries in my last. Poetry never really worked for me, but I read Eliot and dutifully signed up to the doctrines of Leavis's *New Bearings*. The head of English, Ralph Nixon Curry (nicknamed WKLPB — well-known local poet and broadcaster), was, despite his scornful nickname, a distinguished South African versifier: almost in the Roy Campbell league. He had little time for me, but even those he didn't think much of, learned from him.

Exit Kenneth

The death of my grandfather, I am ashamed to remember, affected me less than that of Bird Parker. And I would myself rather have died than have my sixth-form classmates know I had for years shared a lavatory with a council labourer, and former presser of gentlemen's trousers.

Nor, to be honest, did he want me, or anyone else, to know about his death. It was, like everything in his life, shrouded in angry, silent privacy. He went missing. So uninserted was he into others' lives that it was only after his daughter, Ivy, had knocked on the West Street door for three afternoons running that it was realized something might be wrong.

My grandmother had been in hospital — a false alarm, she was informed. (In fact, she had cancer of the kidneys, but they simply removed one and discharged her, to live out a few years in relative comfort on the other less tannin-rotted organ.) For some time Kenneth's life had been more pointless than ever. He would occasionally, of an evening, go to the New Inn, at the top of his street, for a half pint. He and his wife had rather taken to the West Indian pianist, Winifred Atwell — particularly when she played on her 'old Joanna'. They listened to her quarter of an hour's medley every Saturday night on Radio Luxembourg. (The station, down in the low hundreds, was marked on their Bakelite, cylindrical, pre-war wireless, which required virtually a quarter of an hour to warm up.)

There was what was un-euphemistically called 'an old people's club' in a Nissen hut, on the last remaining bomb site in Essex Street. But he didn't like old people — or any people. He went there only for the free afternoon tea and biscuit and left before the knockout whist. His favourite occupation was to go down to the bypass and look at the traffic on a summer weekend, as it pounded down the A12 to Clacton and back. His last recorded words, to my uncle Bill, who had brought him a cooked meal clamped between two dinner plates, was 'Everyone rides in cars nowadays.' Not him. If I was the outsider, he was the nowhere man.

While his wife was in hospital he simply disappeared. He had never visited her, relying on bulletins from his daughters. The supposition, later, was that he assumed (not without justification) that anyone going into the pre-op ward was probably going to come out, as they said, feet first: down to the refrigeration plant and then on to Mersea Road. He had no intention of living by himself. Or, as it turned out, living.

My mother was out — 'doing books' — when my uncle rapped, with the recognizable family knock, on the door of Wellington Street, early in the evening. A soldier who had served through the war, been decorated for gallantry, killed for his country and scrapped like a terrier in the ring, he was too unsure of himself to make the necessary phone calls. We went down together to the nearest box, by the Regal. He embarrassedly gave me twopence, with a muttered 'You do it.' I duly did the necessary with Buttons A and B, and informed the police that Kenneth Salter, of 12 West Street, was not to be found. Would they report him missing and put out the necessary alert? Details were supplied. I was embarrassed at how little I knew of a man I had lived, if not with then alongside, for most of my life. (Age? No idea. Close relatives? No idea. Friends? No idea.)

Bill's military bravery had all been under the command of his superiors. My voice now had class and the tone of authority. Nelson was right: I was a leader. It was, of course, a front. To the sensitive ear my accent rang (and still rings) false. But Bill took it for real currency. I was, in my arrogance, more pleased with that than I was, at the time, concerned for my grandfather's whereabouts.

His body was found, two days later, when it rose to the top at Middlemill Pond, in the Castle Park, less than a hundred yards from Maidenburgh Street. Decomposition had brewed the lighter than water gases which gave the corpse buoyancy. He had always had a peculiar horror of that particular stretch of water and told me once that he had a childhood friend who drowned there, in the rushing water and weeds. It never looked all that wild to me, but he was referring to a time when the mill was still working, and that much more dangerous. And, of course (being my father's son), I could swim; he, I believe, could not — he must have put stones in his pockets. The fish he had caught over the years had their short-lived revenge as elvers, roach and perch nibbled the rotting surfaces of his body. He left no note; told no one about what he was going to do, or why. In a world where 'everyone drives nowadays' he could, like the suffragette Emily Davison, have thrown himself under the wheels of some car down at his favourite spot on the bypass where it meets the Sudbury Road. Middlemill Pond was his protest.

My mother, who now had influential

contacts, insisted on an autopsy; she was curious. Much later on, she told me, in passing, that a 'growth' in his brain had been discovered. If so, it must have been the only growth in that organ for many years. The coroner's verdict was the traditionally kind one, 'Misadventure'. It was, of course, suicide.

I didn't go to his funeral, neither did my grandmother. My mother went and, as she reported, had burst out laughing as the wizened shrimp of a clergyman (who knew no more of the corpse at his feet than that it was next in line for the dirt) warbled out his ritual 'Oh Death, where is thy sting?' — like Billy Cotton's band show, she said, only less jolly. (She was thinking of his 'It ain't the cough that carries you off, it's the coffin they carry you off in.') The sun momentarily shone, she informed my grandmother, who replied — with a flash of eloquence rare on her part — that it was 'nice' that it had, since it hadn't shone much during his life. She took his going equably. The bank notes and property deeds found in his trunks enabled her to install a bathroom in the West Street house, get a little Norwich terrier for company, and have friends round for tea and tea-leaf reading at all hours. Her last two years, until carcinoma called back to collect the other kidney, were probably the happiest since she had been a girl, and a local beauty. The terrier, Sammy, had died a little earlier from corpulence.

My uncle Arthur, who had been more ashamed of his father than even I, decided that this was the moment to get married. The guest list now had its necessary blank. The old trouser presser would not be there to embarrass him — or me — any more.

Rebels Without Wheels

The year which, as Virginia Woolf said of 1910, changed the world for young men of my age, and straightened things out for me personally, was 1956. I was eighteen. Twenty-one was still majority, the vote, and the key of the door, but this was, effectively, the start of adulthood. It was the summer of Suez and Osborne. I was already drinking heavily, regularly and — at this stage of life — joyously and without remorse.

I saw Osborne's play at the rep. It was an angry evening, both sides of the footlights. One of my teachers, 'Languid' Lennox (so named by one of the school's more eloquent expressions of discontent), got up during one of Porter's tirades, shouted back 'This is an outrage' and stalked out, fist waving. The display of bourgeois indignation was a regular thing with him. The year before he had walked out of *Godot*, with the exclamation, for those still waiting, 'This is balls!' Some in the audience must have wondered if it was a Pirandelloesque *coup de théâtre*.

I disliked Lennox — a tall and laconic man, with a line in sarcasm that had earned him his epithet and masked an ineffable self-importance. A maths teacher, he had been principally responsible for down-setting me. If they got Languid's goat, Beckett and Osborne were the playwrights for me. Balls to him.

Nineteen fifty-six (it must have been around January, looking at the film's release date) was the year that my particular friend, Rick Simms, and I bunked off one afternoon to watch *Rebel without a Cause*. We discarded our blazers and ties and (still a month or two short) lied about our age to get through the 'A' certificate barrier. There followed a baffling couple of hours. The LA high-schoolers depicted in Nicholas Ray's movie (James Dean, Dennis Hopper, et al.) were as alien as George Pal's Martians in *The War of the Worlds* (another bunk off).

These alleged schoolkids drove to school in saloon cars. ('Buzz', you'll remember, slashes Dean's tyres with a flick knife on a school outing to the Griffith Park Planetarium — would that scene work, I wondered, with a Hercules bike?) They were arrested and thrown into the drunk tank. They hung out with vastly breasted, tight-jumpered schoolmates like Natalie Wood, before shooting each other to smithereens in gardens with private swimming pools as large as

Colchester's municipal bath. They drove stolen cars (the kind that Britons would have saved years for) over cliffs, for fun. They wore what later times would call designer clothes: red windbreakers, chinos, coloured socks (a key scene, with Sal Mineo, depends on his getting his socks mixed up). And these, one gathered, were *sixth formers*? What did they have to rebel against? What more could life possibly give them? Causeless indeed: ungrateful bastards.

But among it all, Dean's 'mixed-up kid' moodiness came through strong. I pouted, imitatively, over the next fortnight. My jaw, someone was kind enough to say in the Bamboo coffee bar, rather resembled the actor's. It jutted the more proudly for an hour or two (the fact was, due to universally uncorrected over-bites, most Essex people are weak chinned).

Complex things were happening to British youth. It would have been possible that one of the books in my saddlebag, that day in October 1956 when Mr Jaguar vented his feelings about 'fucking Eden', was *The Outsider*. Nowadays the London Library sardonically shelves its copy of Colin Wilson's first will and testament in the 'Genius' shelf, between 'Gas' and 'Geology'. There is, alas, no adjoining 'Guff' section — though that is where posterity has firmly relegated it. It was different in 1956.

In its day *The Outsider* was that rare thing — a super-selling work of philosophy. In its first few months of publication it raced through sixteen editions, selling 40,000 hardback copies. Eat your heart out, de Botton. When he burst on the scene Wilson was 'a genius, and only twenty-four', as the *Daily Express* headlined it. Colin had left school at sixteen, with less than genius exam results. His father was a Leicester shoe-factory worker who never earned more than £5 a week. Neither, until fame struck, did Wilson Jr. He odd-jobbed and was discharged early from his National Service on grounds of sexual neurosis (invented, he claims: although in his autobiography he confesses to being a 'devoted underwear fetishist').

Young Wilson married injudiciously, separated, and to avoid paying maintenance slept rough in parks and lived off bread and dripping. By day he cycled to the British Museum, where he read and wrote manically. Like the other angries, he coincided with the first adult wave of grammar school graduates, emancipated by the eleven-plus and the 1944 Butler Education Act. We urgently needed writers to voice our dim discontents. Wilson was our man. In H. Rider Haggard's *Nada the Lily* there is a wonderful scene in which — to impress the white colonizers — Chaka, the Zulu Napoleon, orders his impi to charge into a bonfire as large as a small mountain, and extinguish it with their bare feet and bodies. Regiment after regiment is incinerated until, at last, one warrior — charred and smoking — staggers through, alive but charbroiled, to the other side. I always thought of Wilson as that unknown Zulu — vaguely crossed with the comic-book Wilson winning the Tour de France on his humble roadster.

The London literary world of 1956 was, as Wilson put it, 'mothbally' and due for a shaking up. Wilson with his polo-neck sweater, duffel coat, wild hair and geeky horn-rims — 'the sleeping-bag philosopher of Hampstead Heath' (Osborne's snide description) — was heaven-sent for the part of shaker-up in chief. The opening sentence of *The Outsider* was, that summer, as famous as that of the Communist Manifesto: 'At first sight, the Outsider is a social problem. He is the hole-in-corner man.'

On publication the book received rave reviews. The *Observer* proclaimed it 'better than Sartre'; the *Sunday Times* thought it 'remarkable'; the *Listener*, not to be outdone, declared it the 'most remarkable' book the reviewer had ever come across. Intoxicated by success, Wilson gave reckless interviews, picked fights with fellow angries and, at the height of his brief celebrity, was threatened with horsewhipping by the father of the young woman he was currently shacked up with.

Would-be outsider

The philosophy establishment — from the fastness of their Oxbridge high tables — were quick to put the upstart in his place.

Britain's most famed living philosopher, A. J. Ayer, proclaimed Wilson a 'dancing dog', a jumped-up oick who'd infatuated himself with difficult books he didn't understand. Those hacks who had raved in July, dutifully sneered in December. The author of *The Outsider* was, within months, a busted flush; beyond redemption — in history's trashcan with Billy Fury.

To understand why *The Outsider* flamed so brilliantly in 1956 you really needed to be there and of a certain age. What Wilson did, was to impose order on the Pelican and Calder & Boyars paperbacks one displayed so ostentatiously in the coffee bar. After dipping into *The Outsider* you had, at last, a frame to put round Sartre, Camus and Nietzsche and those other thinkers the pronunciation of whose names you'd never been entirely sure about because, unlike Racine or Molière or Dante, you'd never heard them mentioned by masters.

If there were a Guinness record for immodesty, Wilson would walk it. He declared himself, unblushingly, 'the most important writer of the twentieth century' and an 'intellectual Elvis Presley' (who himself burst, seditiously, on the scene at the same period). But the key sentence in *The*

Outsider is buried in chapter 5: 'The Outsider is *not* a freak, but is only more sensitive than the average type of man.'

Every romantic adolescent in summer 1956 could see themselves as that more sensitive kind of soul. I was one of them. I carried *The Outsider* down to the Bamboo's underground tables, and ostentatiously drank my cappuccino behind it with a sense that, after all, life might mean something. The Rive Gauche had come to Colchester. Existential angst was common sense: one could see the point of it all. I would not, however, wear a duffel coat or an Aran sweater. The charcoal grey suit was a new acquisition which not even Wilson could induce me to discard.

Substances

There were, for me, three exits from the CRGS madhouse and the emptiness of my home life: books, booze and jazz. I would have embraced drugs as eagerly as espresso and bitter beer, both of which I gulped down enthusiastically in my seventeenth year. But the closest I could come to illicit substances was what I read — about jazz players in the music magazines, in Beat fiction, and Aldous Huxley's mystical nonsense. Newspapers were forever rabbiting on about a terrifying 'threat to our youth' which, maddeningly, never menaced me.

I turned, in law-abiding desperation, to the mind-altering substances that were available from the chemist's. 'Oblivon', as it was trademarked, was a 'confidence' drug, a first generation tranquillizer — you could get the large, ovoid, rather beautiful pills off-prescription for a year or two. I bought vast supplies and overdosed myself hopefully. The effect was disappointingly sedative. One could, with a bit of effort, conceive it as a kind of Baudelairean ennui but, in truth, one might as well have drunk Horlicks — the sovereign remedy of the time for 'night starvation'. (Its strip-cartoon ads all began with the line, 'Doctor, even after eight hours' sleep I still feel tired . . .') There was enough ennui round Colchester without paying for the bloody thing.

More efficacious was Preludin — an amphetamine which, in the mid-1950s, you could get off-prescription as a slimming aid. The drug required going into a chemist's and lying that one's fat sister needed it (if necessary, one could take a photograph of somebody else's fat sister). Most chemists would refuse a skinny schoolboy. In Long Wyre Street, oddly enough, there was a pharmacist who would always come through — our pusher.

For a while, somewhat later, I dated a chemist's daughter, whom I fell in with at Colchester's new-founded jazz club. She had access to purple hearts: a higher grade of amphetamine. But, after a few fumbling encounters, hyperdriven by Dad's pills, we split up and the supply ceased: I regretted the loss of the purple hearts more than the fumbling. A friend was, for a while, going out with a nurse at the Colchester General Hospital who could get stimulants of an illicit kind; but she raided the poison cabinet once too often and was fired. It was back to the fat sister and 'Prels'.

The pills got the brain racing, and popping them made one feel daring and doomed. But after many nights' sleep starvation (not even the Oblivon helped) I came to the conclusion they weren't really for me; they mixed badly with alcohol, I found. I used them, along with Pro Plus, for exam revision and the exams themselves. Reading the set texts, rather than Kerouac and Ginsberg, would have been more helpful.

Rick and I went up to London that year, 1956, ostensibly to visit Studio 51 in Great Newman Street. (Benny Green, then a tenor saxophonist, later a blue-plaqued writer, was playing — I was particularly taken by the cool way, while soloing, he placed his cigarette, smoulderingly, between the instrument's keys.) Between sets, we went to Brewer Street with the aim of buying 'reefers'. The Afro-Caribbean pimps and pushers we saw lurking in doorways were so frightening we retreated, pure and empty handed. We had, earlier, tried the experiment (sure fire, we were assured) of dunking Wrigley's chewing gum and aspirin in boiling water, to get a powerful mind-altering substance. It altered the stomach rather drastically. Thank God we didn't know about Benzedrine inhalers, banana-skins or nutmeg; we could have killed ourselves in the cause of escape from Colchester.

Even when, years later, it was freely available, cannabis never worked for me. In small amounts, I felt nothing, and disliked the sensation of smoke in my lungs and the dopey conversation. In large quantities (I only tried the experiment once or twice) it tipped me over into a quasi-schizophrenic derangement which, on one horrible occasion, lasted for days. Alcohol was my drug of choice. That worked and seemed, at that period of life, actually to enhance my sanity.

In Alcoholics Anonymous, it's called a drinking career, which is just the right word. First, because it suggests the fact that (for a man at least) it's a very, very important thing in life; up there with family, job and country and, for many alcoholics (all eventually), the most important of the four. Secondly, because it conveys the idea that drinking, like other careers, is progressive. You're never the same alcoholic this year that you were last year; long-term drinking has its ups and downs, successes and failures. All careers end badly, Enoch Powell said, none more badly than the drinker's. But getting there, however badly, can be interesting. Thirdly, career is the right word for long-term drinking because it also conveys that sense of something out of control: a driverless train careering down the track, as — more apposite — does the car driven by a drunk driver careering along the highway, always in danger of cutting short the careers of sober citizens.

Drinking, like other careers, gets more serious and intense, the more of your life you invest in it. And, more interestingly, that career(ing) is going somewhere. In my case, the destination was solitary drinking, the pure experience of alcohol. Alcoholics in my view, having attended innumerable AA meetings, know very little about very little and love to talk a lot about what they don't know. But one thing they know more about than any whitecoated specialist: the bottle. The secret drinker, 'pure alcoholic', was what I wanted to be and where I was going — alone, in the wasteland of the life I had created, with a glass. I was, AA later reassured me, not alone: merely in a cell of my own making, surrounded by tens of thousands of solitary drinkers in their self-made cells.

The best literary description of this drinking pattern which I've read (I've heard innumerable descriptions of it in AA meetings) is in Charles Jackson's *The Lost Weekend*, a drunkalog novel feebly, but Oscar-winningly, filmed by Billy Wilder. In one episode Don Birnam, who has contrived, with all the alcoholic's cunning, to get rid of his two minders (brother Cliff, fiancée Helen) out of town, stands at last in front of the drink which will kick off his weekend binge. And, paradoxically, he does not drink (at least for many minutes). He simply stands alone, with the sense that he can drink whenever he wishes. He is, at last, by himself as he wants to be — in charge of his own self-destruction.

Gradually he worked up a subtle and elaborate pretence of ennui: stared at himself in the dark mirror of the bar, as if lost in thought; fingered his glass, turning it round and round or sliding it slowly back and forth in the wet of the counter; shifted from one foot to the other; glanced at a couple of strangers standing farther down the bar and watched them for a moment or two, critical, aloof, and, as he thought, aristocratic; and when he finally did get around to raising the glass to his lips, it was with an air of boredom that said, Oh well, I suppose I might as well drink it, now that I've ordered it.

For me, in its last stages, drinking recreated the conditions of childhood. Solitude; myself alone. In my last desperate years as a drinker, I would finish a tutorial five minutes early, dash out of the office, elbowing the student out of the way if necessary with some excuse about rest rooms, and rush through the labyrinthine tunnels that wormed under Gower Street's thundering traffic to emerge, mole-like, opposite the University Arms in University Street (it's now the Jeremy Bentham, and it's where Henry Perowne has his car accident in Ian McEwan's novel *Saturday*). I'd belt in, get a quick two pints, and be back — only minutes late — for the next tutorial at five past the hour. Little time to do more than the most cursory Birnam dawdle in front of the glass on the counter. But this was the point of it all. I was, however temporarily, in the endless white space Jack London describes every alcoholic yearning for.

That was the end point, or destination. It didn't begin that way. Decades of social drinking and antisocial behaviour had to be got through, by way of prelude. I associate my first drinking with occasions when moderate amounts of gin were drunk at various family revels. I recall one in which half a bottle of Gordon's Dry was bought from Last's the off-licence (where streaky bacon was the more usual purchase), and another sent out for. It was so unusual in East Street as to become legendary (the time when we all got tipsy). There was an inherited evangelical resistance to such events becoming common-place, or frequent, even on holidays. But, to my young eye, it looked so much fun I could not understand why it wasn't more frequent.

Doubtless in the army my uncles drank their proverbial one over the eight. My departed father certainly drank his, and his father, as dim legend had it, even more. My mother liked to refer to certain heroic figures as 'real drinkers'. My father was one, and somewhere in my mind I associated real drinking with filial duty. In drinking, as the twig is bent, so the tree is shaped.

A formative moment happened when I was a still unrazored sixteen. I had escorted my mother to the Mersea Regatta. It was an annual summer event at the small seacoast village at the mouth of the Blackwater, nicknamed by locals 'Mersea on the Mud' (radioactive mud after the first-generation Bradwell power station was built there). Mersea has been famous, since Roman times, for its oyster beds (greenly glowing by night, doubtless, after the 1960s). The actual sailing was followed by a wild drinking session, with licence extensions far into the night.

My mother had arranged to meet her former typist friend — 'La Fotheringham' — at Mersea's large pub, the Victory, which doubtless took in more on this one warm night than in whole weeks in winter. The place was heaving. By this stage of her career La F was blowsier. But she was still startlingly, and chemically, blonde, with lots of life in her. In a year or two, she would settle down as a rich farmer's mistress, surrounded, in her 'luxury' bungalow, by expensive, Tretchikoffian tat — including a state of the art TV-ogram (TV, radio and gramophone combined, in something the size of a beach hut). As a kindness to me (she was impulsively generous) she bought an LP of *Parker with Strings*, for a visit I made to her. We sat, awkwardly listening to the over-engineered arrangements, on the overstuffed sofa. Parker, with a violin section behind him, sounded awkward as well. She dreaded, I suspect, the bedroom duties that paid for the luxury — an alley cat in a gilded cage.

Still later, when evicted from her bungalow for drinking, declining looks, and infidelity to her protector — and fixated on Marilyn Monroe — the poor woman gassed herself, after a wretched last few months drinking herself into squalid destitution, at a riverside pub frequented by gypsies, the White Horse. She stuffed the statutory wet towels under the doors of her lodgings and took her cat with her — a detail that upset my mother.

At this time, she was still vibrant, reckless,

and only newly separated from her bohemian photographer husband, who lived on a houseboat on the Mersea mudflats, decorated with nude shots he had taken ('don't know where to cast your eyes,' joked my mother, after a strange lunch there). At the regatta, La F had with her a shrivelled, neatly blazered, wholly bald partner, called Basil. I was informed later that Basil had drunk his way through several inheritances. It must have been hard work: his head was wrinkled and brown, like a walnut; it looked like cirrhosis of the pate. He sipped his short drinks ferociously, paid for everyone else's drinks, and said nothing. He doubtless paid for some after-regatta service from La F. He was younger than I am now, an alcoholic husk, dragging legends of epic drinking bouts behind him like Marley's chain. I would come to know the type well, wreckage on the alcoholic tide.

My mother and Fotheringham drank to a merry, conversational condition. Liz was keeping her distance. She had brought me along not as my debutant entry into the drinking world but to protect herself. I was, as they say in American football, running defence for her: keeping unwelcome people away — men, that is. I was serving the same function that the portrait photographs of my father and me had served in Long Wyre Street. Her current partner, Mr Handlebar Moustache and Motor Trade on the Make, would not have approved of the company she was keeping that night: I was the substitute.

Not that I cared, any more than I had about the photographs, aged five. I was enjoying the experience — adult for a night. Ominously, the half-dozen gins I drank made no impression on me at all. I was not inebriated or even warmed by an intake which, for an unseasoned drinker, should have left me legless and speechless. I said very little, although a lot more than Basil, and quite articulately.

The next day, I had no hangover or cause for remorse. One pool of vomit, some blush-making public foolishness on that night, might have saved me ten thousand disastrous over-indulgences later in life. As it was, I formed that most dangerous of illusions — I had a 'good head' for drink. The next stage? I too could become a real drinker. I should, of course, have meditated more on that death's head, Basil. He too had been real once.

I graduated a year or two later to the party circuit. This, the mid-1950s, was a period when the youth of the country was breaking out. Money was being earned, freedoms grudgingly granted, others nervously snatched. Drinking was companionably antisocial and would frequently climax with some (tame by Booze Britain standards) orgy or riot, in which everything would be let go — within reason. No one was knifed, raped or badly beaten.

The companionship was welded by the round system — one for all, all for one. In drunkenness, if one were drunker than others, the all (or those who remained competent) would look after the one. Like the dispossessed of the American cities and their gangs, alcohol created fluid communities in which one could feel at home — the kind of home life one had never had. Pubs closed at the excessively early hour of 10 p.m. in winter, 10.30 p.m. in summer. Hence the parties. They were, usually, nothing more than after-hours drinking sessions in someone's flat or bedsit. Forget Fellini.

From the first I earned credit for being able to hold my drink. I did not 'drop my ring' (spew), I was no two-pot screamer. I was, proud to say, a ten-pint man. There should have been something like a Boy Scout's badge for it, to wear on my drinking arm sleeve. I could always get up the next day. I did not (until years later, when my tolerance collapsed) suffer blackouts. My strong head may have been a Scottish thing (God knows,

243

being able to survive alcohol is essential in that drink-sodden place: if it weren't, the Scots would have gone the way of the Neanderthals).

Clinically, one is told, there are four kinds of alcoholic. I see myself as being one of those for whom the attraction was moral disinhibition. At a certain stage of drunkenness self-punitive disapproval would dissolve — my disapproval of me, that is. Alcohol rendered me comfortable with myself. Drinking overthrew the tyrants of my sobriety: shame, conscience, nervousness. It didn't necessarily involve doing anything. Five pints of bitter and one stopped beating oneself up. Cheap at the price, or so I thought at the time: 5,000 pints down the line it was different.

Drinking also put one on the edge: just outside Orwell's whale, but still within rejoining distance of the monster next day. My drinking mates (my drinking 'school', as the term was) were all contemporaries who had left at sixteen. I was, at this stage of life, in school, but not of the school. It involved a continuous flirtation with boundaries. Drunk, and wholly irreligious, I would find myself on Christmas Eve (the pub extension ending at 11 p.m.), thick head, bladder aching, at the Roman Catholic church, listening to Midnight Mass in Latin (which, unlike my fellow drinkers, I could haltingly follow). Like Hardy's impercipient, I was 'among the bright believing band' where I had 'no right to be'. (It would be four years, and Monica Jones, before I came across Hardy's poetry. It was not to the taste of WKLPB.)

There were other moments of early alcoholic strangeness. During Suez there was a protest meeting, large by Colchester's standard, and highly unusual given the town's torpidly conservative character. The meeting was held in the grandly named Moot Hall, a large auditorium within the Town Hall. Why I drifted in there with a few friends I cannot precisely recall, but I assume it was out of curiosity. One passed the Town Hall on the way from the George to the Cups bar, and an interval between drinks might have seemed, at the moment, a good idea. The night was young. Whatever the reason, political indignation against Eden or Nasser was not it.

In the balcony of the imposing hall (it was where the school speech and prize days were held) I was sitting with a satchel. It contained a half-dozen or so pipe bombs. We had discovered (as the IRA had) that there was nothing easier than making deadly explosive devices. Step one: go to Cramphorn's, the seed merchants in the High Street (a relic from market days, when the Corn Exchange was the corn exchange), and buy a few pounds of ammonium nitrate ('for the lawn'). Step two: dissolve fertilizer in warm water, and soak toilet tissue in the fluid (not brass-plated Bronco). Step three: dry out the soggy pulp in an electric (never gas) oven, on its lowest setting. Plumbing was still lead-work, not plastic: one could get lengths of tubing as easily as the fertilizer, and from the hardware shop three doors away. One stuffed the pipe with the dried explosive (very carefully, friction could ignite it) and nipped both ends of the soft metal tight, having inserted a length of Jetex ignition wire as detonator (Jetex made tiny jet engines for model aeroplanes: the highly inflammable and intoxicating glue used in this hobby also had its uses).

The speaker at the town hall was the Labour MP Konni Zilliacus, a lifelong USSR stooge. He had quivering, fat jowls. Forgetting rule one in the public speaker's rule book ('never give a heckler an opening'), in his Finnish accent he asked rhetorically: 'What must a British soldier feel, as he drives his tanks against Egyptian women and children?' 'Make the buggers run!' shouted back a member of the Young Conservative claque, who had taken over several of the front rows. Uproar ensued.

To H. G. Wells's Martian, I would have seemed the classic anarchist, sitting as I was in a political meeting with enough bombs to kill or maim scores. That would have been the moment to light the Jetex and run: it would have been a day that lived for ever in the annals of the town.

In fact, the reason I had the bombs was — so to speak — wholly innocent. The invasion of the Canal Zone by Britain and France had been launched on 29 October. This was 5 November. I was no Guy Fawkes. The bombs were prepared for a monster firework display, after hours, in the vast empty car park in front of the town library. It would be a *feu de joie*, not a terrorist outrage — and pointless. We sidled away early (me clankingly), leaving the still noisy meeting, and had our bangs. Very loud they were. But no one lived nearby, the watchmen were uninterested, and the police, it transpired, had other things to do that night than chase up illicit firework displays. Eden was deposed without the need of any pipe bombs, a couple of weeks later.

The defining epithet for the forties had been austerity; for the sixties it would be liberation. For the 1950s, between the two, it was rebellion — but with a still lingering sense that one might want, at some future point, to get back on board (like James Dean, at the end of his film). But just for the moment one was defecting — judiciously. One was not quite an outsider, but what Tony Gould calls Colin MacInnes (an influential writer of the time), an inside-outsider.

Rebellion was deeply half-hearted. The short back and sides was still in order. The DA ('District Attorney' if you had one, 'Duck's arse' if you didn't) was generally, although not universally, avoided; the 'Tony Curtis' likewise. Ties were still worn — although slimmer, or marginally more knotted than previously. Creased flannels, or cavalry twill, was universal, but with narrowed drainpipe bottoms round the turn-up. 'Jeans' belonged to that despised sect, square dancers. Leather shoes alternated with suede chukka boots. Like twill and the houndstooth check jacket, the distant (and deferential) sartorial allusion was to a world of hunting, Indian imperialism, polo.

The opening of Alan Sillitoe's *Saturday Night and Sunday Morning* catches the new dress rebellion riff, describing the stylish-oafish hero putting on his tweed sportscoat, smart slacks, and slim-jim tie. Fully blown neo-Edwardian outfits were despised. Teddy Boys, like Cosh Boys, were creatures of the abyss: savages who tore up cinema seats and danced in the aisles at showings of *Rock Around the Clock*, who got girls pregnant, got married at twenty-one, and were worn-out wage-slaves by forty. Arthur Seaton himself was a notch too low in the social scale to serve as any kind of role model — although, as with Brando in *The Wild Ones* (which I hitchhiked to a private cinema in Cambridge to see), one liked the pugnacity. Vicariously.

Seaton was, with his ten pounds a week, also better off — certainly than me. I had the ten-shilling notes ('half bars') left on the kitchen table, which could easily, with beer around a shilling a pint, see one through an evening. But money was a problem for me, still at school, drinking with wage-earners.

To keep the drink flowing, I worked, on Saturdays and in the Christmas holiday season, on a fruit and vegetable stall. It was owned by the father of a friend — Mort. Every Thursday the father and son would trundle up to London by truck (it left at 5 a.m., but was always good for a free ride). Mort was one of those who had conscientiously objected to the eleven-plus, and failed it deliberately. He was naturally witty, effortlessly spooling out a surreal running commentary on the world (he was also a cartoonist of untutored genius). I was once waiting with him at Colchester's North Station for the up train to London: some provincial adventure in the smoke was in prospect (perhaps Count Basie, or Lionel Hampton, or just a visit to the jazz record shops on Shaftesbury Avenue). As, far down the track, the steam engine puffed in I heard him murmur to himself, 'Just my luck. It's on fire.' There was no attempt to get a laugh, or even be heard. Gags spilled out of him like water from a washerless tap. He deserved a Boswell. And he paid me thirty shillings every Saturday. It meant I could pay my way along the path I'd chosen.

Jazz

Jazz was for me, as for other cultural malcontents of the 1950s, one of the quicker ways out of Colchester. What made that exit possible was a piece of technology which was, by the time I came across it, already antique: the wind-up gramophone. The devices were first introduced into the marketplace at the turn of the century. They depended on (for the time) advanced technology: the needle-pointed acoustic amplifier and the high-tensile steel spring, capable of keeping a turntable moving at a steady 78rpm for three minutes. There was a macabre mythology surrounding the springs. If you were foolish enough to open the works and uncoil them, they would leap out, snake-like, and could cut your throat. Such things, one was assured, had happened.

The stored energy of the spring could sustain the performances caught on 10- and 12-inch shellac discs (with the latter, there was always the danger of slowdown during the last few bars). Archaeologically, the wind-up survives in the current length of the standard single pop number. You can connect

Franz Ferdinand with that steel spring — as important in its development as the other steel wire that made the electric guitar possible.

The first electric-powered gramophone I encountered was owned by the married couple who, just as my mother and I were leaving, bought the East Street house (for a song). They were sophisticates, with a boxer dog called Pooch, and a car on which they also bestowed some coy name. He was an architect. They had books and magazines and bottles of sherry all over the living space they were expensively doing up, preparatory to taking over the whole house after the tenants (me and my mother) moved on. He loaned me Hornblower books. I was amazed to come on the pair of them canoodling. In my frigid world, embraces were ritualistic and rare, and never overtly sexual. As part of their modernity, 1950s style, they had an electrically driven gramophone with wooden needles (kinder on the shellac). Their music was all classical. But I lusted after the electric motor.

Jazz was not, like reading (or the other thing), a solitary vice. One shared it with friends, masonically, and it opened gateways to new friendships — as with drinking, friendships outside the school. There was no home for the Devil's music at CRGS. The headmaster resolutely refused to sanction a jazz club (stamp clubs and debating societies were permissible). He had, earlier in his career, taught at Sir George Monoux School, in Walthamstow, and had turned down the request for one by a pupil called Dankworth — Sir John Dankworth, as he now is, by a nice symmetry.

The outsiderness was an added thrill. It was, however, generally tame, going little further than a Wilsonish wildness of the hair and sweater. A daring fellow jazz-lover, for a short while, donned a Dizzy Gillespie beret and shades: it didn't go with the pushbike. Lady Godiva could scarcely have drawn more astonished attention in Colchester streets. 'I laughed so much, I pissed myself,' I heard one unsympathetic onlooker say. The beret and sunglasses were soon lost; the bike was all right.

The first 78 I bought, from Mann's music store in the High Street (soon to enjoy a bonanza with the pop revolution), was Earl Bostic's 'Flamingo'. Like other music created by blacks, it has not dated in the same way that, say, the big band hits of Jack Parnell or Ted Heath have. That opening shriek of the rough-tongued alto still works. In the background, one learned decades later, was sideman John Coltrane. Charlie Parker, on the night he died, had been listening, appreciatively, to Bostic on TV.

Out of this excessively sentimental 'standard' (typically sung at funereal tempo) about birds flying who knows where, Bostic creates a poundingly laconic, laid-back line. His riffs hardboil the sentimentality. I loved the record, even down to the crimson Vogue record label at the centre of the disc which, as the table turned, blurred into pure colour, merging with the sound. Steel needles quickly tore out the more delicate fringes of sound, and I was forever buying new copies — the more to enjoy, particularly, that opening wail. An alto in exquisite pain.

Bostic was the real thing. Bill Haley's 'Shake Rattle and Roll' ('the Rock Revolution starts here') which came out in the same period is, by comparison, double-distilled ersatz — and filched shamelessly, and inexpertly, from the Chicago blues shouter Big Joe Turner. I saw through the embarrassing hoax the first time I heard the hit. I would no more have bought Haley's record than Anne Ziegler and Webster Booth singing 'Come into the Garden, Maud' (not that one had to buy it: the duet could be heard every Sunday on *Family Favourites*).

Jazz re-energized my love affair with

America. Films, though I still watched them, had become less important in my life; they were a diversion. One couldn't drink and watch a film. Jazz, booze and girls converged into exciting wild times; film had too many social boundaries and restrictions.

My addiction to jazz fed on a nostalgia for a time and place I'd never known, but believed in overpoweringly. Al Alvarez begins one of his polemical books (very influential they were in the 1960s) with the observation that America 'is the only country wholly in the twentieth century'. That, for me, was confirmed every time I listened to Getz, Young, Hawkins, Jacquett (the tenor always seemed to me the essential 'twentieth-century' voice).

There was, at the time, a fierce conflict between the boppers and the traditionalists. To be honest, I never had a discriminating ear, and ideology in jazz interested me as little as in politics. But I knew, as they liked to say, what I liked. Gerry Mulligan's croaking baritone and Chet Baker's anaemic, vibrato-less trumpet, the quartet daringly piano-less, on 'Walking Shoes' had it every time over Bunk Johnson's piano-less (you can't march with a piano) and sax-less 'Didn't He Ramble'. West Coast, not New Orleans (revivalist), was my preference. I liked the idea of Mulligan's heroin habit, which slotted in quite comfortably with 'cool', but Johnson's new set of false teeth (something he needed to be supplied with, before, after decades, he could take up his trumpet-playing career again) put me off. Too West Street. It was a small thing, but I also preferred the charcoal grey suits that modern jazz fans affected, rather than the baggy sweaters of the other lot. They did rather sweat.

Modern was sharper and cooler. It merged, seamlessly, into the new technology: velvety vinyl, sapphire-headed stylus (lovely word), EPs and LPs along with early hi-fi (assembled from Heathkit sets) which turned a bedroom into a music lab. But I could not claim to be a connoisseur. Those who were looked down on my affection for Bostic, Krupa's crazed percussion (in reverent remembrance of *Sing, Sing, Sing*), and the disorderly jam sessions of Jazz at the Philharmonic. For me it was never the music, but what the music signified.

I made the necessary, and wholly disastrous, experiment with a trumpet, which I bought for £15, hire-purchased over nine months from a friend who had given it up in despair, after hearing Armstrong's 'Potato Head Blues'. Old satchel mouth did not deter me. The monthly payment was taken, I am ashamed to recall, from the drawer in which my mother carelessly saved money for the Wellington Street rent (there was usually plenty there, and she never noticed).

I just about mastered the main line of 'September in the Rain'. But I was no more a musician than I had been at St Mary's, when I got over-excited on the tambourine. I gave the trumpet back, in lieu of the six quid I still owed. The neighbours were relieved; and so was I. Other of my friends, more diligent and tuneful than I, became competent instrumentalists and, in one case, a gifted trombonist. I could see playing, as opposed to enjoying, jazz took up a lot of time (better spent reading) and entailed a lot less drinking if one was to do it well. Sobriety was not a sacrifice I was prepared to make, even for jazz.

There was, until the mid-1950s, a feud between the British and American musicians' unions which meant that one's only contact with jazz was through recordings and the Voice of America. One was in the same camp as the Russkis. When, finally, union differences were resolved Stan (The Man) Kenton, wonderful to say, came to play the Regal, in 1956. It would have been too conformist to buy tickets and sit where one would, next week in the 'one and nines', watch the latest Martin and Lewis.

Rick and I broke in through a fire exit, and

listened, standing, to 'The Peanut Vendor' (twenty cement mixers, going full blast), 'The Concerto to End all Concertos', and the rest of the ludicrously over-orchestrated Kenton repertoire. We loved it. Afterwards, we went on stage and talked shyly to the excessively civil drummer, Mel Lewis: the first American jazz musician I'd been physically close to. 'Where are we?' he asked at one point. 'You don't want to know,' I shot back, feeling very cool. I felt a pang, thirty years later, when Lewis died — prematurely — of cancer. It was good that the first American jazz musician I ever met was nice to me.

School-Leaver

My last years at school were unsettled and, while actually *at* school (absence and dilatoriness were as frequent as at St Mary's), unhappy. My A-levels did not go well. How could they? I did not read the books: not the exam board's books, at least. Other stuff I read voraciously, but it was consciously counter-curricular.

I learned about my results in a way which my currently favourite Victorian novelist (George Meredith) would have thought too far-fetched for fiction. It was high summer. Rick and I had cycled down to Stratford St Mary, a couple of cider bottles and pork pies in our saddlebags. We were not there to fish, but to swim, drink, swim, drink. The water was clean, if earthy to the tongue. The only unpleasantness was the fine, squishy mud which, when one put one's feet down, oozed siltily through the toes. One vaguely felt the need of toilet paper.

As we sat on the bank drinking, the headmaster and his family, incredibly, floated slowly by in a rowing boat, hired from the yard by Dedham Mill. The family was there, like so many ladies of Shalott: beautiful wife, children destined (inevitably) for Oxbridge and effortless academic distinction. Looking at us, on the bank, the head recognized my naked form. 'Two threes and a four,' he shouted (it equates, in modern A-level grades, to two Cs and a D).

He had no shout for Rick. We got on our bikes and skeltered back to the school. So it was. My results were wretched, but at least passes. Rick, who had taken the exams stoned and sexually exhausted (lucky swine, still virginal me thought), had wiped out disastrously — all Ds. Cool as ever, he was not particularly fazed. He had expected nothing.

The grades I earned would not get me looked at, let alone accepted, by any of the university departments in which, over the last forty years, I have taught. Every one, I would bet, of the thousands of undergraduates I have instructed over the years got more creditable A-level results than their instructor. I'm unsure whether it seems to reflect badly on me, or on the examination system. I would like to think the latter.

Looking through my CRGS reports — as dreary as kicking wet leaves in winter — provokes serious self-questioning. All those B minuses, C pluses, and worse: what did they mean? WKLPB was particularly severe, not least in his comments: 'Sometimes interesting', 'Occasionally promising', 'Does not apply himself'. Add them together, mix well, and what do you get? 'Second rate.'

And yet, mysteriously, I have never had difficulty making my way in academic life. How could I fail abysmally at school, and be successful, at a main school subject, outside the place? A number of explanations suggest themselves: none of them flattering and only one (the fifth) which does not do grievous harm to the ego. First, I am a fraud (an unpleasantly persuasive explanation). Second, I am a lucky fraud (ditto). Third, the subject I gravitated to, English, is a very soft option ('squish', as the Americans say) and a natural home for fraudulence. In a hard subject, like physics or anthropology, I would have been found out (ditto). Fourth, I wasted my opportunity at school, and only applied myself later (not persuasive — like the 'late developer' thesis, too easy on my early failures, which are consistent and thoroughly documented). Fifth, consciously or unconsciously, I pissed off the teachers and consciously or unconsciously they paid me out with low grades. Sixth, the system was wasteful, and simply did not take trouble with pupils who didn't comfortably slip their foot into the school's glass slipper (true, I know,

261

for others, if not for me). Seventh, really clever kids perceived academic life to be a dead end, and took their talents elsewhere. Success in academic life is dud's gold (deuced persuasive). Eighth, who gives a damn after fifty years?

★ ★ ★

Despite the appalling A-levels, and some frank, man-to-man discouragement from WKLPB, I decided to stay on for a third year in the sixth form. There were a couple of hopeful peaks in the run of English marks. The two modern language papers (French and Spanish) were poor right across the board.

To put my performance in context, I got much worse results than Rudge, the 'thick sod' in Alan Bennett's (insufferably snobbish) *The History Boys*: a character whose brains, what little there are of them, are in his golf clubs and testicles. Like Bennett's crew, I would try for Oxbridge — or, failing that, some respectable second-best university.

Rick decided it was time to earn some money, faked a bad knee to get out of National Service, shed his purple, and went his own way. He got a job clerking with a small business. I continued to drink with him, but in a rather different relationship, now that he was out and I was still in. He would, ten years later, get a first, in his own time, and in his own way, from Birkbeck College, studying by night. He was clever, but always unwilling to put his cleverness out to hire or to anyone's use but his own.

It had been an intense friendship — one of the two or three most intense of my life. But I never saw him entirely naked (was he circumcised like me? I never knew). We never farted in each other's company or shared a woman. We took drugs together, got drunk together: but there was always an ineradicable shyness, or edginess. I like to think that the quality of the friendship was all the better for our avoiding the excessive intimacy of Lawrentian *Blutsbrüderschaft*. Or perhaps it was just Essex timidity. If we were youthful gangsters like the Chicago Blackstone Rangers, or the Los Angeles Compton Crips, we would have gone all the way.

My mother did not understand the magnitude of my flop and had paid little attention to the ominous school reports. I easily persuaded her that, at the end of the year, I would be placed somewhere which would bring honour to the family, and my father's name. The ten bobs kept coming. But so, now and then, did looks.

Oxbridge, however, did not look — no interviews. On the basis of my A-levels, I was turned down by Bristol, Nottingham, Manchester and London — by standard letter; sometimes, humiliatingly, by return of post. The only place which gave me the time of day was Leicester, a University College (outpost of London University) recently chartered and now an institution in its own right. A very inferior institution. I was interviewed in the converted lunatic asylum buildings by the moss-covered head of department (himself sacked later that year). Dryden came up; C. P. Snow — the one famous product of the place — was asked about. I knew enough to make sensible-sounding comments. They, and they alone, offered me a place. It was an insult, not to be borne.

Leicester was, in grammar school preju-dice, so low in the scale that it is not even thought worthy of a sneer by Alan Bennett. Bristol, Hull and Loughborough get theirs in *The History Boys*, but not the institution down cemetery road (Philip Larkin and Kingsley Amis, unlike Bennett, thought Leicester worth a sneer). A friend, picking up the brochure Leicester had sent me, made some slighting comment about the 'Harry Peach Library Room' along the lines of 'not quite Duke Humphrey's' (he, I can still recall — so deeply etched is his sarcasm into my memory — had secured a place at LSE).

Ralph Nixon Curry (WKLPB) commented, as if I were something to be taken out like the garbage, 'At least you've got a place.' He was, apparently, surprised that anywhere would take me. But who was he, an Oxford man, to pass judgement on Leicester? There was no accounting for taste.

It was not a place I wanted. I made a Colin Wilsonish decision. Sod Leicester. I would go into the army — even though they were trying, desperately, to end National Service, and didn't really want me any more than Balliol College did. Salisbury Plain, I resolved, would be my Hampstead Heath, my 'Outside'. At least it would get me outside of Colchester.

Hauling Down the Flag

The Queen's shilling was, by 1957, wholly optional. National Service was winding down. Deferment (with the prospect of never having to serve) was there for the asking. You could get medical disqualification with a hiccup — fake or real. It was reverse Kitchener: Your Country Didn't Need You. Macmillan's winds of change and the Suez debacle had blown away the empire. 'If it lasts a thousand years', prophesied Churchill, 'this [1940] will be its finest hour.' It lasted all of eighteen years (my age: was I, obscurely, to blame, the albatross of British history?). There were no more huge garrisons in the Far East, no more finest hours, no more durbars. No wars on the horizon — apart from some internal security business in Cyprus which the politicians were in the process of sorting out.

NATO had adopted a defensive, hi-tech, hull-down posture in Europe. The game plan was that the British Army on the Rhine should (despite its name) fall back to the River Weser. There it would (temporarily) obstruct the Red Hordes' advance, like an old age pensioner on a zebra crossing, creating the biggest tank-jam in military history. Enter America with its nukes. Air superiority would, by this stage, have been wholly lost. But the US Army had the nifty little Davy Crockett mortar, and artillery which could lob atom bombs as easily as snowballs. It was a mad strategy (not least because the Russians knew all about it); but it had no role for bolshy, ill-equipped, lumpy, amateur cannon-fodder — or failed grammar school boys trying to find themselves.

My closest friends dodged their call-up with trick knees which miraculously cured themselves as they skipped away from the medical centre, and cunning hints at homosexuality (the peeing in the bottle business was said to be good for a histrionic collapse). I could certainly have got out on infantile ear damage (that onion again) had I directed my Medical Officer's probing light down my lug-hole. It looked, another military doctor informed me, when abscesses flared up, like the Chamber of Horrors at Madame Tussaud's waxworks.

But, against the tide of history, I wanted in. It was the first significant decision I had ever made about my life.

There duly arrived a postal order for 7s 6d (the Queen's shilling had inflated, moderately, since Waterloo) and a rail warrant to get to Gibraltar Barracks, Bury St Edmunds, home of the Suffolk Regiment — the Silly Suffolks, soon to be amalgamated with the Royal Norfolks (a superior regiment) and thence into extinction. Once again I was embarking on a sinking ship.

No handkerchief fluttered at North Station. I could not hide from myself that my mother was relieved at my vacating a living space in which my nightly return, half or fully pissed, and bearish behaviour in the morning over the Fry's chocolate spread was, increasingly, a strain on our relationship.

When I was a child, my mother would, when I was lucky, come to my room and peck my cheek by way of bedtime kiss. I would get a fragrant whiff of gin, perfume and her. Now, when I blundered into her room at night, God knows when, she could smell the booze. She had never liked having grown men around the house (her house) — they threw their weight about too much. I think, too, she slightly resented the fact that, despite the dire exam results, I was infinitely better read than she, surer in my grammar, and had the more accomplished 'voice'. I still admired her to distraction. She, on her part, had become rather uneasy about what she had made. A sacrifice or two too many, perhaps. I was off-script — less Deeping than Braine.

Added to this was the increasingly evident fact that, despite all the sacrifice, I had not come through — at least, not according to the family plan. I was not boastworthy, like that little prig, Michael Whatever, at the far end of Wellington Street who had got a place at Oxford to 'do' chemistry, and might well end up a surgeon like Kit Sorrell. She was not quite sure that I had not 'let her down'. National Service would get me decently out of the way. As had Edinburgh — with the difference that the Queen would now be paying the fifteen shillings a week.

So, no tears.

A stern corporal was waiting at Bury Station and took me, and the other rookies, off in the depot's lurching three-tonner. One could feel the disapproval, heavy as custard. The shepherding corporal and duty driver were 'thick' regulars. We were the smart-asses who would, for the rest of their lives, dine out on stories of how quaintly uncouth the military life was — and write things like this. But, for ten weeks, we were theirs.

Bouncing on the truck's hard benches (suddenly British Rail upholstery seemed luxurious) the three of us who had been picked up observed a wary silence. Comradeship would come later. Without time to think (something strenuously discouraged over the next ten weeks) we sprogs were kitted out: small packs, large packs, ground sheets, great coats, mess tins, mugs, eating irons, enough straps, belts and lanyards to tie down Houdini. The quartermaster NCOs didn't quite shout 'Schnell! Schnell!' and there was no 'Arbeit Macht Frei' inscribed over the barrack gates — but that's what it felt like.

We were allocated to two platoons, programmed to be deadly rivals for the next ten weeks. They were named after Suffolk battle honours: Gaza and Minden. The second was the more significant. At Minden, in 1759, the Suffolk Swedes (then the 12th Foot) had, for the first time in European battle, not merely defended their line against a superior force of cavalry, but charged and defeated their horsed foe. It was, historically, a players versus gentlemen match in which the lower orders came out top. Mel Gibson should have done a movie about it: *Swedeheart*.

The regiment, soon to be disbanded, bore its swede (sometimes a mangel-wurzel, sometimes a turnip) with pride. It had done particularly well in the Malayan insurgency where the poaching and scrumping skills of the East Anglian countryside adapted seamlessly to the jungle. Regiments like the

270

Suffolks won that little war.

Living on the border, I had always, since my fishing days, felt closer to Suffolk than Essex (whose county regiment was full of Kray-like thugs from Romford — and currently in a state of seething mutiny). I liked the sedative traditions of the regiment, when I came to know them, and I resent all those alien local traditions which have been blended together to form the new 'Anglian' Brigades — units with no more regional character than the Ruritanian Light Infantry. It's not something I'd make a fuss about, but I feel the same kind of impotent disquiet as about the wholesale grubbing up of hedges in Suffolk. They're some of the oldest man-made artefacts in East Anglia: vegetable Stonehenges, destroyed by some Brussels incentive bonus and agro-industrial greed.

Regimental history was not in the forefront of my mind on the evening of 19 July 1957. As my number (23578919) was being stencilled on my gear (but not, thank God, on my forearm), my nose suddenly gushed with blood. 'If you were a fucking Yank', said some sardonic sweat, 'you'd be awarded a fucking purple heart for that.' We were given tea and a doorstep sandwich and put to bed in a dusty barracks room, smelling of rifle oil, toilet disinfectant, the lingering sweat of the just passed-out intake and a century of misery before them. I sniffed myself gorily to sleep, wondering what was to come over the next few weeks.

Basics

Basic training was to come. Boots were bulled (toecap dimpling flattened with red-hot spoons, the smooth surface spat at and polished until — the final test — you could see your face in it). Webbing was blancoed. Buttons were brassoed. Battledress was pressed into creases sharp enough to cut the finger. Rifles (Lee-Enfields, hardly different from what my uncles and grandfather had discharged at the Hun) were lovingly oiled, 'pulled through' and the butts polished; likewise the bayonets. Brens were dismantled and reassembled in seconds.

'Your weapons', one's paybook grimly instructed, 'are given to you to kill the enemy.' And fifteen shillings a week was given with them as killer's fee. The pittance was the measure of what we were worth. Nor, willing as one might have been to lay down one's life for Queen, country and Suffolk, was killing what rifles actually seemed to have been given us for. They were decorative lumps of wood, leather and gunmetal, to 'slope', 'present', 'shoulder', 'ground' and — from time to time — aim at cardboard squares, 300 yards away, with the hope of getting at least a magpie.

Recruits were bullied, screamed at, run ragged. We were taught the higher skills of marksmanship and warned against VD. The notorious film, by hallowed tradition, was shown just before the evening meal; so ravenous was one that not even a parade of rotted cocks could dampen the appetite for the nightly doorstep and jam and pint after pint of oversweetened tea. And anyway the film was, for these ten weeks, unnecessary. Sexual desire evaporated entirely. One was, effectively, neutered.

Potassium in that pint after pint of tea was darkly suspected. Physical exhaustion was more plausible. One fell into bed after deconstructing the intricate blanket pack, which would have to be reboxed the next morning. Often, since it took the cackhanded like me ten minutes, it entailed the most difficult of dilemmas: canteen or lavatory? Hunger or constipation? At least one recruit slept on the floor occasionally, to spare himself the morning chore.

I would sometimes bribe a skilled mate to do my blankets for me. A double Coke and a Mars bar in the NAAFI, that evening, would buy the service and allow me the comfort of starting the day with full stomach and empty bowels. My mother was still sending me ten-shilling notes, with her weekly letter. I took the one and kept the other to read later; or not.

I read nothing except the Orders of the Day. I had brought with me a novel which I fondly expected to occupy my leisure hours: Meredith's *The Amazing Marriage* (a knotty narrative, even by that writer's perverse standards). The training corporal came in one evening and saw me lying on my 'wanker' (the Indian word 'charpoy' was preferred by regulars) reading. 'You'll be playing with yourself before the fucking night's out,' he shrieked, to sycophantic laughter. 'Let me see your fucking boots.' On being shown my dress boots, he scraped a nail across the toecap, with the remark, 'Fucking filthy. Get cleaning.' Exit Meredith; enter Cherry Blossom. It was not the literary sensibility which was being trained at Gibraltar Barracks.

As with every army in the world, the institutional stupidity eventually took you over and remade you in its stupid image. But not quite everyone. Some broke. There were two deserters (easily done) and one suicide. The motive I never knew. A country boy who suffered silently the disciplines he probably could not understand, he swallowed a bottle of Thawpit — cleaning fluid; fatally toxic, as the label warned or, in his case, promised. I recall him lying palely on his blanket-boxed bed — but I was late for a parade, or dinner, or PE — whatever. Camaraderie had its limits. Had it been a battlefield, it would have been the same. There was nothing I could do. The higher-ups and medics had it in hand. The court of inquiry would clear everyone. It did.

The Gibraltar Barracks in Bury, where I and generations of recruits before me sweated, groaned, and occasionally topped themselves, is now a municipal leisure centre. Its massive, slightly sloping and asymmetrical parade ground (nothing was ever quite squared off in the Suffolks) is a car park. The huge, castellated front wall is, like the ruined Abbey (despoiled by townsfolk furious at having to pay tithes in the fourteenth century), of archaeological interest only. Something was once there.

Character eventually protruded through the anonymizing khaki, fatigue overalls and scalping haircuts (day two of training's ordeal). There was the Scot who knelt by his bed to pray, aloud, every night — 'Holy Jock'. A graduate of St Andrews, he intended to do missionary work for his church. His pieties were politely not noticed. I hope, when he carried the light of his Caledonian God into the dark continent, that he had better luck converting the African heathens than the East Anglian.

There was the local yokel who claimed to have a nine-inch penis that no one wanted to see. He was, inevitably, nicknamed 'Knobby' (otherwise reserved, no one knew why, for the surname 'Armstrong'). One was not keen to stand next to him in the shower. Not that time was allowed to stand around. A clever fat man (graduated from Liverpool), with the surname Newton, was nicknamed Isaac — and sometimes 'Tub', after the jellied eel merchant, 'Tubby Isaacs'. He dropped out after impaling himself on a spiked iron fence which, to save time (everything was at the double), the platoon had been ordered to clamber over to get to the next training ordeal. I thought of Moby Dick (at last read) as he feebly struggled, and the point dug further and further into his gut. He spent five weeks in hospital and picked up his training with the next intake.

There was the slow-witted Bury lad in the bed next to me, who would slope off every night to kiss his girlfriend through the wire at the back of the camp, where it merged into changeless Suffolk countryside. I caught sight of them one evening, mooning unhappily like a couple of flank-rubbing cattle, incapable of making sense of the barrier 'they' had put between them. His name was Rodwell ('Oi do,' he said proudly: it was, I guessed, his only joke). He was one of the deserters. He was recaptured after a few hours and was doubled off to the Colchester glasshouse (a place of horrific legend) where there was lots of wire but no more kissing.

There were a couple of extremely wretched recruits who had failed to complete their training in elite units (one a para, the other SAS). They'd signed up for six, and would now have to serve out their time in a very unsexy regiment of the line. They knew all the ropes and swanned through the training, wondering how they could eventually buy themselves out. They were ruthlessly picked on by the NCO staff. 'Errol Flynn' outfits didn't win wars. Slogging foot soldiers like them did.

County regiments depended for morale on local recruitment. Unlike the American army, they believed that men fought and died better, if they had grown up together. I knew three of my Suffolk intake from childhood. One I knew better than I cared to. In an ugly incident I never like to think about, he had been the leader of a street gang round East Bay that had caught me (by what I would later recognize as a classic flanking attack), tied me up and gleefully lit a fire under me, on the railway bank. I had struck them as toffee-nosed. They were, in their brutal way, class rebels; Just William's Outlaws. I was their Hubert Lane.

I was quite badly burned, hospitalized, and the police called in. It never got to court. He had seen me blubber and plead for mercy. After some wary eyeing of each other, Marsh and I became 'mates', although never 'muckers'. Our previous encounter was never mentioned. He was youth club fit, and could do 200 pressups non stop. So beaten down was I by the exhaustion of basic training that I was humbly impressed.

Old habits die hard. He later put a couple of bullets into the back of someone who was his mucker in Cyprus. He claimed to have been cleaning the weapon, a Sterling sub-machine gun — notoriously hair-triggered. The court martial disbelieved him (he was not famous for his cleanly kit) and he returned to his home town Colchester the hard way — via the glasshouse. When I learned of it I hoped the sadistic NCOs at the Military Corrective Training Centre gave him an even harder time than the other bad hats (I did not put poor Rodwell in that class). The burned child, as the proverb says, remembers the fire. But part of me, like Stephen Spender and the rough children his parents never let him play with, would have liked to have belonged to Marshie's gang.

In wartime a reasonable casualty rate is tolerated by the ministry (my poor father was one of that percentage). In peacetime, it was zero. One could not but suspect that the authorities condoned the occasional suicide, or gun crime, or beating up, to 'blood' their men. Even today, the papers report mysterious and suspicious deaths in barracks, like Deepcut. A paranoid part of me wonders if blind eyes are not turned — there, and at every military training establishment in the world. Get the buggers used to it.

Mine was an intake of sixty conscripts, a third of whom were destined to be sergeants in the Education Corps — 'fucking educated goons', as the training NCOs put it in their resolutely uneducated way. Their stripes had been harder earned than by spelling correctly. Quite a few had fought in Korea, Malaya, and seen tense times in the Troodos Mountains and angry streets of Cyprus. They had Active Service Medals. Spelling? The office orderly would do it for them.

The Army Certificate of Education third class, which was the Corps' principal educational programme, was, however, much needed. Of the other two thirds of the intake many were functionally and some totally illiterate. It coincided with bad teeth. The army would, in later life, be the only useful education they got, and the only dental care.

I needed neither. In the verbal aptitude test, I came top — my sole distinction over the ten weeks' square bashing. Meredith (the wordiest wordsmith in Victorian fiction) helped. I was a very fucking educated goon. Official. My oral hygiene was proclaimed, by the camp dentist, to be excellent. Thank you, Eucryl. Two of my intake had teeth rotted to the gum, and got dentures, along with their educational certificate. This kind of social repair-work has always seemed to me the only valid reason for bringing back National Service.

Even more contempt than for the FEGs was reserved for recruits judged OR1 — those eligible for National Service commissions — of whom, with my A-levels, I was one. Second lieutenants were, one was reliably informed, the lowest kind of shit in the British Army. And possibly in the human race. It was something to aspire to.

Futility was the theme in basic training. One did not 'stop' when doing drill: one 'halted' — on a screamed command — with an absurd hop, skip and jump, using five times as much energy as the operation of merely ceasing to move required. Coal was whitewashed. Grass was cut with eating irons. One marched up hills only to march down again. One burnished kit, only to get it filthy enough to clean again. Nonsense was never questioned; the order was always right.

I was, the first time I took to the square, identified as a 'moon man'. That is to say, my arms swung in time with my legs — my right arm, for example, would reflexively come forward along with my right leg. It was common among Suffolk recruits. It was the yokel's gait — quite normal if one spent a lot of time traversing furrowed fields, where moonwalking (forget Michael Jackson) helped preserve the balance on rough ground. It correlated, typically (but not in my case), with gorilla-strong shoulders, from humping bales, felling trees and spadework.

The traditional corrective in the Silly Suffolks had been to put a piece of straw on one boot and piece of hay on the other ('left' and 'right' being well beyond the yokel's comprehension). For a while I was known to the bellowing drill sergeant as 'fucking strawfoot'. It took a while to come down from the moon and join the human race. But eventually I got the knack of it. In later life, alas, the old habit has come back. Fucking strawfoot.

One became inured to the insults, although

the first time the Company Sergeant Major told me that I looked like a great bag of shit, tied up round the middle with a bit of some tart's used jam-rag string, I felt a twinge of indignation. The most irritating thing was that the insult would be followed by the inches-from-the-face question, 'What are you?' and one would have to parrot back the abuse — with the addition of 'Sarn't!' It was important to do so with the requisite obedient inflection. 'Dumb insolence' — that most useful of offences for the malevolent NCO — had been deleted from Queen's Regulations. But it was still more than one's life was worth (fifteen shillings a week, less stoppages) to be 'clever' in one's self-description as a great bag of etc.

The one term of abuse forbidden to the otherwise unfettered NCO foul-mouth was 'bastard' (a prohibition going back to Victorian sensitivity about illegitimacy). There was, as it happened, a member of the Minden platoon by the unfortunate name of 'Barstead'. 'I'd change my fucking name by fucking deed poll,' I heard our corporal say. To John Fucking Smith, presumably.

Feet were a main problem. There was a peculiarly offensive PE corporal, called Huckle (unaspirated 'H'). His kind wore red and black striped jumpers (rather like the ones that burglars had in comics) to show off their muscles. They shouted constantly while running up and down manically. As I lumbered up to the springboard and horse, Huckle liked to put me off my proud vaulting stride with the observation (loud enough for general mirth), 'Here he comes, then — me old mate, Splodfoot.'

My feet have indeed always kippered, Chaplin style. 'Quarter to threes', they were called. They had been deformed by the wartime practice of keeping children's shoes too long — cobbling, metal-studding and rubber-heeling the outgrown pair rather than buying new, larger footwear. The result was what happens to Chinese princesses, but less beautiful — at least to the occidental eye.

Too late in the day my guilty mother had tried to repair the neglect with trips to chiropodists, whose main business was cutting old ladies' toenails. It did as much good as juju. By then, the damage was irreparable: a small toe which curls under its neighbours, and bunions the size of Spanish onions — and an incorrigible tendency to splod.

Army boots completed the work of pedal destruction. You had to 'break them in', they said, as they issued the things; rigid as concrete. In my case, it was my poor plates of meat, not the boots, which suffered the breaking. More specifically, blisters the size of half-crowns exploded wetly, leaving volcanic, suppurating craters. The bastinado could not have been more painful. A fellow trainee, by the name of Sparrow, pulled — with an agonizing wrench followed by a spurt of blood and lymph — an Elastoplast from one of my wounded feet after the day's drilling (I was too pain-racked to do it myself) with the complacent observation, as I shrieked, 'You'll remember my name all your life.' I do. Dunking the feet in urine was recommended as a sovereign remedy. Sparrow, ever helpful, led the way in emptying a barracks fire bucket of its water and filling it with his own. Others pitched in. It doesn't work. But I appreciated the gesture.

Splodfoot I was — like Swellfoot Oedipus, but without the respect. One had to be careful of becoming a figure of fun. Ornithologists identify a practice in birds called 'mobbing': a flock will turn on one of their number, chosen arbitrarily, and peck the luckless bird to death. This ritual murder serves, apparently, to bond the flock. Stanley Kubrick's film, *Full Metal Jacket*, dramatizes the practice and implies, correctly, that armies find it very useful, and encourage mobbing — particularly during basic training.

It was dangerous to be publicly identified as ridiculous; the laughs could turn nasty. There were substantiated legends of recruits being stripped naked, and brushed with bristle-headed bass brooms till their flesh bled, or having their testicles boot-blacked. I was, by now, sufficiently well up in the socio-dynamics of bullying to apprehend the danger, and how to avoid it. I hurled myself at Huckle, like a mad thing — not Splodfoot, but Splod the Torpedo. I enrolled for the boxing team and flailed, indifferent to punishment, so long as I could inflict some hurt on my opponent. I ingratiated myself with the platoon opinion-formers. And some other poor sod was mobbed. His name was Sly — a gravedigger and mute in civilian life. I seem to recall he eventually got a medical discharge. To my shame, I made no protest.

The platoon was awarded a congratulatory 36-hour furlough after three weeks, and passing off the square. One could wear civilian clothes again. They felt like silk. Colchester was only thirty miles away, and I could squeeze in a Friday and Saturday evening there, with old friends. And slake a 21-day thirst. The Saturday was memorable as the occasion when, at last, I lost my long-preserved virginity. Two rites of passage in two days — life was looking up.

It was, after all the years of waiting and furtive blanket practice, excessively casual; civilized, almost. I met her at a party, at someone's house in Shrub End. We drank. Cliff Richard (!) played on the Dansette ('Move It!' — he was a rocker in those days). She was fast, saucy, and rode a small motorbike — with large gauntlets. It was still summer, and there were fields and woods nearby. The night was warm. I rode pillion. Afterwards, we exchanged addresses — a bad move, perhaps. For some weeks after, I trembled in fear of disease or her being pregnant. The second, in those pre-pill, pre-legal-termination days, would have been the more disastrous. But I never heard from her again. Doubtless many men rode her pillion, and I was nothing special.

By the end of the ten weeks one was fit, smart, drilled and ready for 'the regiment'. Like Gerald Kersh's guardsmen we would, should the call come, die with our boots clean, and kill as many of the enemy as we could on the way to bulled-boot death. Whoever the enemy might be — Cypriots, Russians, Chinks — let them come. The Suffolks were, as they had been for three hundred years, ready.

After the passing-out parade, there was the ritual massive piss-up with the NCOs (including the odious Huckle), now self-proclaimed 'mates' not tormentors. A final pay parade had filled pockets. The platoon was ferried to a country pub by the ubiquitous three-tonners, and several newly qualified soldiers of the Queen passed out for the second time that day.

Good drinker that I was, I was able to adopt a quizzical, Jamesian view of the orgy. With my skinful warm inside me, I went off to the local church. 'Been spewin'?' asked the leering Sergeant Bates (the inventor of the 'great bag' simile). 'No, Sergeant,' I replied, 'just admiring the Norman tower — unusual in this part of Suffolk.' Score one for the FEG. Except that he laughed good-naturedly: he'd known hundreds like me, and another sixty would be coming in next week.

Officiering

After a week's leave, the education goons went off to their bookish depot, and the bulk of the intake was shipped to Cyprus, to join the battalion. They could start their chuff charts ('days to do'). I and four others were destined for another three months of basic training, as officer cadets.

There were three hurdles to a National Service commission, and the pip on the shoulder denoting lowest kind of shit, etc. The first was the Unit Selection Board (usbee) in which the depot commander made a decision. That was by interview. A higher hurdle was wosbee (War Office Selection Board) in which, over a period of seventy-two hours at Aldershot (armpit of the British Army), one was given initiative tasks (could one get a squad across a surging river with a too-short plank, a hank of rope, and a knitting needle?), physically challenged by assault courses of fiendish ingenuity, and psychologically profiled. Could one be trusted to do the right thing on the field of battle?

It was more complicated than just going

over the top, leading the way, as in 1917. The strategic assessment was that in an irradiated battlefield, soldiers would have twelve hours' fighting left in them after exposure to tactical nuclear weaponry. Which, in Europe, was inevitable. We would all be kippered with gamma rays, before vomiting, paralysis and death. Those few hours were a crucial asset, given the inevitable follow-up attacks, or counter-attacks. In them, wars of the future would be won and lost. The officers would know they were doomed and would do their duty: the 'men' wouldn't know. Questioning revolved, cunningly, around the issue: would one die, gallantly, with one's boots radioactive?

I was taken on one side, afterwards, and told that the board had given my case much thought. My heart, at times, didn't seem to be in it, although I'd scored sufficiently high on every test. The shrinks had not been entirely convinced. Was I, Major Gimlet-Eye asked me, 'going to give it my best?' Yes, I lied — making gimlet-eye contact in return. I was in. On the train back, the successful candidates segregated themselves from the unsuccessful — leaders and sheep, just as Nelson had said.

As the army whittled itself down to an all-regular force, National Service Officer

Training had removed itself from the Sandhurst-like Eaton Hall to a vacant camp slum in Aldershot, Mons — a name which lived in the mouths of soldiers. With that peculiar British preference for celebrating disaster, the phrase 'biggest fuck-up since Mons' (military lore, in the ranks, disbelieved the official version that it had been a great victory) was still current slang for anything that went even mildly askew. Even at Mons camp. Perhaps in the Belgian town, as well.

It was now winter, and bitterly cold. The black wooden 'spiders' (eight dormitory 'legs', attached to the central block containing washroom, toilets and drying room) were effectively unheated by token stoves and unignitable coke. Aldershot was a garrison town of even less attraction than Colchester; and officer cadets were not popular with the other troops based there. The training areas (principally the vast Salisbury Plain) were of an ugliness that would have defeated even Constable's beautifying palette. Bury St Edmunds, in high summer, was a Butlin's by comparison.

I found myself part of what was substantially a 'Guards' intake. These were officer cadets with private incomes (the Brigade wouldn't look at you unless you had £300 a year) with public school backgrounds and exquisite manners — except when they chose not to be civil. Several had sports cars and wardrobes to match. They probably got their fatigues tailored in Jermyn Street. They would tool off to 'Town' at weekends for parties and popsies. (One informed me, the Monday after, that he'd twice arrived, doing the party round, 'just after Eddie Kent left' — Prince Edward, Duke of Kent, that was.) Their barracks were in the West End and their duty, as household troops, would be close protection of the sovereign and her entourage of people like themselves. Sloane Clones. No soldiers were more the Queen's than they.

I could not get travel warrants, Colchester was far away, and I was always wretchedly unlucky at hitchhiking. I would mooch around Aldershot, catching the odd movie (Hammer horror was big at the time). Or reading. There was a lot of good Angry Young Man, second-generation stuff around. I particularly liked bolshy books, like Sillitoe's *Key to the Door*, Osborne's *The Entertainer*. David Lodge's *Ginger, You're Barmy* I came across later. Simon Raven's *The Feathers of Death* is good on the mess and regimental culture as experienced by the short service officer (which he was, until drummed out). The best of all novels in the genre are Douglas J. Hollands' *The Dead, the Dying*

and the Damned (1956), written by a
National Service officer who had taken part
in the Korean War (toff's view), Andrew
Sinclair's *The Breaking of Bumbo* (toff's
view) and Gordon Williams's *The Camp*
(worm's-eye view). The novelist B. S. Johnson
(whose military career is recorded by
Jonathan Coe) put together an anti-National
Service tract, by many hands, *All Bull*.
Perversely, some of Johnson's contributors
evidently enjoyed the experience. It was never
easy to get national servicemen to march in
step.

Aldershot had a good library for the troops:
I read the whole of Dos Passos's *USA* trilogy
over one 48-hour period in the NAAFI
canteen (the only warm place at Mons) while
most of my fellow cadets were over the fence
hobnobbing with Eddie K., or whatever. I've
always liked empty flats, barracks and (during
the long vacation) universities. The emptiness
gives a sense of ownership.

As comrades the Guards-cadets were toler-
ant and amiable, because wholly unthreatened
by the likes of me. They seemed, in fact,
threatened by nothing. For them the sergeant's
'Sir!' was as natural as sunshine in May. They
inhabited an enviably stable world. There would
always be an England, and it was their England.
They hurrahed — literally hurrahed — when

it was announced, among other news of the day, that the Queen 'would undertake no public engagements over the next five months' (Andrew — another royal parasite, as my mother put it, in her weekly letter). I muttered something Osbornian about a 'gold tooth in a rotting jaw', but inaudibly. Audibly, it was the consensual hip-hip; it was the Queen's Commission one was training for, not the Order of Lenin.

I saw the film version of *Look Back in Anger* with one of the Hurrah Henrys, called (amazingly to me) 'Montague'. No parent in my background would have named a child after the 50-shilling tailor. For him, though, 'Montague' recorded a family which came across in 1066 to lord it over oicks like me. Nor did he feel threatened, even by the bloodiest flights of John Osborne's rage. 'What an absolute cunt!' he ejaculated softly, during one of Burton's rants about how rotten old England (Montague's England) was:

> I suppose people of our generation aren't able to die for good causes any longer. We had all that done for us, in the thirties and forties, when we were still kids. There aren't any good, brave causes left. If the big bang does come, and we all get killed off, it won't be in aid of the

old-fashioned, grand design. It'll just be for the Brave New Nothing-very-much-thank-you. About as pointless and inglorious as stepping in front of a bus.

The obscenity 'cunt', as Montague muttered it, had none of the ugliness it has in working-class mouths. Only now, I was conflicted. Whose side was I now on? And Montague was unruffled; amused, even — and no more threatened by John Osborne's sansculottism than Sir Percy Blakeney.

I had always admired the cool of musicians like Miles Davis or (more to my taste) Jimmy Giuffre. But these men were even cooler. Cool blood coursed through their veins; there was always firm ground beneath their feet. While I, and others like me from unglamorous corps or regiments of the line, feared, above all, 'RTU' (being returned to unit, uncommissioned, a candidate for mobbing), the only thing that they feared was being turned down, at selection time, by their preferred regiment.

One unlucky fellow, who committed the wholly unpardonable sin of losing his rifle bolt, was offered nothing in the Brigade of Guards but was informed the Inniskilling Fusiliers would take him. He would rather have joined the Foreign Legion, and faked a medical discharge on the spot. Why, I asked (thinking that a Queen's Commission was, whatever the cap badge, worth having on one's CV). He just looked at me and went on rehearsing his nervous breakdown. Anything but the Brigade was the Pioneer Corps — those latrine diggers (where the British Army, in a supreme gesture of contempt, consigned the uppity philosopher Arthur Koestler).

What is it Othello says?

> I had been happy, if the general camp,
> Pioneers and all, had tasted her sweet
>   body,
> So I had nothing known. O, now for ever
> Farewell the tranquil mind! farewell
>   content!
> Farewell the plumed troops, and the big
>   wars,
> That makes ambition virtue!

That afterthought about pioneers firmly puts Othello (descended from 'men of royal siege') among the toffs. Hard luck, Black Watch.

I suspected that one of his kind had thrown the wretched cadet's missing rifle bolt in the canal, because, after caballing secretly on the subject, they did not really want him in their exclusive club. He had been blackballed. Let the bogtrotters have him.

In his memoir of the 1950s, Frederic Raphael rhapsodizes about his National Service experience as an amusing prelude to the real thing, Cambridge:

National Service was the public school of those who might never have escaped from the provinces. How else would X have screwed the queen of Mogadishu or Y the wife of his company sergeant major? Would Z have had a shot at some Mau Mau in Kenya — and never known whether he killed a man or not — unless he had been conscripted to maturity, if that is what it was? Would a maths scholar have been disposed to say 'up your gongah!' as often as Tony B., if he had not gone from Cheltenham to Cambridge via Camberley? 'Just because you've got a penis and two testicles, that doesn't mean you're a man,' the drill sergeants used to yell. Getting some service in guaranteed manhood.

It's nicely turned, but very Lord Snooty and his Pals. What is most striking about it is that for a Carthusian like Freddy R., National Service was salutary degradation; an instructive dip in the sewer which, like baby Achilles and the river Styx, made the child stronger, and the Cantab, thereafter, more the Cantab. For me, and those like me, it was promotion: going up in the social world, not down on some voyage of discovery to the lower depths.

They were everything that one resented, in one's pseudo-Porterish way, about England; but it was impossible to hate these toffish officer cadets — more so as they were so civilly accepting of oneself. And their manners were perfect. They were, of course, unlike me and my kind, to those manners born (as to much else). I was, at best, an impersonator. Spell that p.h.o.n.e.y.

The National Service commission, for such as me, was a kind of brevet membership of the upper classes — on the king-for-a-day principle. There was a cynical reason behind it: there always is with the British Army. Nowhere more should one fear gifts than when they come wrapped in khaki and crimson lanyards. In wartime the casualty rate among second lieutenants, given the army's tradition of young officers leading from the front, is fearsomely high ('follow me, men — aargh!' Next, please). Junior officers die like flies, and swarms of them are needed — more than the traditional officer classes can supply.

One was politely accepted, as one passed

through. It was a luxurious corridor, on the way to the kind of military cemetery in which my father peacefully rested. Accepted, that is, so long as one did not make waves, or expect to overstay one's welcome. Had my father survived to make Squadron Leader, he would, for all the length and splash of his medal ribbon, have returned to civvy street as a police constable, where the likes of him belonged — unless their country needed them.

Existing class rules outside the army were in no whit changed by temporary pips on the shoulder, or modulating one's accent and jargon to harmonize with theirs ('Yah', not 'Yes'), knowing to ask for a 'glass of beer' not 'a beer' in the mess (even if the drink were served in regimental silver). Even bravery and gallantry would not do it. There were, in the regiment I eventually served in, NCOs who had won field commissions for extraordinary performance in battle — only to find themselves back in the sergeants' mess when the firing stopped. That was where the tattooed arm belonged.

Officer cadetship (the rank in which my father died) was confusing and ambiguous. One was, as ever, shouted at by the NCOs but they had been handpicked as the best instructors in the army (like those at

Sandhurst) and they had to attach a 'sir' to their tirades. One was the same old bag of shit — 'Sir!' They jabbed the monosyllable into you. And they had the power of RTU — which made them doubly fearsome.

I was good at taking orders and giving them with the requisite mimicry, smart enough to do the classwork, and willing to charge in any direction on command, at whatever risk to the person. That was all the training asked. One spent whole days in muddy holes (no 'fox' would have been so stupid) in freezing weather. This was 'battle training'. At the end of it, I felt rather good. If this was war (it wasn't of course) I could take it. I was always more frightened of displeasing my superiors than incurring personal pain, discomfort or humiliation. It helped that, apart from the occasional weekend revel, there was no drinking; or, at least, not regular drinking. I had been in training now for getting on for twenty weeks, and was fitter than at any time in my life.

The uniform improved with the physique: riding macs, skintight leather gloves, dress shirts with detachable collars and ties, white chevrons on the battledress. One dressed like a gentleman and was soon to be an officer — with a 'servant', no less; one's 'batman'. It was generally regretted that there were no good wars. We were already talking like mess heroes.

I suddenly realized, at a freezing muster parade at an ungodly hour one morning, as I was being inspected by the platoon commander like a dubious side of beef in a cold store, that I was happy — even though some minor blemish was found that morning on my webbing belt and it would mean a tedious night's guard duty or being confined to barracks that weekend. This was a world I had chosen. And, for the first time in my life, as an officer cadet, I was my father's equal. And, amazingly, I was doing all right. No one had made any 'sacrifice'. It was all my own work.

Protecting England

I was accepted, after commissioning and much terminal stamping of feet on the Mons parade ground, back into the Suffolks. Less successful cadets were slotted in, 'greenlined', wherever there was a vacancy. It was a proud moment: more so as the same NCOs who had made one's life miserable now saluted and took one's orders. Life rarely supplies such revenge. They probably despised one as much as ever, but dared not show it — great bags of shit that they were.

Not all of one's officer comrades in the mess were well disposed. Career officers often disliked National Service officers; here today gone tomorrow johnnies, pressed men who, they suspected (quite correctly), would make scornful dinner-party fun of them when, a few months later, it was safe to do so and they, the regulars, were still chained to their machine guns, defending the rights of ex-NS officers to ridicule them.

At the Bury depot, where I was ordered to stay a few weeks in transit, there was a scion of one of the Suffolk brewing dynasties who was a particular pig to NS oicks. I was a particular offence to him (ungrateful, since I'd drunk more than my share of his family beer). I hope he failed his staff college exams and ended up, a passed-over, premature release major, drinking himself to death in some God-forsaken East Anglian rectory between blasting aimlessly at birds. Other career officers were nicer, but saw no point in investing much in transitory comradeship.

I finally worked out how to fit myself in. After my stay in the depot (where I was, briefly, officer in charge of tennis courts — but no longer expected to weed the grass with my eating irons) I was posted to the battalion. It was now back from Cyprus, the London Agreement having settled that hash, and stationed in Germany — the Ruhrgebiet, not that far from where the Dam Busters had bounced their bombs so bravely in 1943.

British audiences loved the 1953 film, but the country's soldiers were particularly loathed round Möhne, as they were at Wuppertal, where thousands died in an RAF phosphorus bomb attack. Flood and fire had ridden through the industrial area, like riders of the Apocalypse. The surviving residents would, one was warned, spit on our boots. Why not? A regiment of the Waffen SS goosestepping through Coventry would probably have got the same treatment — particularly if accompanied by a Luftwaffe-glorifying movie entitled *Blitz über England: 1940*.

I thought of it often. One couldn't avoid the topic in that part of Germany where whole cities like Essen had been flattened. I could never quite make my mind up about the ethics of the RAF bomber: even Guy Gibson's heroics were, to my thinking, of doubtful morality. Was it necessary to drown all those civilians (something the film does not linger on in its tearful attention to the death of Gibson's pooch, Nigger)? Did it really shorten the war?

Mess life in Germany suited me. There was plenty to read (there were even subscriptions to *Encounter* and the *New Statesman*). The conversation was often interesting. There was horseplay on mess nights. Most importantly, there was, at last, a huge amount of licensed drinking. The night tray, loaded with help-yourself liquor, in the anteroom, was a particular boon — you could drink for as long as you could legibly sign the chit and keep your chin off your chest. And, there was some discreet whoring. Germany was, and is, very rational about that kind of thing; the British Army (as Simon Raven eloquently lamented in his novels) less so; hence discreet. Drunkenness could be flagrant and bravely done.

Often one would not bother with sleep, but simply bathe, shave, and put on the clean clothes laid out by one's servant. Regimental life was so active, and one was in such good shape, that the nocturnal dissipation was shrugged off and one was as ready for the early 'musketry' practice before breakfast as any pure-in-mind-and-body Boy Scout would have been.

For those with a gentry background, equination was an early-morning alternative to the musket (by now semi-automatic self-loading rifles — great lumps of junk that the Belgian-made crap was). I tried it just the once. The horse, doubtless resentful of the lower-class knees pressing against its barrel (there was the ritual 'naming of parts' before getting on the beast), bolted and carried me — a Second Lieutenant John Gilpin — across the rifle range. Luckily, my fellow officers were sufficiently awake, or well disposed to me, to hold their fire — more effectively than I held the reins. It was, I would later realize, the only time in my military service I was destined to be shot at — or mounted. It would have been an ignominious death: into the valley of death rode the idiot horseman. After that I stuck to the rifle practice, which I was good at — oddly, at my best with a hangover, a condition which, somehow, seemed to still the hand-eye relationship.

The fact that I had some command of idiomatic German made me popular when we took to the German bars by night. A photograph from the period (it's in Berlin, where the regiment was later posted) shows me holding a beer glass big enough for a dolphinarium. For reasons that were obscure,

The Wannsee. Note the glass

I was nicknamed 'Jock' by fellow officers. I had carefully bleached out all tartan from my accent, replacing it with toff inflections, since likewise bleached. It was the first generally accepted nickname I'd had since 'Stinker' (an attempt at CRGS to get myself known as

'Sudsy' had failed). I was proud to be Jock, and grateful. Nicknames indicated institutional affection — and, even if they alluded to stench, belongingness.

My National Service messmates had, in the main, been to better schools than me, and the regiment's career officers had roots in the East Anglian gentry. My closest friend ('oppo', in the slang of the regiment) was a good-looking wild man called Mackay. He was less Scottish, despite the Caledonian surname, than even I was: his Italian family had prudently changed their vowel-laden surname during the war. His brother was regular RAF, and piloted a Vulcan. Mike was drunken, dashing, handsome, and reckless — everything I aspired to be. I followed in his wake.

I was lucky not to die with him. Driving back drunk one evening, he overturned the car. Trapped under the vehicle, I felt a liquid dripping on me. Petrol, I thought, in panic. In fact, it was battery acid. The next day my suit (which had cost me a hefty £28 from Alkit) had decomposed into its constituent wool. Mike talked his way out, as always, from the subsequent inquiries. It was, as he called it, a 'shunt'. He survived many such episodes, shunting his way, stylishly, through life. He'd failed his accountancy exams many times

— which was why he was now in the army. Doubtless he eventually shunted his way to qualification and carelessly accounted his way to Jaguar-driving prosperity in Virginia Water.

There was an excellent battalion library: I still have, on my shelf, Henry James's *The Reverberator*, with the Suffolk Regiment stamp on it (not a theft, I tell myself — just a long loan). I had moved on, in anti-militaristic fictional territory, from late Meredith to early James. I turned to late Trollope at around this time, which spoke to me more directly. The fact is, I read as much in the army over those two years as I had in the sixth form. And more thoughtfully. Trollope's anatomy of what he liked to call the 'hobbledehoy' (a kind of Victorian schlemiel) — in *The Claverings*, for example — seemed to explain a lot about myself to me. As Trollope saw it, one didn't really become oneself — throw off the ugly duckling — until well into one's twenties. It is a kind of *per ardua* philosophy, and socially generous in a way that Dickens (dependent as his plots are on providence) isn't.

Jock, Champion of the World

I achieved some glory in my last year — although not the kind that would get me on the CRGS honour boards. For two weeks in late September 1959 I was a world champion. There was at the time a craze for long-distance marching — long distance being 110 miles. Two marines did it in thirty-three hours, winning themselves and their unit headlines, with pictures of the knackered heroes and their yet more knackered feet. There was even the dizzy prospect of a paragraph for them in the newly launched *Guinness Book of Records* — assuming their time stood.

BAOR (the British Army on the Rhine — an embarrassingly melodramatic name for what we were) was an army waiting for something which, because we were waiting for it, would never happen: a stand-off, as it would later be called — and arse-achingly boring for the quarter of a million British soldiers doing the standing off. I suspect the Roman legionaries on Hadrian's Wall (RAOW) felt the same, fifteen hundred years before. Roll on death, demob's too far away.

There were, we were informed, 200 Red Army/Warsaw Pact Divisions, tank engines revving, poised for imminent attack. But they wouldn't ever attack, because of the paralysis of MAD (mutually assured destruction). Any move of a military kind would bring the whole pack of cards down. The two greatest, most fearsomely armed, military goliaths in the history of the planet did not dare throw a pebble at each other.

It wasn't entirely the fearsome battle-honoured record of the Suffolk Regiment that kept the red wolf at bay. As one later learned, around 199 of those Red Divisions were needed to keep Poland and other satellites from doing a Hungary. The Soviets were, in a phrase being bandied around by Mao at the time, paper tigers. Despite the apocalyptic warnings of the *Daily Express*, Moscow was in no position to launch World War Three: at least, not on the European front, staunchly defended by Second Lieutenant Sutherland and the hard men of 8 Platoon.

This geopolitical stasis looked set to last until the end of time — or until some idiot in Moscow or Washington pressed a red button, giving humanity four minutes to put its affairs in order before incineration. No role for BAOR in that eventuality, either. One beer and it would all be over.

BAOR was desperate for anything, any stunt, which would keep their bored conscripts from mischief, venereal infection, and in physical condition. 'Adventure Training', it was called. The only proviso was that the adventures should cost the British taxpayer nothing except, at a pinch, leather and a gallon or two of petrol. Long-distance marching was warmly approved. The clodhopping infantry, whose soul had always (homophonically) been in its boots, took up the marines' challenge.

I — representing the Suffolks (regimental march, 'Speed the Plough') — would make the attempt on the world record with my (I loved that possessive) platoon sergeant, and whatever members of my (ditto) platoon were willing to tag along. Not many, it transpired. Schweikism ruled among that crew. I doubt 200 red divisions could have got them off their wankers.

Even over the flat borderland between Germany and Holland, 110 miles, non-stop, is a challenge. It was also very, very boring. Conversation lasts about three hours. After that, the brain switches on to automatic and the mouth is transferred to breathing operations only.

Every hour or so, we would stop for five minutes, gulp pints of lime juice (which I have never been able to drink since) and gobble sweetmeats. Starting again was agony. Knees would audibly creak. After ten hours, the blood stops circulating and pools in the extremities. It is like walking on liquid bladders, with a couple of sausage balloons (and ten overstuffed chipolatas) hanging by your sides. Feet one did not dare think about.

As we tramped across the Dutch-German borderlands we were accompanied by a couple of Champs (Jeeps) — Champs for would-be champions. The vehicle (as did I) summed up much that was wrong with British materiel then and, I suspect, now. It had been introduced as the replacement for the Land Rover — a simple box on wheels judged to be insufficiently sophisticated for modern warfare. The Champ could winch itself out of the Grand Canyon and you could have mounted Big Bertha on its chassis. It had ten gears — both forward and reverse. It could actually do 70mph going backwards, powered by its mighty Rolls-Royce engine. That reverse speed could well have been useful when the red hordes poured over the wire. The maximum forward speed of the T54 tank, one gathered, was 55mph.

The Champ had a couple of shortcomings. It was so overengineered, only a couple of wraith-thin personnel could get inside it.

And, cornering at anything over 20mph, moving forwards, it would overturn, killing those wraiths. It was a TSR2 on wheels. After spending hundreds of millions, the Army went back to the bog-simple Land Rover, which it uses to this day.

Only two of us, the sergeant and I, made it round the great loop to where we started. Our time was 29 hours and 10 minutes — a world record. Unfortunately, the next day, I discovered my legs were still in a condition of elephantiasis. I could actually not get my trousers round them, but had to slit the legs of a pair of fatigues. Another world record, perhaps — the fattest calved officer in British military history.

The battalion Medical Officer (a physician of legendary incompetence, who was later nearly lynched after he misdiagnosed the Colonel's beloved daughter into a near-death crisis) recommended a week's skiing to dissolve the clots. After an agonizing 100-mile journey (another one) to the ski-camp (designed, principally, for cold-weather training) its MO, rather more competent about haematology than our battalion prat, bleakly informed me that death, from heart or brain stoppage, was certain if I so much as sneezed — thus dislocating the lumps of cottage-cheese consistency that currently inflated my unhappy pins.

I returned the hundred miles, in the same staff car, as an emergency patient to one of the huge hospitals that had been set up in the rear echelon, for war casualties. I was, literally, walking wounded. The doctors were wholly unsympathetic. 'How did you train for this?' asked one Canadian specialist (the Canucks ran the place). 'With a couple of beers and a cigarette in the mess?' At least I didn't smoke. The beers I would plead guilty to.

While I recovered from my shameful thrombophlebitis, immobile, under a leg cradle, in a huge, cavernous, empty hospital (its miles of wards awaiting, patiently, the thousands of patients that would come in with World War Three) a civilian, Barbara Moore, clipped two hours off my time for the 110-mile bash. She was fifty-nine years old, and carried no equipment other than a vacuum flask, and a tortoise in her shopping basket. (Why the tortoise? Was it some Aesopian, allegorical joke?) An interesting woman, Moore had been an aviatrix in the Soviet Union. She was later, I seem to remember, revealed to be a fraud — she and me both. She is remembered as a pioneer breatharian — believing that the human body could be sustained on a diet of air, without the need of that 'filthy tube', the gut. I too was eating little at the time — to avoid bedpan indignities.

The sergeant with whom I had marched brought me ironic grapes. He marched, heel-toe, through the long, empty ward, with its gleaming 'buffed' floors, like El Cid, the rapping of his steel toecaps mocking my bedpan. My bedbound condition, although he was too tactful to say so, confirmed all that he and his kind had ever suspected about National Service officers. In the final test, however much spirit they showed, they were never 'hard' enough for soldiering.

His background, unlike mine, was 'real'. He had been posted with his regiment in Palestine, as the mandate came to its messy end. He had fallen in love with a dazzlingly beautiful Jewess and deserted to fight with the Irgun. On his return, having given himself up, he was sentenced to a year in the glasshouse, the MCTC at Colchester. On his release, he painfully clawed his way up the ranks again to Sergeant. Why was he not, at least, a warrant officer? I asked my company commander. 'Because we don't trust him', was the uncompromising reply. The black mark on his record meant he would never get any higher, in peacetime.

He was the best, and hardest, soldier I ever came across. And, in terms of military morality, the most admirable. He had honestly felt it was wrong to leave the Jews to be slaughtered and raped — again. Had the Russians started a war he would have been given a field commission and, if there were any justice, should have been put in charge of a company over my head. As it was, he clucked (mockingly) over my inflated leg.

Defending the realm

I celebrated my twenty-first birthday in hospital. My mother wrote to say she had a present for me, awaiting my return (a rather nice brown cashmere jumper). It was there when I got home. She commissioned a photograph of me (acutely embarrassed) to show off.

I was back on the mantelpiece.

Berlin Again

By one of the now repetitive circuits of my life (had my pregnant mother been frightened by a hamster in its cage?) the regiment was posted to Berlin. It had now been amalgamated and renamed the 'First East Anglian Regiment' (which historically it wasn't). The former capital, still technically under four-power command (think *Third Man*), and sliced into quarters, was deep inside the Russian Zone. We were installed at Kladow, on the edge of the British Sector. On wire patrol, we would pass our patrolling Russian counterparts, feet away. They looked under-nourished and bemused, unlike the Slavic gorillas pasted on our rifle-range targets.

The barracks at Kladow, in which 1EAR (First East Anglian Regiment) were alien lodgers, had been built for the Wehrmacht. It was five-star luxury compared to the slums of Aldershot or the preposterous imperial kitsch of Bury's Gibraltar Barracks, with its turrets, towers and windy barrack rooms — barns for soldiers. Kladow had large windows, comfortable mess and canteen facilities, and human-sized dormitories for the men. It lacked a large parade square, but had numerous large and small firing ranges (in the UK, one had to go miles by trucks to get one's shooting). In addition to skills, the buildings were cunningly designed to foster company and small unit *esprit de corps*. The whole thing had been thought about by architects in collaboration with military people.

Germans (Prussians in particular) evidently liked soldiers, and the panoply of war — parades, uniforms, shining steel. They still did: station masters on the local Eisenbahn were better turned out than our Commanding Officer who sanctioned a comfortable 'shit order' relaxation about dress. He was also beyond Moonman in his marching capacities.

But then, if one thought about it, something which had kept Britain democratic through the twentieth century, while Germany went goose-step crazy, was its contempt for strongman, Bismarckian politicians; its distrust of standing armies in the home country, and its dislike of military show, except in time of war. This distrust expressed itself in poor equipment, inferior accommodation and the Tommy Atkins peacetime discrimination Kipling complains about so bitterly.

I went into a public-'ouse to get a pint
   o'beer,
The publican 'e up an' sez, 'We serve no
   red-coats here.'
The girls be'ind the bar they laughed an'
   giggled fit to die,
I outs into the street again an' to myself
   sez I:

O it's Tommy this, an' Tommy that, an'
   'Tommy, go away';
But it's 'Thanks you, Mister Atkins,'
   when the band begins to play,
The band begins to play, my boys, the
   band begins to play,
O it's 'Thank you, Mister Atkins,' when
   the band begins to play.

Pity unappreciated Tommy. But pity more the
country that loves its soldiers and looks after
them well. None the less it was good, for a
few months, to be comfortable — more so
since it was at Hitler's expense.

There was a Teutonically efficient bus and
tram service to the fleshpots of Berlin. In his
journals Stephen Spender, who had enjoyed
the last days of the Weimar capital, recalls
returning to Berlin, as a de-Nazification
missionary, in 1946. The first thing he did, on
arrival in the city (leaving his wife in the

hotel), was to beetle off, *ventre à terre*, to the Ku'damm, in whose boy bars and bathhouses he, Isherwood and Auden had so enjoyed themselves in the early 1930s, before Hitler made the place too hot for leftist homosexualists like themselves and Mr Norris.

Spender was appalled that he could not even work out where the Street of Princes and pretty boys had been. A wasteland of unmarked rubble extended from the Wannsee to Potsdam. But fourteen years later, the old metropolitan and bohemian outlines had reasserted themselves — albeit with rather less gaiety than in 1930. In the alleys and sidestreets around the centre there were, again, gay bars, lesbian bars, and high-class whore bars (some with telephones on tables for assignations). One could see women wrestle in mud if one fancied that spectacle which had, somehow, captured the Anglo-Saxon imagination as the epitome of pornochic (Keith Waterhouse's novel *Jubb* is very funny on the subject).

There was, for those wishing for true degradation, a cluster of bars known, among the British soldiery, as 'ten-mark alley' — that being the cost of its women and there (the alley) being where the goods were delivered. I was once there, at the end of a night higher up the debauchery scale, spending the less than ten marks I had left on drink (with something spared for a curry wurst on the way back). Sitting at the bar an amiable and currently clientless lady of the alley informed me that the main thing about the British soldiers was that they didn't rape. 'Nicht so viel, mindestens,' she added thoughtfully — not so much, at least. But the Americans paid more. The Russians raped and paid nothing. History, for her, was an unzipped battledress — rather like Orwell's boot, stamping on a face for ever.

Normally one drank either in the mess or in the Officers' Club in Charlottenburg. That minisector was home territory for me, and I would spend evenings there with Otto (who, an honorary club member, would go through life with an absurd English officer's accent — Herr Terry Thomas) and the Schmidt-Fabians. 'Du bist unser Schutz,' said Mutti fondly — you are our protector. The band was always playing for Tommy Atkins in Berlin. I preened, bravely. She stuffed Braunschweiger sausage and ryebread (which I had foolishly once said I liked) down me, like a Strasbourg goose. I thought of Granny's mince. Feeding and motherhood had never really gone together for me.

There was a splendid British Council library and, for the first time in my life, I was able to steep myself in more contemporary fiction than I could comfortably read. I've always rather resented the caricature Greene and Wilfrid Hyde-White offer of the Council in the film *The Third Man* (1949). As it happened, I pulled quite a lot of Greene from the shelves of the Council's library, nestled as it was near the Tiergarten — the animal park whose beasts were slaughtered for food and its trees felled for firewood in the terrible winter of 1947. It had been much improved since 1953, like the rest of the city — hugely invested in by the Bundesrepublik as a 'shop window' for life in the West. At this period, two years before the Wall, the DDR was losing thousands of its population every week.

It was an easy life, and the timetable (apart from sporadic convulsions when the high command felt the need to get a grip) was relaxed. The biggest thing in the calendar was guard duty at Spandau for Albert Speer and Rudolf Hess, the two life-serving war criminals. The task was taken in turn by the four powers. I saw Speer pottering around in his little plot of a garden like a pensioner on his allotment.

Honey Trap

I could use the city rather more familiarly than most and was as much at home outside as inside the barrack wall. Once, on an early evening bus from Kladow, a girl plumped down beside me asked if, by chance, I knew a Corporal Smith. 'Many,' I replied roguishly. She had come, she said petulantly, to complain about him to his commanding officer. Corporal Smith had promised to marry her, but they would not let her past the guardroom. And they claimed not to know him — which was ridiculous.

There were a couple of odd features about her: she was attractive, in what the Germans call a foxy way, and could speak fluent, inaccurate English. She was clearly not a whore — no queen of Mogadishu, certainly, but a notch or two higher than the CSM's wife.

She forgot all about her errant corporal when she discovered that I was an officer. They didn't normally use buses or trams; there was too much likelihood of friction with drunken Other Ranks. One thing led to another, and I found myself in the apartment she shared with her mother (currently not at home) in Tegel — deep in the French Sector. She, almost before the door was closed, had her blouse and bra off. Would I be quiet, she asked; her young child was in the next room, sleeping.

It was very odd — and inhibiting. I, like virtually every young soldier at Kladow, was starved for sex. Like my messmates, I knew where the houses of convenience (for officers) were, and the red-light brothels (for the 'chaps'). Visiting them was no more erotic than the fortnightly short back and sides from the regimental barber.

But this presented a scenario which was, for me, deeply offputting. It wasn't the sex. I felt as if I were Russell, in the Long Wyre Street flat. Incest taboo kicked in — and a kind of self-pity. It was confusing and unaphrodisiac. My being there, with a half-naked woman, dramatized every military occupation in history. I was nervous, like a swimmer on the edge of a cold pool. We cuddled a bit. I took the beer she offered (along with that impressive frontage and whatever else I might take a fancy to) and we talked. I might have taken the plunge (God knows, my genitals were willing) were it not that her mother returned, after an hour or so. There was some scuffling of clothes (the

325

daughter's) and after a few meaningless pleasantries, I left, genitals aching resentfully.

I mentioned the episode to an older Berlin hand at the Officers' Club. Was it, I wondered, the famous honey trap? The Stasi were so obsessed with espionage they even bugged their own offices. They probably bugged their paramount leader, Ulbricht. An officer who spoke German, in a front-line unit, might have been considered an asset. Were there cameras waiting to catch my naked buttocks in action? Would I sometime soon receive a batch of photos in the post, and the suggestion that I should meet someone in a park, and await further instructions? Unless, that is, I wanted my folks back in the UK to get some new snaps for the family album. There would have been nothing easier than for Fräulein Tits to have discovered my identity, name, rank and number, while I was taking the post-coital pee. Was there really a child in the next room, or a Stasi stooge, with his lens to the peephole?

Possible, he thought; it happened. The fact that she was waiting, like a spider in the corner of its web, just outside the camp, was suspicious. I was not irresistibly handsome, or irresistibly anything. To be honest, Corporal John Smith, if he existed, would probably have offered a jollier time — certainly more jolly rogering.

On the other hand, women in Berlin were still traumatized by the mass rape of 1945. There was nothing jolly about it. They wanted out from a place which was indelibly stained with their sex's suffering. For them, the city was a massive crime scene. Deep in their wombs, they just knew it was going to happen again. A husband was a passport not to anywhere desirable, but out of the rape zone. It was less the honey than the tender trap. She was not Mata Hari, nor Lily Marlene under her street lamp, but, as it might well have been, a canny woman like my mother wanting to get a little bit ahead.

Thanks to Otto, I'd seen Helene Weigel do Mother Courage at the Theater am Schiffbauerdamm, the house of Brecht. It was often revived, not merely because it is a great play but because of its relevance to what women had gone through in Berlin. Whichever it was that night in Tegel, I'll never now know. But it was another circuit. I had returned to where I had been fifteen years earlier, a child in Long Wyre Street, but on the other side. To be absolutely congruent, that child (if he — and it had to be a 'he' — existed) in the other room, like me, should have been brought in to admire me, and be admired by me, the foreign officer. But things are never quite that shapely in life. And, of course, the child may have been a dirty-minded East German hired voyeur, with a fag drooping from his slobbery mouth. And, I can't help thinking, it was only my morbid imagination that created these shapes in the first place. I should have shagged and run, like Corporal Smith, leaving sperm and a false name behind me.

Two years, at that time of life, seemed a long time. But by now it was 'days to do — and a greasy' (the traditional fried breakfast) as the National Service slogan had it. During my last few weeks in Berlin I made efforts to get a university place. I was again turned down everywhere (those damned A-level results) except, inevitably, Leicester.

It was humiliating, but clearly kismet (the Anglo-Saxon 'doom' was perhaps the better word). A messmate (destined for his family farm) advised me to look in the advertisement columns of the *Telegraph*. There were always jobs on offer for blokes like me, he said — men, that is, 'who knew how to handle men'. I looked, in a desultory way, and made no applications. I was seriously tempted to sign up for another three years, or six. I liked the army — not because it was the army, but because it was an institution which had shaped me well enough to fit in.

It represented security and an unearned measure of privilege — things that had been in chronically short supply in my life. They would, I think, have kept me on. Like Leicester, they seemed to have faith in me. But there was no interesting action. The whole great machine was demoralized by the clumsily executed switch from conscription to all-regular. And, in my heart, I knew that if I did stay on I would probably never make it to Staff College.

There was a lieutenant in the regiment who, I'd been told, had been put on a very-secret list at the War Department for 'flyers'. He would have a jet-propelled career. Which, indeed, he did. Thirty years later, in a TV dispatch from Bosnia, I saw him with general's insignia on his lapels. I would have been in the other category, which there was no need to list. They weren't flying anywhere. Plodders. Officer Atkins.

So I took my discharge from the colours (with the prospect of five years on the reserve, and promotion to full lieutenant) equanimously. My mother picked me up, in my uniform, from the railway station. She was impressed, as we passed the garrison barracks in Mersea Road, when the sharp-eyed soldier on guard at the gates snapped a salute at me. My last. That fraudulence was over.

Hard Labour

My mother was now living (unmarried, and on and off) with her man in the motor trade who was coming up in his scummy line of work — by being scummier than the rest, I sometimes thought. The stuff rises. But he was always civil to me and would sometimes give me cast-off clothes — usually virulently checked sports jackets faintly smelling of Senior Service and Brut. I would occasionally wear them to please my mother. I still had my room at Wellington Street, until I moved on. As would she, I understood, quite soon: it was a way station, not a home. I was used to that. My old kitbag had by now seen many stations.

I came out of uniform, as I had entered it, in high-summer July. It was three months before term started at Leicester. I had saved nothing from my time in the army. Mess bills and clothes (one had to dress like a gentleman) wiped out the weekly fiver, even at the giveaway rates at which booze was supplied to the troops in Germany. My mother, any umbilical connection being now well and truly cut, could not be looked to for anything other than the now traditional (but traditionally infrequent) ten bob. I would get an Essex county grant of £200-odd a year to keep me at university: but the first instalment was months away.

I had a bank account but in those days, without collateral or guarantor, a loan or overdraft was out of the question. I had nothing substantial to pawn although I had come to know Markham's pawnshop in Priory Street quite well. My watch, brought back to me from the Argentine all those years ago, had been 'pledged' many times over the years. Fifteen bob was what it usually got.

I would have to find work.

I went to the Labour Exchange in Stockwell Street. My grandmother, I recalled, had once cleaned the steps there, thirty years before, when it was the town library. That was during the depression. We were now, as Macmillan never tired of telling us, living in jammy full employment — never so good, and all that. I would test the Macmillan thesis.

I don't know what I expected — something, I daresay, appropriate to my superior station in life and my proven ability to handle men: a management position, perhaps, in some go-ahead firm's personnel department showing them how to do it. The only thing they had, after much shuffling of index cards, was casual work with a firm called Terson's. They were subcontracted to lay rail and did so by recruiting unskilled labourers. All that was required was physical fitness for humping, digging and hauling, and the ability to understand three words of English (hump, dig, haul). A month before, I had been up there with my pilot-officer father. Now I was down in the pits, with my council-labourer grandfather. Fucking circuits.

I took the Terson's job. I would be, I romantically thought, what the blues singers called a steel-driving man. The pay was good — as high as £20 a week, with overtime, and long summer days. But, the girl behind the desk warned, the work was very hard. The employer wanted that point pressed home urgently. The prospect of toil phased me not at all. I was fit, I could march 110 miles, and could — if I psyched myself up — do 200 press-ups, without stopping. Was I, who had faced down the Red Wolf across the wire, frightened of a pickaxe or a shovel? Hell, no. I would show them how to do it.

The ganger, when I reported to the meeting point at 5.30 a.m. the next morning, took one scornful look at me and said, 'You're not used to real work, are you?' (He was, I later discovered, a former RSM in some

Welsh regiment: it took him seconds to decode me.) I had made the mistake of wearing a sports jacket; it was not a good choice. Over the next two months I came to understand what the nature of 'real' work is. It is not being in tip-top condition; it is not hard exercise, even if the exercise involves marathons, Snowdons, or bench-pressing 300lbs.

Real Work is the wearing down of the body until the body is worn out — usually in middle age. Those of my early friends who did it (punching HGVs, construction, marquee erection) were crocked by fifty — if they made it to that age. Typically the back went first. 'Back-breaking work' is not a metaphor, it's a promise. The term 'soul-destroying' is often used in describing manual labour. It should, more properly, be termed 'body and soul' destroying — in that order. There is absolutely nothing noble in it. It should be banned.

The Terson's gang I was in was made up of those who, for one reason or another, could not do 'regular work' (very different from the real variety). There were surly Poles (at least two of whom had been in Eastern Bloc labour camps). There were yokels, who in earlier times would have sped the plough in the muddy Essex fields but whose age-old crafts had been mechanized, pushing them out into vagrancy and casual labour. There was a chancer called 'Nigger', just out from jail (and hence unemployable in any respectable line of work, like bricklaying or scaffolding). He was nicknamed in recognition of his swarthiness. There was also, as it happened, an actual West Indian negro. 'Do you like being black?' I once heard him asked. 'Fucking no,' he replied.

There were, inevitably, Irishmen — a race which had been navvies on the English railway for a century. The name, one of them told me (I haven't checked), originates with the steam-driven 'navigators' used to lay Victorian railroads. One of them brought a transistor radio wrapped carefully in a plastic bag and loved Acker Bilk, whose syrupy clarinet was big that year. They were courteous and good talkers. In other circumstances I would have liked to drink with them.

There were womanizers — Colchester Romeos — who, as we bumped along in the tilt (the canvas cover over the back of the truck), would flick-comb their hair and entertain the company with lurid descriptions of screwing on the Hilly Fields or some other wild place.

It was a human bag of nails. A soft-handed

ex-officer was no big deal, so long as he didn't try anything on or, in my case, reveal where he'd just come from. I listened and said little: if that. There were some superb storytellers, but whatever pleasure I took in demotic narrative was submerged in constant physical pain. In basic training, it had been my deformed feet. In Terson's, it was those soft hands. After one day's shovelling, they were a bloody pulp. ('Stick them in the chamber pot tonight,' a fellow labourer advised. Where had I heard that before?) I eventually found that coarse leather mittens minimized the agony, although taking them off at night was like peeling ducktape off open wounds.

I found myself hopelessly clumsy at 'hogging out' (scraping the cinders from under the ties) while a bent and wizened neighbour (probably all of thirty-five) did it as easily with the clawed tool as picking teeth (of which he had fewer, and much blacker, than me). If I swung the ten-pound hammer, to drive the rail clips into the wooden sleepers, I was as likely to miss and hit the steel rail itself; something that infuriated the ganger, because it was likely to snap the wooden hammer-haft. The shock to my wrists — which were continuously sprained — was of no account.

I was similarly clumsy with sleeper dogs, and rail dogs (gigantic tongs, for communal lifting of the larger pieces of railroad ware). The gang would yelp, like hounds on the scent, when the call 'Dogs' went out. I would add my canine cheep and do my clumsy, unhandy best with the tools. 'This,' one of the Poles told me after I dropped my end of a three-hundredweight sleeper, 'is not a job for children.' It was my lowest moment.

There was a fifteen-minute break for sweet tea, brewed in a bucket, in the morning. Exhaustion rendered it as delicious as nectar. We had thirty minutes at lunch — sandwiches (my mother had discovered the utility of Heinz sandwich spread and, on good days, the old standby, scrambled egg). The faster the jobs could be done, the more profit on the fixed payment from British Rail for Terson's. The ganger was instructed to jack up the work rate to Stakhanovite levels. During the hot afternoon hours of work, someone (often one of the recently injured, who still wanted to work for the pay) would walk up and down with a bucket of water and cup.

Cool Hand Sutherland.

It was dangerous work. A year before, a score of workers had been killed as they worked on the line because the warning flag system had been neglected: they were mowed down like weeds on the bank. Flag and klaxon duty was sought after, but went to the gangers' favourites, not me. Hardly a day went by without someone being hurt or badly bruised. There was so much jarring metal flying around, so many things that could be dropped or mishandled, so much hurry. And, if you had to take time off, there was no pay. Married men, with families to support, worked through physical damage that ought to have seen them in hospital. They lived from pay packet to pay packet and speculated endlessly, during tea breaks, about how much overtime there would be that week.

The girl in the labour exchange had been right. The money was good: often, as promised, £20 a week, delivered in cash and coin, in a pay packet, no stoppages — the only time I have been so paid. The cash nexus, I realized, symbolizes total social irresponsibility on the payer's part. 'Our duties towards you cease for ever with this envelope.' Take your cash and bugger off; if we need you next week, we'll let you know. Meanwhile, of course, behind all those envelopes soft-faced men were getting rich. There was blood on their hands too, but of a different sort from mine.

I stuck it out for a couple of months until I

had a sufficient stash for a holiday (Spain — boozy and hospitable, pre-package tour and playa vandalism) and my 'going up' to university. Except, of course, Leicester wasn't up. That dark cloud on my horizon got darker and larger every week that brought me nearer October and, horrible prospect, Leicester.

But I never thought of dropping out — even though, with the start of the sixties, braver spirits than me were doing it. (My stall-owning friend had already left for Nepal. He would come back three years later a shattered man.) The open road was not for me. Neither was labouring. Working on the railroad had cured me of that (and of any lingering, blues-derived romanticism about that line of work). Leicester might be degraded but it was, potentially at least, a skive. No blood-stained mittens. Ever since graduation from Terson's my motto has been, as the joke puts it, 'I love work, I could watch it all day.' Fishing, as a child, had brought me close (as close as he would allow) to my grandfather. Terson's, as a man, brought me close again. To think of doing this kind of shitwork all your life! I would have thrown myself into Middlemill Pond long before he did. Or joined the revolution.

In the space of six months, I had drunk chilled beer from regimental silver, and had a servant to lay out my clothes. And I had sweated, manually, in conditions barely better than those of Ivan Denisovich, in a labour gang, my hands so bruised and sore I could not have got them round a goblet if I was dying of thirst. Whatever else, the Terson pay packet knocked out whatever amour-propre the Queen's commission may have instilled in me. I was what I was, not what any uniform (whether mess kit or soiled overalls) said I was. Not much.

Leicester

Could one, I wondered in September 1960, sink lower than Terson's — lower than the world of tilt, bucketed oversweetened tea, and rail dog? Yes. Leicester University. When I arrived there, the campus air was porridge-thick with inferiority complex. The university on cemetery road (immortalized in *Lucky Jim*) was, if not of last resort, then at best the hopeful undergraduate's third, 'safety net', choice. Unlucky Jims, all of them.

To be accepted at Leicester was to have failed everywhere else in academic life. You didn't 'come up' to Leicester, as Oxonians and Cantabridgians said (toffily), you ended up there. For decades before my surly arrival, Leicester had been a lowly 'university college' — an outrider of the University of London, which, Kremlin-like (how right Orwell was to make Senate House the Ministry of Truth), superintended its activities — as it did, for example, the university colleges of Hong Kong, Kuala Lumpur and quite possibly Wagga Wagga. Faceless committees in Malet Place, WC1, administered finance, teaching and exams for places like Leicester.

Leicester, like other unvalued colonial outposts of the London academic nexus, got its 'charter' (independent university status) in the 1950s — about the same time as Ghana's University College (the White Man's Grave College, as was). Leicester seized its new freedom as an opportunity to ape not its parent London, but Oxbridge. For a couple of years, there was an unhappy experiment with gowns, 'college houses', maces, high tables and dry sherry, which merely served to remind luckless Leicestrians that Leicester wasn't Oxbridge.

Ede & Ravenscroft, purveyors of academic garb, profited. The wearing of the gown (and the prohibition on women students wearing trousers) petered out in my first term at the university. There was no edict on the issue — nothing equivalent to a Victorian surplice riot — the absurdity simply hiccupped to a stop.

Coming from the Officers' Mess, where I drank my beer from regimental silver, I felt all that was missing was the leper's clapper and the shout, 'Loser, loser!' In subsequent years, American colleagues would ask me, on glancing at my CV, 'Is Leicester College, Oxford or Cambridge?' Fuck off, I would explain (silently, in my head).

I was, in 1960, two years older than most

who entered Leicester. Virtually all the males had sensibly taken deferment or were now too young for National Service. At that period of life, a couple of years is a gulf. I felt like the proverbial uncle — as the 'old for their rank' are called in the army. I wasn't a virgin. I had read Goncharov, Sartre, Kerouac and Wyndham Lewis (all his work — he was then a favourite). I had, in fact, read about ten times as much as the other twenty or so incoming English under-graduates (and at least a couple of the junior faculty). I could put a magazine-full of Bren rounds into a 9-inch grouping at 300 yards. And much good that would do me. I had got drunk in five countries and had had the services of a batman to help me straighten out on hungover mornings. And here I was, sharing a room (during my brief experiment with one of the pseudo-colleges) with three school-leavers one of whom I'll swear I heard sobbing on his first night away from home.

The city of Leicester was proud to have been named the second most prosperous city in Europe. The football team (at that date) was in the Second Division — halfway down. If I really worked at it I might become a top-rate second-rater. The great subcontinental immigration had just started and the city could claim to have the best curry houses in the country; but Bolton, I suspected, could probably have edged it out of first place. 'Numquam primus' should have been the city motto.

I read *Lucky Jim* around this time — a novel which distils the Leicestrian inferiority complex into bitter comedy (bitter, that is, if you were there — sidesplitting if you were lucky enough not to be). And I very soon picked up Larkin. Amis's novel is loosely based on his poet friend's experience as a junior librarian at the university down cemetery road (as Larkin later identifies Leicester in his poem about the 'toad work'). Jim Dixon's escape from fictional Leicester is as happy as Monte Cristo's from the Château d'If. Nor is the depiction of the place in Malcolm Bradbury's *Eating People is Wrong* flattering. Bradbury, of course, was a fellow graduate of the English Department. 'A well-aimed kick in his alma mater's fanny', I heard someone describe the novel. He too, judging by his subsequent career and writings, was glad to escape. He never, as far as I know, wrote nostalgically about the place in later life. Another blank in the CV.

Facing the municipal graveyard (haunt of toads — which inspired Larkin's poem) the central buildings had been, in former times, a lunatic asylum. (UCL, where I spent twenty years of my working life, housed its English Department in what, in a previous incarnation, had been a mattress warehouse. Fate, I assume, had determined to keep me as far from any Dreaming Spire as was architecturally possible.)

Leicester's redbrick still had that generic Victorian institutional feel. Barracks, hospital, school, prison, asylum — what's the difference? My first impression confirmed my worst expectations. This was one of the circles of hell: the second (rate) circle. No really distinguished sinner would be seen dead there.

In fact, I was wrong — as wrong as could be. For reasons intimately connected with Oxbridge snobbery — its hidebound traditionalism, nepotism and physical smallness (and of mind, I would argue) — large overflows of British cleverness and intellectual heterodoxy had been diverted into redbrick channels: no greater stream than into Leicester's English Department.

Looking back, with the experience of a now complete career served out in many universities, I would assess that Leicester at this period (late 1950s, early 1960s) was, pound for pound, the best English Department in the country. It had, for example, Richard Hoggart, riding high on the recently published *The Uses of*

Literacy, and destined to rise to national fame with his testimony at the November 1960 Chatterley Trial. A graduate of Leeds (a cut or two higher than Leicester in the redbrick league), Hoggart had asserted his class credentials by working on a building site, before writing his thesis on Auden. He mixed Leavisite austerity with a pioneering interest in what would later be called media studies.

The department was run by Arthur Humphreys. He has a cameo appearance in *Lucky Jim* and is the model for Professor Treece in *Eating People is Wrong*. Humphreys was scholarly, puritanical, wide-ranging in his expertise, and dutiful — a stewed prune with all the fruit's desiccated virtues. He was, I would guess, (with a monograph on Melville) the first senior academic in the UK to take a serious interest in American fiction. Another member of the faculty, G. S. Fraser, a Poundian and high journalist, did likewise for American poetry.

The list could be extended. But a particular influence on me was Philip Collins — arguably the greatest British Dickensian of his age. There was a lot of Lawrence purveyed in the department — Hoggart and R. P. Draper were card-carrying Lawrentians. Strange as it may seem now, he was regarded as a writer of Shakespearian stature; possibly greater. It created a rather lofty sense that one had to be life-affirming, and a rather confused conviction that the phallus was very important in that affirmation. And sex in the head should be avoided. I was all for that.

Malcolm Bradbury had graduated a year or two before me. Although his degree was in English (and, famously, he was writing for *Punch* while still a student), he had been infected by another richly endowed department. The 1960s was the decade of sociology. Leicester, under the archetypally rootless cosmopolitan head, Ilya Neustadt, had recruited on to its staff the exile Norbert Elias, a developmental sociologist to rank with Weber or Durkheim. Elias's classic work on socialization had been lost, with his other papers, when the Nazis invaded Poland. It was (about this time) rediscovered, as was he as the greatest living sociologist in the country. His accent was reminiscent of the radio naturalist, Ludwig Koch, and when he became excited (as, for example, when delving into the intricacies of Durkheimian 'anomie') he was both comic and incomprehensible. But one felt in the presence of intellectual greatness. I suspect Oxford undergraduates felt the same about Isaiah Berlin.

Among junior members of the department

was Anthony Giddens — the thinker credited with the invention of Tony Blair's Third Way: the doctrine that put the 'New' into 'New Labour'. Now Lord Giddens he was then, to put it euphemistically, a 'dashing' figure on campus. He could also be breathtakingly rude to male undergraduates (me, once) — perhaps because, dark haired and slim, he was so often mistaken for a student.

Dashing was the flavour of the time. Among its other achievements, sociology — with its commitment to relativism and distrust of absolutes — was loosening and relaxing morality. Its undergraduates, snuffing the first reverberations of swing in the decade, pioneered the wearing of denim shirts, leather jackets (en masse, the department fairly creaked) and Beatle haircuts. It was, no questions asked, the best sociology department in the country — and the trendiest in any subject.

I took a subsidiary in sociology and would have transferred to it as my major had the intellectual competition not been so fierce and my essay marks so middling (they gave no credit for fine writing). There was, at the heart of the discipline, a way of thinking I could not quite master — epitomized in the writing of the structuralist Talcott Parsons (a decade later post-structuralism would invade

English, and I would feel the same again). I could not, in the last analysis, 'do' it. Or, at least, I could do it in the same way I could do French: I could read, but not speak the stuff.

I was also put off by Neustadt. One evening he invited me back to his house for a discussion of T. S. Eliot and a nightcap. He had picked me up, drinking moodily by myself, in the Marquis of Granby — a friendly pub at the end of Cemetery (aka University) Road. I was developing a taste for soapy midlands bitter. It was a cool evening in my first term and I was wearing a donkey jacket (working man's gear, £5 from Millett's — my feeble Terson's protest against denim, leather and Lennonism). Neustadt, people told me, liked young men. He took me back to his flat to discuss, as he proposed, T. S. Eliot and recent experiments with poetry and jazz. He had some LPs — Christopher Logue, it turned out, with, I recall, the Tony Kinsey Quartet. He made what I construed as a pass at me — although why, with so many pretty young school-leavers around, I can't think. It may have been the donkey jacket and still hardened hands: rough trade (I flatter myself). Or, quite possibly, I got it all wrong.

After some rumination on the subject I decided sociology wasn't for me, although I could see it was the coming subject. I was more interested in expressing myself (as a kind of act of self-love) than in changing the world, which is what most of the young sociologists were burning to do. Marx's eleventh thesis on Feuerbach ('The philosophers have only interpreted the world in various ways; the point is to change it') was holy writ with them.

I was quite happy to philosophize — or waffle, chunter and dabble — for the next forty years. English was the subject for the wafflers of the world — scholars happy not to lose their chains (as long as they came with a pension after forty years). Let the world change itself. It had done enough of that, over the last twenty-one years, without my help.

My closest friends, and girlfriends (happily emancipated by the new libertarian doctrines emanating from their department), were none the less mainly sociologists, and their ways of thinking influenced my way of doing my waffly subject. 'A literary sociologist', I liked to think of myself over the following decades. It helped mask the fact that I wasn't much of a critic. Particularly for poetry, I had a tin ear (Granny's onion again?).

My arrival at Leicester, fortuitously, coincided with a great revival of provincial culture, in which Hoggart was a heroic pioneer. The Woodfall version of *Room at the Top* hit the screens at around this period. With only a smattering of sociology (and the subject was spread, thick as marmalade, over Leicester) one could see the film both as a defiant validation of social mobility (why shouldn't an oick have it all?) and of places outside London; indeed, that were anti-London.

Colin MacInnes, and his metropolitan infatuation (think *City of Spades, Absolute Beginners*), was ousted by Sillitoe. There was black pride, and gay pride (although not yet so called) and — wonder of wonder — provincial pride. There was something reassuringly symbolic in Laurence Harvey, in that not very good film, overlaying his upper-class accent with, not very convincing, Yorkshire (Harvey, of Lithuanian origin, must have had more linguistic layers than a Battenberg cake).

Leicester, alas, did not have its laureate; its Braine (Bradford), Sillitoe (Nottingham), Stan Barstow (West Riding), Shelagh Delaney (Liverpool) or Storey (Wakefield). Unless, that is, you counted C. P. Snow. But he was too infatuated with his damned corridors of power and Cambridge masterships to click with the forward youth of his home town (and his university, as it happened). Bradbury was too satirical; Orton was too eccentric (although his papers, along with Sue Townsend's, now reside in the university's rare books room).

Top of this literary second division would be Roy Minton's 1967 play, *Death in Leicester* (Minton is better known as the screenwriter for the film *Scum*). Minton's Leicester is a kind of pinstriped zombieville; urban living death, Beckett crossed with Bootsie and Snudge, not quite important enough even to be existential. It's a pity the play is never revived. In fact, as I recall, it was effectively stillborn. I note, from Wikipedia, that I am listed among Leicester's distinguished alumni, along with John McVicar (once Britain's 'most wanted man' — by the police, that is).

The teacher who had most influence on me at Leicester (though in no sense was she of Leicester) was Monica Jones. Why that should be so, I can best convey by paraphrasing the obituary I wrote for her in the *Guardian*, when she died, in February 2001 (she hated the twentieth century, and I rather fancied she felt the next one would be even worse). Writing the obituary was a guilty experience for me, since I had neglected her in the last years of her life when, I suspect, she probably most needed contacts. But I tried to put into it what she had meant for me, and a few others she affected.

The principal feature in her professional character was sceptical non-conformity. An academic for four decades, she published absolutely nothing. None the less, she will be remembered long after the manic over-producers of her trade as the career-long companion and aide, occasional muse and intermittent bed-mate, of Britain's most acclaimed post-war poet, Philip Larkin. His acclaim would have been a lot less had he never taken up with her. In a smaller way, my life would have been very different had I never been taught by her.

She was, in her youth, striking. When I first encountered her (in her mid to late forties) the strikingness verged on alarming. She had fine bone structure, a good figure, a mane of blonde hair, and wore thick dark-rimmed glasses which, *pace* Dorothy Parker ('men don't make passes'), had done nothing to diminish men's interest in her. But, when she smiled, a row of magnificently crooked (and in later life, tobacco-tanned) teeth would give a suddenly vulnerable look to her face. Garbo became Grenfell.

She lived in a small flat on the corner of Stoneygate's Springfield Road and Cross Street. There was a tiny farm nearby and the

352

congenial Clarendon (a Bass pub), which she and her drinking friends favoured at Sunday lunchtime. This flat would be her home for twenty-five years. I would be a regular visitor there. And at the pub.

Her position in the department was the traditional one of Miss Bluestocking — with the difference that she was smarter, wittier, and (not infrequently) better read than many of her colleagues. She was, to complicate things, an object of male desire. Many undergraduates, well into the 1960s, fantasized — hopelessly — about an affair with her. I did.

The ambivalent reactions she provoked are evident in the two representations of her in fiction. Margaret Peel in *Lucky Jim* is a malicious portrait which, inexplicably, Larkin allowed his best friend Kingsley Amis to put into print, with the proviso that he change the character's name from the libellously close 'Margaret Beale' (two of her first names). Malcolm Bradbury (a former student) offers a friendlier, but equally cross-grained, depiction of Jones in his Leicester *roman à clef, Eating People is Wrong*.

Jones's position in the department, where she would work until 1981, was tricky. She surrounded herself with a small coterie of trusted friends in whom she could confide

— often scathingly, always wittily. Her colleagues were uneasily aware that, behind their backs, they were, perhaps, being mocked. Meanwhile, her public demeanour was inscrutably demure.

I encountered her as a teacher in 1960. Her first lecture to the first year of English students at Leicester was on *Wuthering Heights*. She came in, dressed to the nines under her Oxford gown, slammed down a Timex alarm-clock on the lectern and tore into Emily Brontë for her incredible perversity in giving so many of her characters the same Christian and surnames. Wholly inconsiderate. It was very funny (and meant to be). For *Wuthering Heights*, she wore a woolly sweater. When lecturing on *Macbeth* it would be a tartan skirt and for *Antony and Cleopatra* a string of swinging pearls. I never heard her lecture on *Hamlet*, but would not have been surprised to see her plunk a skull down alongside the Timex.

The essence of Jones's teaching was the personal relationship (as she conceived it) with the writers she admired. Those she admired most tended to be clubbable males: Scott, Thackeray, Trollope, Crabbe. These authors were, she would tell students who shared her enthusiasm, 'gold in your pocket for life'. Jones despised the dour doctrines of

Downing College, Cambridge, which were, during most of her career, dominant in the country's English departments ('lead us, heavenly Leavis, lead us' was one of her favourite jibes). Her approach to her subject was marked by dislikes fully as passionate as her literary loves. She had a peculiar contempt for Yeats ('imagine — a grown man wanting to be a clockwork bird on an emperor's tree!'). She had as little time for Sylvia Plath (whose name she consciously mispronounced 'Plahth') as did Larkin (privately) for Ted Hughes.

Of Larkin's harem, Jones was the woman with most claim to be his intellectual equal. To her friends, at that time, it was evident that many of Larkin's famous perversities chimed with hers, and may well have originated with her. She, like him, felt that 'in this age, it is more distinguished not to publish'. She, like him, was defiantly insular ('I'm sure I should not like to travel abroad — the dust!'). Women students who came to her with 'personal problems' were quite likely to be told that scrubbing floors was a sovereign remedy (it worked for her). Men might be told to try the local pub. That evidently worked for her as well. She liked the company of the male undergraduates she trusted, drinking halves for their pints. At home, she favoured gin and tonic in goblet glasses the size of small goldfish bowls.

On favoured students, like me, her influence was strong but, arguably, risky for those more ambitious than she for the baubles of academic life. She fostered a kind of marching out of step which guaranteed that — like her — one would never get on in career terms. To sign up with Monica Jones for the full duration was, in effect, to commit professional hara-kiri — honourable, elegant, but suicidal. Shamefully, she was never promoted beyond the rank in which she entered the profession. It demonstrated to me that the profession was unworthy of her.

From the *Guardian* I got £300 for my stuffy obituarese. From her, as she promised, I had got gold in my pocket for life. On the emotional level, there is no mystery as to why I should have come under the domination (willingly dominated) of a woman of her age, blonde hair, and dashingly controversial sexual activities. The absent lover — Philip over the hill, the picture on the mantelpiece — also slotted perfectly into the grooves of my own fatherless childhood.

Monica Jones was a version of my mother if my mother, instead of cleaning the students' rooms at Bedford College, had been taught there; triumphed there. She too was chronically at odds with her environment — but an environment in which, by guile and superior intelligence (the American 'smarts' is the better word), she could survive.

Monica it was who supplied a rational explanation of how one could be 'in' a subject like English, love it, and yet have a healthy scorn for what it had become in the hands of experts. She was a criticism of academic life as it was now. (The phrase 'criticism of life' reminds me that she loathed Matthew Arnold, seeing him as a Victorian Leavis; her favourite Victorian poet was the comedian Praed; her favourite novelists the clubmen Scott and Thackeray — I would later write books on both of them.)

Monica advocated a permanent marginality. I would not follow her example and do a Lysistrata — decline to publish on the grounds that, things being what they were, silence was the more dignified option. I would follow her elsewhere, but not down that professional dead end. None the less, I reserved the right, like her, to nip the university hand that fed me; more so when it turned itself, as it did in the 1960s, to high-flown theory.

My undergraduate friends at Leicester all had things in common. They drank a lot, they didn't fit in easily, and they were unusually clever: by which I mean clever in unusual ways. They are all alive (although one, a heavier drinker than even me, I'm not entirely sure about). They would not want me to talk about them. All of them took what one might call early retirement (in their mid-twenties) from professional lives in which their talents could, had they worked at it, have taken them to the top.

Looking back as one who was unwilling to go all the way down that route (satisfying myself with feeble subversion) I wonder, now, if they were not merely braver, but more right in their life-decision, than me. Why, as Larkin asked, looking around Leicester, should we let the toad work squat on our shoulders? I, like him, accepted the squatting reptile.

Exit Mother,
Exit Grandmother

Two big events coincided while I was coming to the end of my time at Leicester. They ended a large phase of my life: what I might call my formative years. Over the following decades I would age, and alcohol would exacerbate the erosions of age. But, after this point, I was, effectively, made; what I was.

My mother finally married — which was, from my side, a kind of divorce: the 'amicable' kind. She had never, since being widowed, cared for commitment, believing that in the troubled times in which history had dumped her, it was prudent to adopt what, in the army, is called a position of all-round defence — preparing, flexibly, for surprise from every quarter. Her life had been turned upside down by war and widowhood in 1942. She would not let it happen again.

But part of her was, as she hit fifty, tired. She had achieved enough. Her flexibility was not what it was. She was now a JP, sitting on the bench in the town hall whose steps her mother had scrubbed. She could, as it were, take a rest from her own life; sit on her laurelled bench. She would alternate the remainder of her life — twenty years or so — living over a fume-laden garage on the Mersea Road and on a yacht in Cannes. I saw relatively little of her in either place. And even less of the man in the motor trade — for which I was grateful (as, certainly, was he). Whether, in her heart, she thought I measured up to my father I would never know — and, with the years, ceased to worry about.

The other event was the death of my grandmother, less for the emotional wrench than its quaint symbolisms and circuitry. Daisy Hamilton had been born, I think, in 1890. I don't remember ever knowing, or celebrating her birthday. Anniversaries of any kind were not a big thing in her class of life. She was among the first in her teeming family (eight siblings, as I was told) to benefit from Forster's 1870 Universal Education Act, just as I, two generations later, was the first to benefit from Butler's 1944 Education Act.

Her own grandmother must have belonged to that semi-literate mass of women who could read fluently, but not write or 'figure'. Historically, reading has been something that mothers from all but the lowest classes taught their children, even their daughters. Like the needle and thread, it must have been something of a powerful bond between women in the family. Men, of course, had the pub.

Since writing and numbering were marketable skills, they were taught at school and, for most of the nineteenth century, were the exclusive property of men. In her late twenties my mother had become (thanks to the Pitman school and my father) a shorthand typist. It was a Promethean gift, one of the best things my father left her — along with me, of course.

Sewing, knitting (without bothering to look down) and silently obeying male voices ('taking dictation') were perfect preparation for the girl typist. Exit Bob Cratchit with his goose-quill, enter Miss Jones with her 100wpm. Later on, my mother taught me five-finger touch-typing, for which I am every day grateful — more so as she added little idiosyncrasies of her own, such as reaching the right-hand index finger over for the 't' key on the left-hand rank. Pitman's was my mother's university — the exit door from the class in which she had been born.

My grandmother wrote painfully (around 3wpm, I'd guess), her lips working harder than her hand, often licking the tip of the pencil (disastrous if it was an 'indelible'). She was infinitely more dexterous with a needle or the treadle-driven sewing machine which, like the massive mangle, had come to her in 1909 as a wedding present, or dashing away, as the song had it, with a smoothing iron. She had no role in the small West Street garden — the shovel was a man's tool — other than rushing out with the coal scuttle when any passing horse dropped its useful waste.

Her script was an imperfect copperplate — man's writing, badly done. There was no connection between the way she spoke (or, I suspect, thought) and the way she wrote. The only letter I ever had from her — a one-page note during my National Service — was probably a replica of what she dimly recalled writing to her husband while he was at the front in the First World War and was assembled from working-class epistolary Lego: 'Hoping this finds you as it leaves me', etc.

In the house clearing after my grandfather's suicide in 1957, 300 stolen books were discovered in various cupboards, drawers and crannies. All had been lifted from Fincham's 'twopenny library' on Colchester's North Hill by my grandmother. Her modus operandi was simple. A regular and trusted customer, she would take the latest romance to the counter to be stamped (later inscribing her mark on the back endpaper — she didn't want unwittingly to take the same one out again, thus wasting her little fee). In her shopping basket her swag, swiped furtively from the shelves, would be buried under the groceries.

It was difficult for the family to know what to do with these books. Isobel Barnett killed herself after being prosecuted for lifting in kleptomaniac despair a few shillings' worth of tins from a corner shop. Barnett had a title and powerful friends. She had been a celebrity on *What's My Line?* ('shoplifter', with appropriate mime, was the joke at the time). Barnett lives on as the subject of David Bowie's song 'God Knows I'm Good'. God knows what the authorities would do to a hardened, inarticulate sneak thief from the lower classes. And even if the Colchester magistrates (one of whom was my mother) were in a forgiving mood, what about the shame? My grandmother had neither a lucid explanation nor repentance to offer.

When Faustus said 'I'll burn my books' he can't have thought how difficult that is. Books are hard to dispose of without leaving, so to speak, a paper trail. You can't incinerate them, or not in any quantity, in a domestic grate. Bonfires are too public. The damn things don't sink into river water. My grandmother's hoard — all two hundred-weight of it — was finally deposited by night, batch by batch, in ditches across the deserted Essex countryside. Perhaps a few nestle to this day, mysteriously discovered booty, in attics in Tolleshunt D'Arcy, Great Bentley and Stratford St Mary.

A fine public library had opened in Colchester in the early 1950s. The town was inordinately proud of it (even though there was a cash crisis and only half the planned structure was completed). The building, decommissioned and turned into a cavernous bookshop, now stands in the Culver shopping precinct, stolidly handsome, unlike the California-lite architecture of the depressing mall that surrounds it. The Roberts Report of 1959 and the subsequent Library and Museums Act had promised 'an efficient and comprehensive' service to every British citizen. Colchester's new public library rose to the challenge magnificently (better than Chelmsford — unfairly, we locals thought, chosen to be Essex's county town).

I spent whole days in that library. My grandmother would never have dared join it. Apart from anything else, its previous site — founded as a 'penny on the rates library' in the 1870s — had been in an annexe of the town hall, next to the municipal labour exchange. During the slump years my grandmother had got up at dawn to clean the High Street town-hall steps and those down Stockwell Street, where the old library was. During the same grim period, my grandfather was employed, for next to nothing an hour, sweeping leaves in Colchester Park. The 'public' library, however attractively remodelled, would always stink to them of the dole, the 'exchange', the means test, and the scrag end of everything.

Colchester's public library served me, swot and bookworm that I was, as efficiently and comprehensively as its remote Westminster architects intended. It had an extensive reference room, where a copy of Joyce's *Ulysses* was kept (with the offending pages razored out by an official blade), and a well-stocked newspaper reading room where even the *Daily Worker* was available (rumour had it that a plainclothes policeman was always on hand to see who read it). It was a major municipal asset, but the apparatus of tickets, hard-faced, uniformly aproned assistants, application forms and punitive fines was a deterrent to the uncertainly literate. And the stock of popular fiction (anything lower than, say, Dennis Wheatley or Ursula Bloom) was minimal. It was, essentially, a paternalistically 'improving' institution with an educational mission.

Some of the books my grandmother stole from Fincham's were oddly different from the romantic tripe she borrowed. My copies of Hemingway's *Fiesta*, Warwick Deeping's *Sorrell and Son* and John Braine's *Room at the Top* (a first edition no less) have the faint purple imprint of Fincham's rubber stamp on their flyleaf. These volumes did not go into the Essex ditches. I also toyed with keeping Kathleen Winsor's *Forever Amber* (recalling it as being 'hot'), but let it go. At this stage of life I had other sources of heat. I kept some Gilbert Frankau, which I threw away after sampling it (the name had struck me as somehow distinguished). The prize item in my theft from her thefts was Norman Mailer's *The Naked and the Dead*, which Colchester public library would have consigned to its poison cabinet.

I never asked my grandmother about the stolen books, although she survived for three years after their discovery; reading still. As far as the family were concerned, nothing had ever happened. But in retrospect it seems clear that the thefts were inspired by intellectual aspiration. If the celebrated Isobel Barnett's shoplifting was a cry for help, my grandmother's library-lifting was a mute cry for education. She would never, I think, have stolen tins of condensed milk or cabbages, even if her family were starving (as, at bad times in the 1920s, she may have feared they might). She did not need what she stole. She could not have sold the books. She couldn't even let anyone know she had them. She couldn't risk taking them back. All she could do, as best she could, was read the damn things.

When I knew them, she and her husband did their reading with the aid of massive magnifying glasses, swivelling like two light-house beams as they covered the page; she noticeably faster than him. He would have the *Daily Mirror*, the *News of the World* or the 'Green 'un', the local sports paper. As her husband trawled slowly over his paper my grandmother would devour 'her book'. God knows what she made of Hemingway or Braine. As I raked through her stolen books I was horribly contemptuous of her pretensions. I remember once having come on her reading a novel called *Dr Chaos*. She pronounced it, when I maliciously inquired, as 'chayos' — the 'ch' softened, as in 'choose'. (The book, I now learn from the British Library catalogue, was a 1933 romance, *Dr Chaos and the Devil Snar'd*, by George R. Preedy, the pseudonym of Gabrielle Margaret Vere Campbell.)

I mocked her mispronunciation with all the harsh intellectual superiority of the newly, but insecurely, educated. I now hate myself for that. She wanted something more than class, place and history (forces over which, unlike me, she had absolutely no power) allowed her. Hence that heart-wrenching boast, 'I have seen both my girls at Bedford College.'

Fincham's was, in Gorky's phrase, my grandmother's university. Not, alas, as prestigious as Bedford College: but at least it had two departments. From the street it was a genteel, obsolescent circulating library for the culturally unambitious. In the back, it was the unofficial centre of Colchester's spiritualist activity. Together with books (licit and illicit), my grandmother would bring back from Fincham's copies of the *Veil*. Spiritualism had by the 1950s declined from its grand days in the 1920s, when vast numbers attempted to make contact with loved ones lost in the Great War, but it still had followers. My grandmother read, in order of importance, tea leaves, the 'cards', and books (I am fairly certain she did not read palms).

As a 'good' (unnaturally silent) child I was often present at a typical afternoon meeting. Friends — women who were going through bad times (cruel husbands, wastrel children, sickness, debt) — would drop by in that interval after domestic duties and before the men got home from work. After some gossip and ritual observations on the way of the world (days drawing in or drawing out; the price of this or the scarcity of that), the reading would come. Cups would be swirled and the dregs drained to uncover what the leaves revealed — something legible only to the tassologist. That, of course, was my grandmother, suddenly an oracular presence.

I was not privy to the more dramatic readings, but it was clear that whether or not she had 'powers', she certainly had the tricks of an accomplished bunko artist. Her predictions with the leaves and the cards (a standard pack, thinned down to the pictures) went far beyond the platitudes of fortune-telling: meeting a man in black, crossing water, receiving a parcel. They were, on occasion, startlingly outspoken: prophesying loss, bereavement and much pain.

I was told by my mother (as prone as others in her family to gilding lilies) that my grandmother was, in her heyday, consulted by local businessmen such as the proprietor of the auction showrooms and even, it was rumoured, 'Old Fincham' himself. I am inclined to believe this. Whether or not she really was clairvoyant, 'reading', whether of books or tea leaves, was associated for her with power: it was a means of achieving some sort of control over her narrow and culturally impoverished existence. The leaves and the cards, and perhaps the books, also connected her to a world of magic.

Daisy Salter, the year of her death

Possibly I inherited from her a primitive reverence for the book as something magical — an illusion that would have encouraged obsessive reading in early life. But I think that is common in lonely children. I probably owe as much to the *Hotspur, Wizard* and *Rover*. My grandmother perhaps did pass on a relaxed attitude to ownership where books are concerned — but lots of people are free and easy in that department. My shelves have probably been robbed as often as I have stolen to help fill them. Books for my grandmother were, I think, a closed door. But she recognized them as a door and, like a cargo cult aborigine, took up her place by it. For me, the door was open. I was lucky.

She died, I believe, from a lifetime overdose of tea. Cancerous kidneys — the revenge of all those leaves whose mysterious ways she had presumed to know. I did not see her during her last week in hospital on her life-support machinery. I was prevented from going into the ward by my blubbing uncle Arthur. He pretended it was a kindness to me — she was so unlike herself in life, and that was the 'picture' of her I should have in my mind. I suspect the real reason was a desire to have her to himself. I did not begrudge him that ownership. He, the youngest and the only son, had always been the 'mother's boy'. And when a parent is dying, strange, powerful and deep-buried feelings come to the surface. My mother, in the interminable week while the pitiless machine pumped air into her mother, played game after game of Patience.

I did not go to my grandmother's cremation. Oddly, the Salters (my mother, her brother and sister) did not, as they made clear, want me there — any more than at my grandfather's funeral. I did not fit in easily any more. And I think they found it hard to 'be themselves' (what they had been, and shared, as children) with me around. Whether the sun shone over that unpleasant corpse-burning manufactory in the Mersea Road that day I never knew.

Afterlife

The remainder of my life, between then and now, can be summarized in fast forward. I drank vastly at Leicester and drew into my little orbit companions who also drank heavily. But I stopped, cold turkey, for the last three months of my undergraduate career as finals loomed. At the same time I put my love life in order — settling down with an intelligent, pretty, and introverted sociologist who made few demands on me. Thus stabilized, and cleaned up, I got a very good degree.

It earned me a state scholarship to do three years' research. Which I didn't do — other than a phenomenal year's reading in which I inhaled hundreds of volumes of Victorian fiction, with which second-hand bookshops round the city teemed. For a few shillings you could (and I did) pick up complete runs of Bulwer Lytton, Charles Lever, George Meredith. It was less reading than total submersion. I was still using the notes I made in that year, a quarter of a century later, when I put together an encyclopaedia of Victorian fiction.

As I looked back to the nineteenth century, the British university system was making a belated lurch forward into the twentieth. The Robbins Report in 1963 had sanctioned a huge expansion of places and campuses. Demographically, it was a knock-on from 1944: there were many more qualified school-leavers. More teachers were needed — and they need not all be dons.

What it meant in the job market was a once in a lifetime, perhaps a once in all-time, balance between demand and supply. There were academic jobs for qualified graduates all over the place. I had only a BA (from *that* place) and a head overbrimming with Victorian fiction. No thesis, no publications. But, encouraged by Monica, I got offers in the same week from Edinburgh (which had advertised *five* posts in the English Department in the same advertisement), Exeter and at Merton College, Oxford. The last was a junior fellowship specifically for candidates from 'non-Oxbridge backgrounds'. I was reminded of the last the other day (23 October 2006) when *The Times* carried on its front page the screaming headline 'Poor but Bright Pupils to be Offered Places at Private Schools' (St Paul's, Cheltenham Ladies' College). I can't recall if Merton called it the Lady Bountiful fellowship.

I took Edinburgh on Monica's advice: John Butt, the Regius chair, was, she said, 'the nicest man' to work with. It would be another circuit. Like Tamburlaine, I would ride in triumph through the Caledonian Persepolis.

I was at Edinburgh for ten years. I drank vastly and read a lot and published very little — so little that I would, by today's standards, be regarded as prematurely dead wood; and very drunken to boot. All that time, I suppose, Victorian fiction was settling, like a sediment, in my mind. The university had distinguished Victorianists on its staff — in history as much as in English. I did a PhD — for no other reason than that I wanted one day to work in the United States. The subject of my dissertation was 'Thackeray at Work' — a study of the novelist's manuscripts and compositional methods. It was a homage to Thackeray and to John Butt's seminal *Dickens at Work* (he, like the older, gentlemanlier generation of British scholarship, had no PhD, regarding it as a Germanic aberration).

I married and bought a New Town flat. Junior lecturers nowadays have no more hope of buying them than a castle in the Borders. But the profession still, in the mid-1960s, had the accoutrements of a profession. I was very lucky and happy. One of the effects of

Robbins had been to suck in a generation of lecturers only a year or two older than finalists and the same age (or in my case younger) than postgraduates. It was a heady mixture.

In all the years I was at Edinburgh I never once went back to Dalmeny Street — in fact, I would make long detours to avoid going there. It was not an inhibition I could make sense of. Nor, to my greater shame, did I keep up with Leicester friends, or Monica. I once, in later, alcohol-troubled years, asked a psychiatrist about this reluctance ever to pick up old strings in my life. He explained it, as psychiatrists always do, in terms of trauma and fear.

I later moved down to UCL, following two Edinburgh friends (who may have fixed things for me), and stayed there ten years. By now I was writing books; first on Victorian fiction, then on modern fiction, then on popular fiction, then on pornography. The Godless Place in Gower Street (the Oxbridgeless place, that is) suited me perfectly. Thanks to the head of the department, Karl Miller, I was also writing what could be called either higher journalism or lower scholarship. I spent some visiting terms (at last!) in America, and loved the place as much as I had loved the idea of it, all those years ago in Long Wyre Street, the Hippodrome, and Mann's music emporium.

I was, by this time, a family man: but letting them — everyone — down by drinking. I would guess that by the age of forty-five I was clinically alcoholic: past the point of no return — reversion, that is, to 'responsible' drinking, as New Labour's new puritans call it. Two things happened in 1983. I was offered a job in America, at the California Institute of Technology, and I got sober. My drunk-alog-pamphlet, *Last Drink to L.A.*, tells as much of the story as is tellable. It was like writing razor blades (as parts of this book has been). In 1992 I came back to fill the vacancy left by the departure of Karl Miller at UCL. Yet another circuit.

Since then my life has been topsy-turvy but I am, at the moment, very happy. The principal reason may be found in the dedication to this book.

Afterword

The Boy Who Loved Booze

I sometimes look at books I've owned during my reading life and think how much more gracefully the things have aged than their owner. Indeed, since most of the volumes I've chosen not to give (or toss) away will outlive me, I consider myself less their owner than a temporary custodian; a leaseholder. In my most bibliomaniac phase, when the owner-ship of books was important to me, I collected a vast number of Victorian fiction titles. Many carried inscriptions by dead owners; some Victorian, even. The inscriptions nowadays speak to me louder than the printed words.

Riffling the pages of my *Brideshead Revisited* (Penguin, 1954) I see a brownish stain blotching some of the central pages. It could be tea, but isn't. It's certainly not 'foxing', battered as the book is. It's beer. If I put my nose to the page, I fancy I can even identify the brand — Bass bitter ('cooking bitter' as we wittily called it — as opposed to 'director's').

Books and booze — my theme.

I can remember how the stain got there. Vividly. I'd taken the book to lend to a friend (the eccentric greengrocer, Mort) at the Castle pub, perched at the top of East Hill by the pompous 1914–18 War Memorial. I was in my literary missionary mode, eighteen years old — Colchester's popular educator, a one-man Diffusion of Useful Knowledge Society. 'You like those books about piss-artists,' I recall Mort saying, somewhat deflatingly, after he'd looked at it (I'd earlier lent him *The Great Gatsby*). Sharp-eyed as ever, he saw through me. Sebastian Sutherland — piss-artist *maudit*. Prat, he must have thought.

In the carelessness of the last-round helter-skelter that summer evening, Bass was slurped about. Hence the stain. In those slurping days, I would, as I recall, knock back some six or seven pints and regard myself as well within the limits of civilized topery — under the proverbial 'eight', that is, which marked the squaddy's drunken Plimsoll line. A gallon of wallop was not that big a deal in the 1950s. Draught bitter was gnat-piss weak compared to what pub beer is nowadays — expensively bottled, labelled and silver-stoppered as the stuff is which I see being swigged straight from the bottle; something that only parkbench winos did in the 1950s. Watery Bass made possible a long, and gradually more convivial, evening before closing time spilled one, bleary and bladdery, on to the streets (still twilit in summer) at ten-ish.

A skinful of Bass also, as we confided knowingly to each other, kept the bowels in trim and did not, inevitably, result in the dreaded brewers' droop. Bowels were, at that period, alas, more exercised than gonads. One drank with a sense of doing oneself more 'good' than even Guinness could (the keg variety of the Irish stout arrived on the scene in the same late 1950s: 'milkshake, beer flavoured' we roguishly called it).

None the less, despite the insipidity of that bitter, hands would get careless, tongues loose, and glasses slippery. I can now see myself better than I could then; through the obscuring glass, so to speak. I was ingenuous, well-meaning, foolish and — did I but know it — on the path to self-destruction. But the crash was so far away in the future as to be sometime-never. Drunkenness was still my great adventure.

By peddling Waugh or whatever to my unliterary drinking friends my motives were mixed. Intellectual snobbery was certainly there somewhere. Pharisaically I liked to see myself not as other drinkers were; no illiterate sot. I was varnishing my low vices with literary veneer. Ever since that inaugural gin and tonic with my mother, I loved to glamorize boozing, enhancing the artistry rather than the piss aspect. Novels helped. I can't admire myself for that delusion. But — more admirably — I genuinely wanted to share what I enjoyed. Books, like drinks, were, I fondly believed, best consumed in rounds. They should, like alcohol, dissolve barriers: put one in touch with the shared conditions of humanity.

I'd enjoyed the Waugh book: millions of social miles away as the Castle pub was from Castle Howard — or whatever pile Brideshead was based on. Conceived in the wasteland of postwar austerity, the novel has a self-confessed gluttony: a nostalgic wallowing in the forever lost pre-war banquet. Vastly luxurious meals, and epic drinking, punctuate the stories of Charles Ryder and Sebastian Flyte. Parts of the novel are less narrated than salivated.

As Waugh later recalled, his narrative was distorted into gastro-obsession by the locking up of the British population for seven lean years within the austere confines of their ration books: two eggs per week, a 'quarter' of butter, six 'ozs' (how well one knew that hateful abbreviation) of bacon; 'marge' that tasted like axle grease. 'The period of soya beans and Basic English', Waugh called it. Auberon, the novelist's son, recalls (at the period when *Brideshead* was being written) how his father grabbed from his son's plate the first banana the little boy had ever seen, and ate it himself — as a kind of *droit de père*. One can sympathize with the domestic tyrant. If you'd never had it, you didn't feel the lack of it as keenly as those who had. Paradise Regained means less to those who haven't lost it. Hard luck, Bron! Most of my generation can remember their first banana as distinctly as their first sexual experience. I took mine out into Wellington Street, I recall, and ate it in the bomb site; no chance of my yellow prize being snaffled. The exoticism of the taste is with me today.

The era of shared social drinking on which I had launched myself (with a bottle of brown ale across my bows) while still at school lasted a couple of decades. The drinking school was, in those last teenage years, more important than CRGS. If not as educational, it was formative of my adult personality. 'Drinking Made Me' — in much the same way that, pre-war, people liked to say 'England Made Me' (slogans absorbed into titles by both Graham Greene and D. H. Lawrence, favourite authors in my growing-up period: I lent them around the favoured Castle clientele as well). It was freedom, rebellion, community — the gateway to jazz, sex and selfhood. Books were in there somewhere.

Later in my drinking career, much later, I would graduate into solitary drinking — guzzling, that is, as privately and introvertedly as my reading became. Schooldays, the happiest days of my drinking life, were, by that point, over and the reckless joyousness of youthful boozing was irrecoverable — although one kept trying, with a glummer kind of recklessness. The stains, thereafter, were on my character.

This dangerous stage of drinking life took many more years to get to than did my three degrees; and enough liquor was consumed to float the proverbial battleship. But, until I was well into my thirties, drinking was primarily a communal thing: happy revel, not lonely dissipation. I would drink more than others, typically, but alongside others. I would no more have thought of buying a hipflask-sized bottle of whisky at nine o'clock in the morning from an off-licence (always a different off-licence from the day before) than I would have worn a sandwich-board saying 'hopeless alcoholic'. In the last five years of my drinking career, that handily concealed phlegm-cutter was as necessary as insulin to a diabetic. It wasn't booze, it was medicine. It was killing me, but I would have died without it.

In the good years I drank companionably. So too with books: they were shared pleasures. I read where others read; I liked libraries and the flyleaves of books, with borrowings registered by date and grubbed on to the pages by thumbs and index fingers (some, doubtless, bespittled). If communal drinking, why not communal reading? There was something comforting in the idea of a 'public' library, as cosy as the public house. In some way which I still do not quite understand, books and booze have run together in my life: and at the root of that confluence is the complicated fact that we are alone, and oddly together in our loneliness. I've never worked out where the line is.

Reading is, like dreaming, a private activity. Drinking, in its purest form, is solitary. I have always been struck by a comment of Conrad's in *Heart of Darkness*: 'We die, as we dream, alone.' Substitute 'drink' for 'dream' and it makes perfect sense to me. Substitute 'read', and likewise it makes sense. I liked to think, late in my drinking career, when glamorization had given way to self-dramatization, that there was something wonderfully self-defining about booze. I was a wanderer — an explorer of myself — in Jack London's 'white waste'. Yet, at the same time, it was London who made that profound observation on alcoholism — that he drank to make other people bearable. At the end of it all, it was not what drink did to him, but to those around him. Drink made him simultaneously social and lonely.

Drunks are boring company and tales of drunkenness, if true, are tedious. Few are true, in my experience — particularly novels about drinking. They are either understated (like the number of drinks the drinker confesses to, when questioned by non-drinkers) or heroically overstated (like the number one confesses to when challenged by fellow drinkers). On the one side denial, on the other James Frey.

I never starred at AA meetings, principally because I never had a terribly interesting story to offer — interesting, that is, by comparison with the maestros of piss-artistry who hold audiences rapt at speaker meetings. Someone (I'm thinking of 'Jim') would get up and reminisce, with clinchingly authentic detail, about knocking back tequila with Kerouac and Burroughs in San Francisco — before they became world-famous beatniks and were merely wonderfully talkative bar-flies. Someone would kick in a few anecdotes about that other legendary barfly, Bukowski, and Los Angeles. He's dead now, and doesn't need the shroud of anonymity, but I was stunned to hear Hubert ('Chubby') Selby Jr (the author of *Last Exit to Brooklyn*) at a participation meeting: I *lectured* on the man's work, for God's sake. A film actor I see on late-night TV reruns all the time would reminisce about waking up one morning, and finding a Swat Team besieging his house. To this day, he wasn't sure why, but a hotshot lawyer to the stars had, somehow, fixed it.

It wasn't just the famous. Someone would pitch in with the comment that they had learned they had incurable liver disease, had been given only months to live, had been to see a death therapist and was surprised at 'how good those guys are'. And no, he wasn't intending to go out in a blaze of alcoholic glory. How could I match that?

At these meetings I was typically the reviewer, watching other drunks' shadows on the walls (walls which were, often enough, physically covered with religious placards, church halls being the usual AA location). I was never the hero, not even of my own narratives. I was no more a champion drinker — practising, abstinent or recovering — than

386

Colchester United had been a first-division team or Leicester had been Balliol College. All I could assert was that my adventures in the drinking world were real to me, however squalid, banal and unimpressive they would surely seem to others. What I had to throw in was barely worth the sharing; too Prufrockian. Coming to terms with that second-rateness was, for me, the hardest challenge of sobriety: harder, by far, than avoiding the deadly first drink.

The other reason I could never star at AA meetings (very competitive affairs, often) was because the words kept on getting in the way of what I wanted to say. I couldn't clamber over the rhetoric and simply speak in my own voice. I couldn't, as the veterans of the fellowship put it, get past my own bullshit. I could lecture (I did that for a living). And I could, when it came to the confessional fifth step, put the stuff down on paper with commendable eloquence, copiousness and style. I could do a masterly 'inventory'. But I couldn't, for the life of me, be honest — 'come clean', as the phrase goes.

Alcoholics know little or nothing about a lot of things. But they do know a lot about alcoholism — more, certainly, than those members of the medical profession who treated me. As part of that disease-expertise, alcoholics have shit-hot bullshit meters. I was, despite all my efforts, phoney — literally. As if, that is, I was phoning in my 'sharing', or 'performing' it (with the expectation of a good grade), rather than speaking truth. I seemed to have lost that ability — whether through drink or living too many falsehoods I don't know. But it came out wrong, even when it came out fine-sounding.

If I'm as honest (now) as I can be I believe there was a moment between my first significant drink (at some point around 1954) and my last (on 22 January 1983) when I became an alcoholic. After this point my downward spiral could no more be stopped than an avalanche can return up the hill. It was a one-way nonstop journey to the end: death, incarceration, wet brain, or AA.

Since then I have been clean and sober. And, on the whole, happier for it; although not entirely. Most addicts find that recovery leaves a hole in their lives which never quite fills up, however fulfilling those afterlives are. I have never been sure whether drunkenness releases the real self, on the *in vino veritas* principle, or whether it is a Jekyll and Hyde thing, as implied by the phrase 'demon drink' — one is, that is, 'possessed' by something alien. The topic is sometimes discussed, with great insight, at AA meetings. But there seems to be no consensus.

To me, who experienced it all, the drinking career is a narrative — a linear progression. I see shapes, themes, turnings, long moods and changing tempos. But I am the only person who will ever see those events as organically connected — a 'story'. For others, who were close enough to witness (or be harmed) by them, during my long, drunken years, they were 'episodes', 'lapses', 'disgraceful behaviour' — snapshots of shame.

In the early 1950s the popular radio personality Wilfred Pickles (copper-bottomed Yorkshire) hosted a programme called *Have a Go*. At its height, it claimed an audience of twenty million — over half the country's adult population. It consisted of a ludicrously easy quiz, invariably terminated with 'Mabel at the Table' being instructed by Wilf to 'give 'im/'er the money' and the 'old joanna' thumping out a triumphal chorus ('Have a go, Joe! you've got to have a go!'). The essence of the programme was Pickles's matey conversations with his working-class contestants. At a climactic moment, much relished by connoisseurs of the show, the guest would be asked, 'Do you 'ave a most embarrassin' moment?' It always struck me that AA meetings were similarly structured round those moments — more embarrassing by far than anything Pickles's people came up with.

Once, alone in a motel in New Hampshire (my then wife having refused, wisely, to accompany me on the summer school I was teaching) and in one of those awful 'periodical' phases, in which I'd be sober for months, then fall off the wagon, I made a list of the shameful things I'd done, said or allowed to happen when drunk — or because of the situations I got into when drunk. The catalogue went on, for page after awful page, scorching the yellow legal pad paper.

What follows are four of my embarrassing moments: one for every decade of my drinking life. They are by no means the most shameful. Those *most* embarrassing moments involve violence, sexual depravity, criminality. The memory of them still burns. But like that inextinguishable radioactivity under the cement sarcophagus at Chernobyl, they're buried and will be until we're both buried. Minor as these moments are, however, they are still painful enough to make me groan. Those who know me (or may feel they know something about me from the previous pages) may judge from the following snapshots whether, in drink, I was more truly John Sutherland or whether — as I would prefer to think — 'not quite myself'.

The first episode belongs to my school days. By the time I was in my last sixth-form year at CRGS I was what could, with some stretch of the term, be called a 'hardened' drinker. Two years' assiduous practice, and a young constitution, meant that I could, as the phrase went, 'hold my drink'. I had a reputation for it, of which I was absurdly proud. For motives of bravado, and perhaps mischief, I recruited three classmates to club together into a fund for an end-of-school-year piss-up. We would put money (a half-crown a week) into a kitty and have a celebratory pub crawl. Balls to the School, would be the motto.

We duly drank our fund away. I was unaffected by what was, for me, a habitual intake — something over six pints. They got smashed. One, unhappily, was a boarder at the school, truanting. He went back, vomited, shouted, raised the housemaster, and was packed off to the casualty ward of the nearby General Hospital (where, oddly, my grandmother was having one of the family kidneys removed). I, coward that I was, had crept back into the school grounds and, like some peeping Tom, observed the highpoints of the drama through a window. Shaking.

The boy — whose name was Jackson (a star on the rugby field) — did not snitch. The opinion was put about that he had been made drunk by some unnamed old boys. I, of course, was the (unidentified) culprit. He was expelled; some of the things he had shouted, in the frenzy of his drunkenness, had hit home. God knows how his life went thereafter. I could, of course, have rescued Jackson with a full and frank confession. But I said nothing.

What I learned from the episode, apart from my cowardice in the face of sobersided authority, was that my ability to outdrink others represented power. I could, where alcohol flowed extravagantly, not merely hold my drink but use that ability to my advantage. At many points in later life I would, sometimes over periods long enough for it to be a distinct strategy, induce people close to me to overdrink. It wasn't just the relief that comes with guilt-sharing that motivated me. It was the realignment of power. In the country of the drunk, the man who can hold his drink is king. Unfortunately, it's not much of a country.

The second episode belongs to 1963. In my pre-university and early university years I explored the Continent. With greengrocer Mort I dissipated myself in Berlin, Barcelona, Paris and Amsterdam. We, the British, had liberated Europe. Now Europe liberated us.

The Dutch seaport capital, which could be reached overnight from Harwich, offered rich debauch. One evening, after listening to some live jazz (Modern Jazz Quartet styled), smoking a 'reefer' (disappointing, and probably ersatz), drinking glass after glass of metallic lager, befriending some Panamanian sailors, I wrapped up the evening with a visit to the naughty windows on Kanal Dyke (or whatever it was called) and spent my last fifteen guilders on a homely girl. She only had to pull the curtains for a few minutes.

Mort, meanwhile, had gone on some quixotic quest for a tawny beauty who, after two hours of his seductive prattle, took the wind out of his sails by saying, sternly, 'my price is fifty guilder' — which he didn't have, because I had taken the kitty. He never forgave me and we never travelled together again.

After my more successful climax, I stood on the edge of one of the dark canals, in deep post-coital gloom, as the alcohol drained slowly from my system, and resolved to kill myself. I did not want bohemian freedom; it made me ashamed of myself. I did not want Anglo-Saxon decency; it stifled me. Id and superego were rock and hard place. I would drown myself, like Martin Eden. And then I didn't jump — unlike Lord Jim. I would, I preposterously resolved, work myself to death; if necessary, read and write myself to death. It was Paul Morel turning back to the lights of the city (my favourite passage in Lawrence at the time). My life was a tissue of literary poses. But, arguably, the right ones won out.

Fifteen years on, and I was settled as a family man in Herne Hill. There comes a stage in alcoholism when physical inertia takes over. One imbibes alcohol with the bovine passivity of a cow being milked — but in reverse; it streams in, not out. At the period of my maximal sottishness I would sometimes sit all night in an armchair, earphones on my head, listening to tapes of jazz or rock, solemnly devouring litre after litre of cheap wine — Soave, Pecs, or supermarket plonk. The booze didn't aid concentration, but I would also read paperback popular fiction. I was writing a book on bestsellers which permitted a lowering of the critical sensibility to the debased level my sodden brain could handle.

While the family slept I was Jabba the Hutt: a slob. The inertia, after an hour or two, descended to a condition of paralysis. So rotted was my will that, rather than ascend the stairs to the lavatory, or blunder into the garden, I would relieve myself in whatever empty bottle was to hand and empty it later. If, at the end of the night, there was any white wine left over, I would put it back in the fridge before creeping upstairs for an hour's sleep before dawn, coffee, and the pains of a new day.

Alas, I mistook the flagons and put a near full bottle of vintage Sutherland pee in the fridge. It came out, the next evening, at a dinner party. Given the levels of alcohol in my system it would probably have proofed at a respectable 12 degrees. But it didn't taste good, as the faces on the company indicated. 'Corked,' I muttered, as I swept it off the table. I never confessed and, I'm fairly sure, no one suspected.

In the turn of the year, 1981–2, I found myself in the Big Apple (as it was beginning to be called) at a Modern Language Association convention. Some 15,000 university teachers of English congregate in a big city annually, in the dead days between Christmas and New Year, when the hotel prices plummet, and even academics can taste luxury. I had got a suite at the Pierre, the hotel on Central Park that features in *Crocodile Dundee* and innumerable other movies.

I had friends, a leading sci-fi writer and his partner, who lived down in Greenwich

Village. We went down there before going on to a New Year party hosted by Norman Spinrad, a writer I particularly admired (if only because his novel, *Bug Jack Barron*, had been excoriated as obscene in Parliament). My village friends, out of mischief or because I was drunk and obnoxious, spiked (as I suspect) my drink with LSD. I had a full-blown psychotic episode and was convinced that I was in hell. I cannot bear even to recall the horror that I felt. On another occasion when, madly, I ate a lump of cannabis resin the size of a decent piece of Parmesan I had a similar psychotic episode. I was, I realized, borderline schizophrenic.

I don't know how I behaved at Spinrad's party: it's blacked out, and no one cared to fill me in later. But it must have been bad. One of the distinguishing features of late alcoholism (along with the blackouts) is its cunning. The drinker, above all else, must preserve his drinking. Which means, perversely, taking care of himself so that he can remain physically capable of rendering himself incapable. I could not, it was clear, follow the path of multi-drug abuse; there is no booze in the asylum.

There was also something else which was very odd indeed. Whenever I mixed with live authors, as opposed to reading their work on the page, I went mad: or, more precisely, I would madden myself with drink or whatever substances were to hand. It happened so often, and so predictably, that — at the end of my career — I would avoid literary parties, even those where writers I particularly admired would be present. I couldn't trust myself with living literature. As with the anatomist, it had to be dead.

These episodes, and thousands like them, many many times worse, were accompanied by a continuous fracturing of relationships, of career, of health, of trust. And yet, to the end, I still loved the stuff.

★ ★ ★

Books of the Day have their flavours and one of the predominant flavours in memoirs of the early twenty-first century is infantile revenge. Familial monsters everywhere. Is it fair? Where family survives to read about themselves, they do not always agree. It is clear — reading between the lines of some recent family memoirs — that all have a different take on their parents. Some may be vilified. In other cases, there have been serious moves towards legal action, on grounds of defamation, by family members.

I do not anticipate litigation. Nor are there

many around, I think, to object to my portrait gallery of the Sutherlands and Salters. There may, I think, be Old Colcestrians who will find my depiction of their alma mater ('may she stand for ever') unfair, and possibly malevolent. I will only repeat that it is, to my eye, a much kinder, and equally high-performing, institution nowadays.

In ending this memoir, I have toyed with the idea of how my mother, my aunts and uncles, my grandparents, would have depicted me, were the tables turned. One phrase would have sprung to their lips: 'He doesn't know he's born.'

In fact, it's one of the few facts I'm sure about. I have the certificate to prove it. But, were they to write their accounts, I would feature (not necessarily centrally) as the fortunate child. My father's and grandfather's generations fought in World Wars. They, their lives and their families were deformed by conflicts which were largely irrelevant to their little existences.

I was never hungry; not (damagingly) malnourished; rarely beaten. I never had to share a urine-soaked bed with siblings. I had access to free medicine, health-giving inoculations and operations. I was not sexually abused (or, to be precise, was so feebly molested that I look back on it with amusement: in flights of erotic fantasy I did more violent things to my penis than ever that wimpish predator did in the blackcurrant fields).

It's wholly unmeasurable, but I suspect I have had more sex than any of my predecessors; and probably, in my thirty-year drinking career, more drink. Most of it was fun — sex and drink both. My family's lives were (with the exception, perhaps, of my mother's) largely funless.

I have already lived longer than many of my immediate family — undestroyed as I am by anything that they would have considered hard work. I had access to books and leisure to read them — the softest and most pleasurable work. I was privileged to join in adult society while still a child. I was the first member of my family to attend a university — not because I was cleverer, more diligent, or more virtuous. I merely coincided with a historical opportunity. I was lucky. And I still am.

It's appropriate that I should end on a note of gratitude: to those described here, and to the Labour Government, 1945–51. Was there ever a stranger valediction to a memoir?

Acknowledgements

I would like to thank the editorial staff at John Murray, particularly Eleanor Birne and Helen Hawksfield, and my agent, Victoria Hobbs. Some names have been changed in the text, for obvious reasons.

The author and publisher would like to thank the following for permission to reproduce illustrations: page 22, above, courtesy of Colchester Museum; page 22, below, courtesy of Patrick Denney; page 129, *The Young Waltonians — Stratford Mill*, c. 1819–25 (oil on canvas) by Constable, John (1776–1837) © Yale Center for British Art, Paul Mellon Fund, USA/The Bridgeman Art Library.

We do hope that you have enjoyed reading this large print book.

Did you know that all of our titles are available for purchase?

We publish a wide range of high quality large print books including:
Romances, Mysteries, Classics
General Fiction
Non Fiction and Westerns

Special interest titles available in large print are:
The Little Oxford Dictionary
Music Book
Song Book
Hymn Book
Service Book

Also available from us courtesy of Oxford University Press:
Young Readers' Dictionary
(large print edition)
Young Readers' Thesaurus
(large print edition)

For further information or a free brochure, please contact us at:
Ulverscroft Large Print Books Ltd.,
The Green, Bradgate Road, Anstey,
Leicester, LE7 7FU, England.
Tel: (00 44) 0116 236 4325
Fax: (00 44) 0116 234 0205

Other titles published by
The House of Ulverscroft:

THE ACCIDENTAL ANGLER

Charles Rangeley-Wilson

Fishing can take you to the heart of a landscape — whether in the world's most outlandish and awe-inspiring places, or just at the end of your road, it will introduce you to the locals, rip-tides, floods, droughts — and, of course, fantastic slippery beasts. In *The Accidental Angler* you'll battle titanic monsters on a tropical atoll; chase inscrutable grayling through back gardens in Provence; dance in Brazilian carnivals, and find secret rivers hidden beneath the streets. Join Charles Rangeley-Wilson — angler, conservationist, television presenter and traveller — on a journey that will make the familiar new, and the strange familiar.

A VERY BRITISH COOP

Mark Collings

Mark Collings had rated pigeons the lowest of the bird family until he met Les Green, head of the UK top pigeon-racing team — known as the 'Salford Mafia' . . . Les, a sharp-tongued ex-gang member, is the author's guide through the weird and wonderful world of British pigeon racing. Pigeons are big business: there are 60,000 pigeon racers in the UK, and rivalry can provoke arson attacks on lofts. *A Very British Coop* is the story of a journey taken from a pigeon loft in Oldham to a shot at the ultimate prize — The Sun City Million Dollar Classic.

CHARLOTTE AND LEOPOLD

James Chambers

Charlotte & Leopold tells the story of the doomed romance between Charlotte, heir to the English throne, and Leopold, uncle to Queen Victoria and first King of the Belgians. Charlotte was the only legitimate royal child of her generation, and her death in childbirth was followed by an unseemly scramble to produce a substitute heir. Queen Victoria was the product. Charlotte won the hearts of her subjects. Yet, she was used, abused and victimised by rivalries — between her parents; between her father (the Prince Regent, later George IV) and (Mad King) George III; between her tutors, governesses and other members of her discordant household; and ultimately between the Whig opposition and the Tory government . . .